the Last Bride

Sandra Landry

BERKLEY SENSATION, NEW YORK

THE BERKLEY PUBLISHING GROUP
Published by the Penguin Group
Penguin Group (USA) Inc.
375 Hudson Street, New York, New York 10014, USA
Penguin Group (Canada), 90 Eglinton Avenue East, Suite 700, Toronto, Ontario M4P 2Y3, Canada
(a division of Pearson Penguin Canada Inc.)
Penguin Books Ltd., 80 Strand, London WC2R 0RL, England
Penguin Group Ireland, 25 St. Stephen's Green, Dublin 2, Ireland (a division of Penguin Books Ltd.)
Penguin Group (Australia), 250 Camberwell Road, Camberwell, Victoria 3124, Australia
(a division of Pearson Australia Group Pty. Ltd.)
Penguin Books India Pvt. Ltd., 11 Community Centre, Panchsheel Park, New Delhi—110 017, India
Penguin Group (NZ), Cnr. Airborne and Rosedale Roads, Albany, Auckland 1310, New Zealand
(a division of Pearson New Zealand Ltd.)
Penguin Books (South Africa) (Pty.) Ltd., 24 Sturdee Avenue, Rosebank, Johannesburg 2196,
South Africa

Penguin Books Ltd., Registered Offices: 80 Strand, London WC2R 0RL, England

This is a work of fiction. Names, characters, places, and incidents either are the product of the author's imagination or are used fictitiously, and any resemblance to actual persons, living or dead, business establishments, events, or locales is entirely coincidental.

THE LAST BRIDE

A Berkley Sensation Book / published by arrangement with the author

PRINTING HISTORY
Berkley Sensation edition / August 2005

Copyright © 2005 by Sandra Maschette Landry.
Cover art by Daniel O'Leary.
Cover design by Lesley Worrell.
Interior text design by Kristin del Rosario.

ISBN: 0-425-20444-8

BERKLEY® SENSATION
Berkley Sensation Books are published by The Berkley Publishing Group,
a division of Penguin Group (USA) Inc.,
375 Hudson Street, New York, New York 10014.
BERKLEY SENSATION and the "B" design are trademarks belonging to Penguin Group (USA) Inc.

PRINTED IN THE UNITED STATES OF AMERICA

10 9 8 7 6 5 4 3 2 1

*This book is dedicated to all of you who
are going through a rough time in your life.
May you find your way to a Happy Ever After.*

*And to my son,
Andrew,
the light of my life.*

ACKNOWLEDGMENTS

I'd like to express my deepest gratitude to all my dearest friends who stood by me and offered me comfort in my time of need. Particularly my editor, Cindy Hwang. My critique partners Elizabeth Laiche, Kathleen Nance, and Maureen Krail. Leslie and Shirley Ferdinand, aka Christine Holden. Judy Cvitanovic, Marie Rihner, and Kathy Linam. And my dearest family. I am blessed with your presence in my life.

Chapter 1

New Orleans
Present Day

CLAIRE Peltier buzzed in her brother, Nick, un-
locked the door of her French Quarter apartment,
leaving it ajar for him, and then ambled to her kitchen to
refill her wineglass. She knew she'd have to face Nick
sooner or later. She just hadn't expected it to be this soon.

She poured another glass of Chardonnay and took a
good swallow. The cool liquid slid comfortably down her
throat and settled warmly in her gut. Thus fortified, she
stood underneath the archway that separated her kitchen
from the living room, waiting to greet her brother.

"Scott just called me," Nick said as soon as he shut the
door behind him.

"Well, hello to you, too. It's good to see you again."

He bent his six-foot-four quarterback body over her not
so diminutive five-foot-eight frame and kissed her cheek.

Then he stepped back and was all business again. "Why, Claire?"

"Why what?" She moved past him and into her living room with a calculated nonchalance. Damn Scott! Did he have to run to her brother not an hour after they parted ways? She was still trying to come to terms with her decision; she didn't need to explain herself to Nick now.

"You know exactly what I'm talking about." Nick followed her. "Why did you call off the wedding? What the hell happened?"

She sat on the sofa, curled her feet underneath the skirt of her dress, and waited for Nick to sit across from her so they could calmly talk. He didn't sit, he paced. She sipped her wine. "It just wasn't meant to be."

"When did you realize that? You haven't said a word to me about having doubts. In fact, you were quite ecstatic—" He stopped abruptly. "Wait a minute! Did Scott change his mind about the in vitro procedure?"

Scott's willingness to seek out alternative methods of conception had been the catalyst of Claire's decision to accept his marriage proposal. A thirty-three-year-old, reproductive-challenged, longing-for-a-family woman couldn't miss such an opportunity. Besides, for a little while, she had truly believed that a happy-ever-after, a certainty only in romance novels and the fate of a lucky few, could be within her grasp.

She should've known better than to believe in fairy tales.

"No, he didn't change his mind," she said.

"Then I don't understand what's going on. Scott is a great guy, Claire. You've said so many times. He's the first guy you've been truly serious about. He adores you. And I thought you cared for him. What happened?"

It was obvious Scott and Nick had bonded. That hadn't happened with any of the other men in her past. Maybe because none of her other relationships had lasted this long—six months, an eternity in her dating book. Still, she wasn't about to marry a man just because her brother liked him.

"That is exactly why I cannot marry him."

"Because he adores you? Or because you care for him? Please, explain that logic to me."

Claire rose to her feet. She was going to get a crick in her neck looking up at her brother, and it was obvious his nervous energy wouldn't allow him to sit and relax.

"I do care for him," she said. "But I don't love him as he deserves to be loved. Sooner or later he'll feel cheated and resent me."

"So you decide not to even try? Shouldn't he be given a choice? You know, he might not share your romanticized idea of love. Men don't think that way."

She spun around to face him. "Oh, Nick, that's a bunch of bullshit, and you know it. You either love someone or you don't. You can't fake it. You can't delude yourself into believing the feeling is there when it's not. It's the same for men and women."

"And when did that revelation come over you? Before or after you agreed to marry him?"

"Whose side are you on anyway?" Claire whirled and found her way to the small balcony overlooking the street. She wrenched the French doors ajar and stepped onto the patio. Nick was her brother. He was supposed to offer her support, not question her decisions. It wasn't as if she had set out to deliberately deceive Scott. She had sincerely believed they could be happy together.

And they probably could have, had the dreams not returned.

Hands gripping the ornate iron rails, she gulped in the sweet fragrance of the potted honeysuckle vine. The scent often took her to the edge of some dormant memory that always remained stubbornly aloof.

Just like the man in her dreams—the culprit in this whole mess.

"You know I'm always on your side," Nick said, having followed her outside. "I just want to make sure you're not making the biggest mistake of your life."

She pivoted. She knew her brother loved her, that he cared for her happiness like no one else. He was just being overprotective. "Things don't always go our way."

Nick expelled a loud breath. "I've been there for you every time a relationship of yours falls apart. Hell, I've had some falling-outs of my own, and you've been there for me as well. I respect your right to live your life on your terms, but knowing how much you want a family and a child, and knowing you care about Scott, I'm a little baffled you've turned him down."

"I can't marry him," she insisted.

"Okay, then please tell me that your change of heart has nothing to do with your dream man."

Her silence was answer enough. Nick knew as well as she what lay between her and her happiness.

"Damn!" He shot his fingers through his thick blond hair.

Greek god, she called her brother in fun. In contrast she was as dark as a witch, albeit a benign one, she liked to think. Nick looked just like their mother. A mother he never got to know well since she died when he was two, but Claire remembered her and missed her every day of her life.

"I thought you weren't having the dreams anymore."

For a few months her nights had been blessedly empty of his presence, lulling her into a false sense of control. It hadn't lasted. "A week ago the dreams returned with a vengeance."

"Wasn't that when you and Scott decided to get married?" Nick asked.

Claire nodded. "Excellent timing, wasn't it?"

"Son of a bitch!" Nick muttered.

"At first I tried to ignore him in hopes he'd go away." Not that that tactic had worked before, but she was determined not to let the man in her dreams ruin her plans again. "But with each subsequent dream I began to weaken and doubt the wisdom of marrying a man I care about but feel no passion for. Oh, Nick. I want to feel this tightening in my stomach when I look at the man I'm going to marry. I want the hairs on the back of my arms to bristle when he touches me. I want my heart to sing when he's around, and I want to miss him when he's not. I don't have any of this with Scott. Never did, not from the very first moment."

Her brother seemed to have no answer for that.

But she knew she had it all with the man in her dreams. She emptied her wineglass. Every relationship she'd had paled in comparison to the emotions her dream man elicited in her. A passion so intense, she usually awoke from the dreams trembling with need, her heart wrenching with sorrow.

Were she to marry Scott, how could she explain to him that her nights were filled with dreams of another man, and her days with thoughts of him?

She couldn't do it. It wasn't fair. It wasn't right.

"Claire, I hear what you say, but this man is not real. He can't return your passion. He can't give you the child you so long for. He's a dream, maybe even a memory from a past life, as you believe, but he doesn't exist." Nick stressed the last words. "You're trading a sure future for a past you can't reclaim, and you're not even sure it truly happened."

"I know," Claire whispered, unable to deny the truth of her brother's words. Yet the man who haunted her nights and unraveled her life, the man she knew nothing about but could never forget, was more than a dream to her. She had only hazy recollections of him and no clear memory of their past association, but she had a soul-deep certainty it was crucial she resolve the mystery of their past together.

Only by setting the past to rest could she free herself from the shackles of his haunting.

This man held the keys to her heart, and she had a mind to ask for them back.

"Knowing he's a shadow of my past doesn't make him any less real to me. I can't forget him, Nick," she all but shouted. "I can't ignore him, nor can I dismiss his interference in my life."

"What you can't do," her brother retorted, "is let this man ruin your life."

"What do you want me to do? He's not going away. My only chance to wrest control over my life is to find a way to exorcise his memory and delete him from my mind and my heart."

"And how do you plan to do that, when you've tried before and failed?"

Frustration knotted her insides. Of course, Nick was right. She'd gone through hypnosis, life regression, medium séances, anything that she thought could help her shed some light on the man's identity, on her past life, but nothing had worked. "I must have missed something. There must be something I can still do."

"I need a drink." Nick marched back inside her apartment, and Claire followed him. While he headed for the small mahogany bar that had belonged to their father, she went to the kitchen and poured the rest of the Chardonnay into her glass. She returned in time to see her brother swirl a couple of ice cubes in the two fingers of bourbon he'd poured in a crystal tumbler. He took a good swig before turning to face her. "Maybe your ghost could help you."

"Ha! You mean the ghost who has visited me since I was a child, and who has never, ever, spoken a word or given me any indication why she comes to me at all?"

"It's not as if you have many options left."

Claire snorted. "Yeah, I can ask her, when I see her, if I

see her again. It's not as if I have any control over when she comes to visit or how long she stays. In fact, I have no control over anything in my life anymore," she cried.

Nick pulled her into his arms, trapping her in a bear hug that almost always made her feel like a small child even though she was nearly eight years his senior. "You're not alone, Claire. Everything will be all right."

Claire smiled sadly against his chest. Those were the exact words she used to tell Nick when he was a little boy and would wake up in the middle of the night, crying out for their mom.

He was right. She was not alone. But this was her problem, and she was going to find a way to resolve it and regain control of her life.

THE DRIZZLE TURNED INTO A DOWNPOUR, PELTING THE French doors with the force of a hurricane. Nick had left a while ago, before the rain began, and Claire stood alone in her living room, watching the water sluice down glass windows.

She was emotionally and physically exhausted and, after consuming a whole bottle of wine, a little tipsy as well. Still, she delayed going to bed, knowing the dreams would come and overwhelm her with emotions, leaving her drenched with sorrow come morning.

Emotions she just didn't know how to deal with.

Maybe a bath would help her relax. Do what the wine had not. She put down her empty glass on the coffee table, ignored the high heels she'd flung off her feet when she'd returned home earlier from her confrontation with Scott, picked up her beloved book of medieval poems, and crossed the scarred pinewood floors to the bathroom.

Coco lay on the windowsill. The stray was so big that she looked more like a poodle than a cat. Claire was surprised to see her; she'd been missing for days. But that was Coco's way. She'd appeared on her doorstep one day months ago and invited herself in. She stayed for a few days and then disappeared, only to return days later. Claire had no idea how she got out or came back in, as the doors and windows were always locked, but Coco found a way.

Tonight, she must have come in with Nick.

Claire wasn't exactly a cat person, but she kept a litter box, food, and water for Coco in the kitchen, just in case. Of course, the cat never limited herself to one spot in the apartment, though she did favor windowsills.

"I see you're back," Claire said, ruffling the long, pristine white fur with her fingers. Coco purred, stretched, and then shot a displeased green gaze at Claire when she quit stroking.

Unknown pedigree but a whole lot of attitude, Claire thought, amused, as she turned on the faucets of her antique, claw-footed tub and dropped in a good wallop of honey-scented bubble bath. While the tub filled, she set the leather-bound, ancient-looking tome on top of a small marble-top table. The book wasn't a first edition, though she'd paid dearly for it; its value to her derived from a more singular worth. On its pages, French medieval poems and their modern translations lay side by side like ancestors' portraits in some fancy historical home.

Fluent in French—she earned her living as a translator—and fascinated by medieval history, Claire enjoyed wrapping her mind around a language no longer spoken, a world no longer in existence. A world that enthralled and excited her imagination. A world that at times seemed oddly familiar.

And why not? She could've just as easily strolled down narrow cobblestone streets in a time long past as she ambled the modern streets of the French Quarter now. Savored the sweet-tart taste of a pomegranate at a medieval market as she did at the New Orleans French Market of present time.

Who could disprove reincarnation? Who could say for certain that past and present weren't connected segments inscribing an ever-changing future?

What more proof did she need of having previously lived with the man in her dreams than the fabric of her soul being permanently marked by him?

Still, it was one thing to be shaped by past experiences and an entirely different thing to be eternally caught in a vortex of past mistakes.

Something had gone terribly wrong between them; Claire was sure of that. Conjectures and speculations swirled in her mind, but as always, no answers came afloat.

Knowledge was power, free will the force that moved the world forward. If she could figure out what dramatic event chained her to the man who haunted her dreams, she might be able to let go of the past. Find a future for herself.

The problem remained, however. How was she to get her answers?

Well, she wouldn't get them tonight, for sure.

Quickly, she undressed, piled her hair on top of her head, and turned off the faucets of her almost overflowing tub before gingerly stepping in. Warm, sudsy, honey-scented water lapped softly against her body as she eased down and leaned back against the cool porcelain. She deeply inhaled the perfumed steam, and, closing her eyes, sought the emptiness of mind that evaded her of late.

What she found was the blurred image of the man who haunted her nights, flashing urgently behind her closed eyelids. Her heart swelled with the same intense, conflicting emotions that made her body quiver every time she dreamed of him. Passion. Anger. Sorrow.

Tension mounted in her gut again. There was no ignoring him. Instead of opening her eyes to chase the image away, she shut them tighter, seeking him out, willing her heart to stop aching and her mind to start remembering.

After long moments of heart and mind willfully disobeying her, all that came to her was the same vague image and overpowering emotions.

Nothing would change just by wishing it. She needed more powerful tools.

Resigned she'd find neither answers nor relaxation tonight, Claire finally opened her eyes and reached for her beloved book in search of distraction. Her body prickled with sudden awareness; her heart skipped a beat and then tumbled into a reckless pounding. The ghost who had visited her since she was a child brazenly stared at her from underneath the archway of the bathroom door.

As the first bout of alarm subsided, the uneven beat of her heart settled on a steady yet still too rapid rhythm. Claire took time and great care in lowering her book to the table while she gathered her emotions.

She shouldn't be frightened by the ghost's appearance. Not after so many years of innocuous visits. But although she had never felt threatened, the sporadic and unexpected visits never ceased to unsettle her.

However, to have someone, ghost or not, pop up uninvited, unannounced, and in the most private of moments was hardly acceptable.

And, until tonight, it had never happened. Before, the ghost had only briefly appeared in the early hours of the morning and then disappeared just as quickly.

Why was tonight different? Had the ghost heard Nick's suggestion that Claire question her about the man in her dreams?

Would she have the answers Claire so desperately sought? Would she share them?

Determined not to miss this opportunity, Claire reached for a thick towel, covering herself as she rose. When she turned to get out of the tub, she gasped. The ghost stood no more than two feet away, closer than she had ever come before.

Knee-deep in water, holding the towel tight against her breast, Claire stared into her deep blue cornflower eyes, startled by the vibrant color. The ghost had always appeared washed out, faded to a smudged gray. Tonight she couldn't look more real. Glorious red-sprinkled golden hair fell in incandescent waves to her waist. Looking to be in her thirties, the ghost wore a long gown in an outdated style.

A strong sense of familiarity took hold of Claire. They had met before, were somehow connected; their paths had crossed at one time. Why else would the ghost visit her?

"Who are you?" Claire asked.

There was no answer, but a strong sense of urgency, much like what Claire had felt last night in her dreams, skittered down her spine. Something was definitely different tonight.

Her heart racing with possibilities, Claire insisted, "Why do you visit me? Do you know the man who haunts my dreams?"

No answer was forthcoming, and yet the ghost didn't disappear, either. Claire shifted in the cooling water, her body shivering with cold and awareness. In all the research she'd done on ghosts, one theme had popped up: there was always a reason for such apparitions. As a spiritual being, her ghost was surely privy to otherworldly matters and very possibly to Claire's past life. If only Claire could find a way to communicate with her.

She looked so real, not at all like a ghost. Daringly, Claire lifted a trembling finger and slowly brought it close to the ghost's face. For a moment she just let it hover there, but before she panicked or lost courage, she pushed through the ethereal form.

Like breaching a winter fog, a chill covered Claire's body. An unearthly feeling possessed her, but if her life depended on it, she couldn't move or avert her gaze from the woman's.

Deeper and deeper she was pulled into the cerulean depths, until she was surrounded by the brilliant color. Slowly, like a dimming light, the sparkling blue faded and darkened until it blackened into nothingness. Trapped inside the pitch-dark, Claire trembled, her breath coming in gasps, until a lone light appeared, and then another, and another. Hundreds of flickering lights surrounded a circle of inlaid stones on a flagstone floor, like candles on a birthday cake, casting shadows on the meandering path. In the center, a man knelt, as if praying.

Claire's whole body jerked. Sensing her presence, the man lifted his gaze in her direction. With the force of a hurricane, her heart slammed against her ribs, robbing her of breath. It was him! The man who haunted her dreams! Even if she had never seen his face clearly, her soul *knew* it was him.

Questions blared in her mind, as if a thousand voices spoke in unison. Her mouth opened. She wasn't sure whether to speak or scream. Before she could utter a single sound, the vision disappeared.

Back again in her home, in her bathroom, weak-kneed and unsettled to her core, Claire stumbled until her rubbery legs gave away, and she perched on the edge of the tub.

Never had she seen him outside the realm of her dreams.

Breath caught in her throat. She struggled to make sense of the vision. Unlike her past hazy recollection of him, she could clearly see his face in her mind's eye. Dark hair framed a strong, manly face. His eyes were just as dark, though she couldn't tell their exact color. His generous, sensual mouth slanted in a hard line.

Not an easy man, not a happy man, but a man with a mission.

With the brief but powerful vision clasping her heart in a vise, Claire was surprised to find the ghost still there, now back again under the archway. She stared at Claire as if daring her to deny what had just happened.

Claire was beyond doubting, though with the exception of the clear lines of his handsome face, she'd learned nothing more of him. Why had everything come to her in bits and pieces? Why wasn't the entire truth revealed to her at once?

A sudden motion distracted Claire. She watched, entranced, as a magazine lifted itself from the rack, as if moved by an invisible hand, and came to rest at the foot of the tub. Its pages flipped of their own volition until they stopped, and the magazine lay flat open, glaring up at her. Claire hunched over and stared at the picture of a circle of stones inlaid on a flagstone floor eerily resembling the one in the vision.

Above it, the caption read: "The Ancient Labyrinth of Chartres Cathedral, France."

If Claire were inclined to faint, she'd have lost consciousness right then and there.

Dazed, struggling to absorb the sudden revelation, questions crowding her mind, again she sought the ghost. The woman was no longer there. She was alone.

Her gaze returned to the magazine, her path clearly delineated before her. Would she have the courage to tread it?

Could she dare not to?

Chapter 2

Normandy, France
The Year of Our Lord 1202

A plume of dust rose from the ground on the unseasonably warm spring day to settle on Aiden Delacroix as he rode down the familiar path toward home. Over the hills where his castle had stood for two hundred years and his family had ruled for generations, dark clouds hovered, hastening the falling night.

For a brief moment, Aiden's heart filled with pride. He had recovered his birthright ten years ago, but the terrible loss he incurred in regaining possession of the castle and the uncertainty of its fate marred what little joy he felt.

Had he known the bleak future that awaited him when he spurned Cherise to wed Jeanne would he still have done it? The question haunted him. Though, in verity, how could he have ignored his vow to his dying father, his duty to his family, his innermost desire to recover what was rightfully his?

Nay, he could have chosen no differently. His oversight had been to expect Cherise to understand. Instead, she refused the only role he could offer her in his life—that of his paramour—and demanded what he could not possibly give her. The path she chose not only shattered her life but destroyed Jeanne's and changed his fate forever.

The bitter reality choked him like bile.

Villagers pouring in from the fields caught his attention, distracting him from his fruitless rumination. Naught would change by dwelling on the past. The future was all that mattered, however uncertain it was.

That he might be the last Delacroix to live within the walls of his beloved castle mattered little to others but meant everything to him. He had sacrificed much to recover it, had lost much to keep it. He could not bear the thought it had all been in vain.

Urging his horse forward, he rode through the narrow streets of the small village resting at the foot of Delacroix Castle. From within the smattering of huts, the tantalizing scents of cooked food drifted in the air, making his mouth water. He envisioned women toiling over cooking fires, awaiting their husbands' return from the fields at the end of the day. Mothers appeared in doorways, calling their young offspring home before night fell and the coming rain began its downpour. The children duly ignored their calls in hopes of stealing yet another play, another run, another laugh out of the dying day.

Aiden's own desolate reality seared his heart like a branding knife. There were no children eagerly awaiting his return, no wife to offer him comfort. Would he be eternally condemned to witness life from a distance, like a prisoner peering through the narrow slit of a cell window?

Fighting the dejection that held his heart with an iron fist, Aiden turned his back on the merry tableau of everyday life and headed for the iron-fortified wooden gates of his castle. The sentries atop the gates' towers signaled to the guards on the ground to open them for him, and Aiden entered the bailey.

He met the inquiring gazes of his men with a blank expression. No need to herald to all and sundry the failure of his mission. Everybody already knew no woman in Christendom was willing to become his wife.

Longing for a hot bath to wash away the dirt of the road and ease his weariness, Aiden approached the stables and, in silence, handed his mount to the groom. He swung a leather satchel over his shoulder, and crossed the bailey on foot, anticipating food that consisted of more than hard bread, jerked meat, and the weak ale of his travels.

The first sight that welcomed him as he entered the torch-lit great hall was of Meredith, Cherise's sister, lurking in the shadows, as usual. Immediately, she spun and disappeared in a flurry of drab black skirts and veils.

Never absent, guilt stabbed at Aiden.

He needed not Meredith's presence to remind him of what he had lost and how he had lost it. That fateful day had been reenacted in his mind a thousand times already, and as long as he drew breath he would never forget the heat searing his face and the acrid smell of burnt wood from the ruins of what once had been Cherise's home, the sight of the grieving Meredith kneeling by the shrouded body of her dead sister, her sobs piercing his ears.

He remembered standing there, unable to muster the courage to pull the covering aside, not bearing the thought of seeing Cherise's charred remains, when Meredith had quietly uttered the words that would haunt him forever.

"She chose death over living without you."

A grief so strong it threatened to rip his heart apart had brought him to his knees then. A grief that even today, ten years later, still coiled tightly inside of him.

Grief and the devastating sense of failure. He had failed Cherise; he had failed Jeanne; he could not fail his family as well.

Despite Meredith's accusations, despite Cherise's own parting words the day before her death—that she would rather die than accept his decision to wed Jeanne—Aiden still refused to accept that she had chosen such a fate for herself.

Intent on setting aright what could never be righted, he had kept the truth of Cherise's demise to himself, thus affording her a Christian burial.

Morally obligated to provide for Meredith, he had brought her into his castle, where she spent her days quietly laboring in the herb garden and her nights curled on a pallet in an obscure corner. Utterly devastated by Cherise's death, she had taken a vow of silence and lurked about the castle, verily as dead as her own sister.

Meredith's refusal to look at him on the rare occasions they crossed paths could either be perceived as silent accusation or unrelenting grief.

Aiden knew not which, but both weighed heavily on him.

Sudden movement dragged him out of his reverie. Realizing he still stared at the empty spot where Meredith had stood moments ago, he pushed his feet forward. The great hall was empty but for Jasper, his late wife's younger brother, sitting at his table.

A weary sigh escaped his lips. *Mère de Dieu!* Would the welcoming cheer ever cease?

Not bothering to disguise his displeasure, Aiden strode to the table, dropped his leather satchel to the floor, and then sank into the lord's chair. Since no female dared approach him, a male servant brought him a chalice of wine, which he gulped down his parched throat before he turned to Jasper. "What brings you back? I thought I had seen the last of you three years past."

Wearing his eternally mocking grin, Jasper sipped Aiden's good wine. "That might have been your wish, but fortune has not been exactly kind to you, has it?"

Aiden resisted the temptation to wipe off Jasper's grin with one swipe of his backhand. "Perchance fortune will grant me this one wish: May your visit be brief so I can be spared of your maddening presence."

Jasper's hand shot to his heart in mock distress. "Why, Brother, such hostility toward your only kin."

"We are not kin!"

"Kin by law," Jasper pointed out, unruffled. "Not that I am any more joyful about it than you are. Still, I am the closest to kin you shall ever have, since you are gaining in years with no apparent heir in sight." He paused, mockingly examining Aiden. "How old are you? Past the halfway mark of life, for certain. So little time left . . ."

Aiden ignored the jab. He might not be as young as Jasper, but at ten and twenty he still had much life left in him. God willing! And yet, the truth of his inability to find a wife and beget an heir frustrated him beyond words.

He would not discuss his woes with Jasper. The young man was well aware of his quandary. "Shall we set aside this foolish banter and speak of what brings you here so you can be on your way, hopefully back to England?"

Jasper shrugged. "As you wish." He handed Aiden a parchment bearing the king of England's seal. "In deference to our kinship, King John has allowed me to personally deliver his orders."

Dread filled Aiden. Few good tidings came from kings.

"Concerned with the future of his Norman lands," Jasper continued as Aiden opened the sealed parchment and scrutinized the document. "And considering your family's troubled history with the Plantagenets, King John thought it wise to ensure Delacroix Castle does not fall into

French hands upon your eventual demise. Which I am certain could happen at any moment in these perilous times."

Aiden lifted his gaze from the parchment for a brief moment. Was Jasper threatening him? He would not dare! But Jasper wore the same idiotic expression of sarcasm that often reminded Aiden of a court jester. Surely a clever disguise, if that was his will.

"As you can read—you can read, can you not?" Jasper's eyebrows rose in mockery.

Ignoring the insulting question, Aiden returned his attention to the document.

"King John has sanctioned my claim to Delacroix in the eventuality you beget no legal offspring of your own. Meanwhile, while I am in Normandy, he asks that you extend your welcome to my person and my men and prepare for your sovereign's visit within a few weeks' time."

Wanting to crush the parchment into pieces, Aiden rolled it with care. Thrice his life had been at the mercy of a king's whims. The first time he was a mere boy. Over false allegations of treason, King Henry—John's father—had awarded Delacroix Castle to Jasper's family. Devastated by the humiliation and loss, Aiden's father's heart had given out, leaving Aiden with the duty to reclaim their honor and recover what was rightfully theirs. As the gates of his home had shut behind his back, Aiden swore he would do so.

Years later, when Richard, another of Henry's sons, succeeded his father to the throne of England, he returned Aiden's birthright with the caveat that Aiden wed Jeanne and foster Jasper, thus in a manner wont to kings, appeasing two warring families.

Now, King John threatened to revert to the injustice of yonder years. John's endorsement of Jasper's claim was no surprise. Unlike Aiden, who kept himself out of the political intrigues of the English court and was content to remain at his Norman holding, Jasper had entrenched himself at the king's side, doubtless hoping to use his close association to wrestle Delacroix from Aiden.

Obviously, Jasper's ploy had yielded the results he sought.

The mere thought of Delacroix falling into the hands of the very family that had stolen it from him in the first place drove a spike through Aiden's heart. When he wed Jeanne, he had accepted their blood would mix in the begetting of a Delacroix heir. He had done so in deference to Jeanne, a gentlewoman, whose prompt acceptance of their forced marriage and kindness toward him upon Cherise's death had greatly endeared her to him. And because he had had no choice.

"In your absence—" Jasper cut into Aiden's thoughts with his customary entitlement.

Bristling, nonetheless, Aiden listened.

"—I took the liberty of occupying my old bedchamber and settling my men in the castle's men-at-arms quarters."

"I see you have wasted no time making yourself at home."

Jasper stiffened. "Delacroix *is* my home. It belonged to my father when I was born, and it shall return to me eventually. It is only a matter of time."

"Only your fanciful mind could conceive that Delacroix might one day belong to you. There is no legitimacy to a claim made by a usurper."

Jasper leaned over the table. "Deny it all you wish, Aiden, but you know as well as I that this castle is as much my birthright as it is yours. And with no legitimate heir in sight—"

"You forget I am not dead yet and can still beget an heir." Aiden knew fully well the folly of such an assertion.

Without a wife there could be no legal heir. He could not even beget a bastard unless he forced himself upon a woman, which he was loath to do. And even thus, the king would not accept an illegitimate child. Aiden had not missed the carefully worded "legal heir" in his decree.

Jasper let out a derisive laugh. "Have you found a witless lady willing to risk her own life to wed you? After what happened to poor Jeanne? And to Lady Marian, who cloistered herself in a nunnery after her unfortunate brief association with you?"

His heart constricted at the thought of Jeanne's death, his face burned with the remembered humiliation of Lady Marian's choice, and his cheek twitched with annoyance that Jasper spoke the truth. No woman with any wits about her would consider becoming his bride.

Particularly damning were the whispered tales that Cherise's ghost haunted him and any woman who dared become his wife. Many thought the stories had proved true when his second bride, Lady Marian, fled the castle in abject horror on their wedding day, before the marriage was even consummated.

To Aiden's utter chagrin and disgrace, Lady Marian's father had demanded and obtained an annulment of the marriage from king and pope.

In a matter of months, he had become the mockery of all of Christendom.

"It is as I thought," Jasper said at Aiden's silence. "You have no prospective bride; therefore no legal heir in sight. Delacroix shall be mine. A just reward, I am certain, for what that whore of yours did to my sister."

"Mind your tongue, Jasper. Cherise had naught to do with Jeanne's death." Aiden refused to lay this added sin on Cherise's soul, though whether for her benefit or his own, he was uncertain. However, as the only witness to the incident,

Jasper's word had been widely accepted as the truth. But why should Aiden believe the man? In verity, a case could be made for Jasper lying to further his claim to Delacroix. Even the tales of Cherise's ghostly appearances could be attributed to Jasper. Many claimed to have witnessed them, but not Aiden. He had only felt her presence in haunting dreams.

"I always knew you cared not a whit about my sister, even though it was through her that you recovered Delacroix Castle, but that you have the temerity to defend the whore who caused her death is revolting. May Cherise burn in hell for all eternity!"

Aiden's fist met Jasper's face with a sickening thud. Chair and man fell to the rush-covered stone floor. Shaking, Aiden glared down at him. *Mère de Dieu!* The man drove him witless. Was it not enough he had to bear his insufferable presence? Must Jasper taunt him at every turn? Remind him constantly of what he had lost?

The few servants about halted what they were doing, momentarily stunned by the altercation between Aiden and Jasper. At Aiden's glare, they promptly returned to their duties. The hostility between the two men was common knowledge—the years Jasper spent fostering at Delacroix had been years of cold and silent animosity—but rarely had it come down to fist fighting.

Jasper slowly pulled himself up. He wiped the blood from the corner of his mouth with his thumb. His lips twitched in a sick grin as if he had expected and relished Aiden's loss of control. "I wonder what vexes you most," he said, "the loss of your whore or your bastard child. Surely not your wife's death—poor Jeanne meant naught to you."

Aiden froze, ignoring Jasper's continuing diatribe. He thought no one knew about the child. "You spout foul nonsense, Jasper."

"Indeed? You mean to say that whore of yours played you for a fool?"

Aiden winced at Jasper's repeated disrespectful address of Cherise, but short of killing him—and the thought became more palatable with each moment Jasper remained in his presence—he was powerless. Aye, he had known about his unborn child. In verity, that knowledge was what gave him hope that Cherise had not taken her own life. He could not fathom her doing so while carrying their child in her womb. The guilt would be too much to bear.

"However befitting and pleasurable that thought is." Jasper broke into Aiden's thoughts. "I know it to be untrue, for surely Cherise would have revealed her secret to you as she had no qualms doing to Jeanne on the eve of your wedding. What she did not count on was that Jeanne, for reasons I cannot fathom, and you, for your own less than gallant motives, would still go through with the wedding, despite her revelation."

Aiden had not known Jeanne was aware of Cherise's plight. That she did and still went through with the wedding only added to his remorse. Jeanne had been another victim in this sad tableau.

A throbbing pain began at Aiden's nape where his headache always started. This one promised to be of great proportion. He cupped his neck with one hand and rubbed it forcibly.

His gaze rested on Jasper, who watched him intently, and he stiffened, his hand falling tó his side. He had no intention of giving Jasper the satisfaction of knowing his words affected him in any manner. "You speak nonsense."

"Indeed? You are a fool to delude yourself. When Cherise's revelation produced no reaction from Jeanne, she warned my sister not to go through with the wedding. Weeks later, Cherise's ghost pushed Jeanne down the stairs. I shall never forgive you for having brought Cherise into my sister's life. And I take great pleasure in knowing her wretched soul suffers greatly in hell. I will bide my time till the day I shall take possession of Delacroix, mayhap whilst you are still alive. It would be a fitting reward indeed."

Waiting for no answer, Jasper stalked out of the great hall.

His insides trembling, Aiden stood precariously on his feet. He had meant for none of this to happen, and yet he was the catalyst of much pain and suffering. Jeanne, Cherise, his unborn child.

He had much to atone for.

Struggling to control his emotions, he left the great hall for his bedchamber. Inside, the lit hearth sparkled and crackled, but no warmth reached his heart.

He fell to his knees. Cold from the stone floor seeped into his body, but he ignored it. After a while, he lost the feeling in his legs, but he did not rise. He remained prostrate in fervent prayer until exhaustion overcame him.

Hours later, he was awakened by the light of dawn filtering through the shuttered window. Someone had stoked the fire and added logs while he slept on the floor. Shame careened through him that he had been seen like this. He despised knowing he was feared by some. He could see it in their eyes, in the way they carefully avoided being around him, the way they crossed themselves when they saw him.

Delacroix used to be such a happy place. Laughter had filled its walls when he was a child. He remembered minstrels and troubadours enlivening the evenings, visitors and guests filling the great hall. He remembered his mother's merry singing while she occupied herself with her daily chores. He remembered sticking to his father like a tick to a horse, delighting in learning a lord's duties, proud to know Delacroix would be his to command. His to pass on to his children as it had been passed on for generations before him.

Nowadays Delacroix resembled a mausoleum. People skulked in dark corners, speaking in quiet whispers, as uncertainty and unease filled its walls. Visitors avoided the place like the plague. And who could blame them? Who would wish to spend the night in a haunted castle?

When had all gone so wrong? When had fate stepped in to transform his paradise into a living hell?

Aiden rose from the floor, stripped off his clothes, and performed his ablutions with cold water. The servants had left food for him, but he felt no hunger. He filled a tankard with ale, drained it, and then replenished it.

Would that he could let go of the past, but it clung to him like stench to a garderobe. Would that he could change it, but he could not.

However, whether or not forgiveness for his sins could be obtained, he would still seek it. Whether or not a bride and an heir were part of his future, he still had to believe they were.

Amends had been made in the past. Much prayer and alms had been given. But naught had changed, proving his stand with God was precarious to say the least. Could a full confession to Father Aubert aid him in his plight? And yet, remembering the old man as a most pragmatic and unforgiving priest who seemed to enjoy condemning people with much lesser sins to eternal flames made Aiden shrug off that option. The priest would surely excommunicate him instead of giving him the absolution he sought.

Had he the time, he would go on a pilgrimage to the Holy Land, but with the king arriving in a few weeks he could ill afford such a long absence, particularly with

Jasper comfortably ensconced inside his castle. He could not easily dismiss the veiled threat in Jasper's words. Perchance the man would not be content to wait for Aiden's natural death to take over Delacroix Castle.

Flopping down on a chair, Aiden drained the cup again. There must be something he could do.

His weary gaze drifted until it settled on the flickering flames licking the blackened wall of the hearth. He stared at them until his eyes glazed over, until his thoughts muddled into fogginess.

And then, quite suddenly, from the depths of his mind emerged a memory.

On his last fruitless journey in search of a wife, he had stopped for the night in a small inn in Brittany. In the common chamber, he had heard a man speak with undisguised awe of the rapid and miraculous reconstruction of the *Cathédrale de Notre Dame de Chartres* after a fire had almost completely destroyed it less than a decade ago.

The man, a recently returned pilgrim from Chartres, swore that the Blessed Mother had a direct hand in such achievement, for never before had walls been erected in such a speedy fashion. Miracles were attributed to the *Mère de Dieu*, and it was believed blessings would be bestowed upon those who aided in any manner the rebuilding of the shrine. People, noble and peasant alike, flocked from all corners of Christendom, eager to pay homage to the Blessed Mother of Christ, willing to make whatever contribution they could, be that of silver, labor, or prayer, in hopes of receiving a grace.

And to facilitate the lives for those who could not undertake the perilous and arduous journey to Jerusalem, a labyrinth of stones symbolizing the journey to the Holy Land had been recently inlaid on the cathedral's floor.

Aiden leapt to his feet. For the first time in years, hope unfurled in his heart. Whether it was serendipity or destiny that such a memory had sprung to his mind at this time of need, it mattered not. It was clear, however, the path he must tread.

The Holy Land was out of his reach at this moment, but Chartres Cathedral was only a few days' ride from Delacroix. He could be there and back home in a matter of a week or so, long before the king's arrival.

Perchance all was not lost, after all.

Chapter 3

France
Present Day

THE twin spires of Chartres Cathedral dominated a sky so blue no one would say sunset was only an hour away. Claire stood on the steps before the immense portals of the cathedral's west facade admiring the beautiful end of day.

Funny, she thought with little humor, in the two weeks it took to take care of her personal and professional affairs before making this trip, not once had she doubted the wisdom of following a hunch suggested by a ghost. Not even when her brother had politely doubted her sanity, only relenting when she explained she'd be visiting a church and not some macabre center of occult science, did she hesitate.

But now that she was actually here, on the threshold of possibly unveiling her past, doubts began creeping in.

Some secrets are better left buried, her brother had warned. Claire preferred to ignore Nick's skepticism.

Surely, knowing would be infinitely better than questioning herself forever. As she saw it, even if this trip ended up being a total waste of time, she still had done the right thing by coming here.

Prepared to accept disappointment, she prayed for resolution.

And that was what made her hesitate. What if the answers didn't set her free? What if, even after learning the truth about her past, she continued to be haunted by it?

But what choice did she have? She couldn't ignore it. She had to know!

Her gaze swept the intricate carvings on the portals and the sculptures above them, resting on the majestic image of Jesus Christ above the Royal Portal. He seemed to stare straight at her, his face loving and peaceful. His right hand raised as if blessing her and welcoming her to enter His mother's domain.

Have faith! He seemed to be telling her.

Though her mystic beliefs conflicted with her Catholic upbringing, Claire understood faith. It ruled her life. Early on, she had embraced a belief in reincarnation, in the eternity of souls and the spirituality of beings, and had never regretted the path she'd chosen. In matters of faith there was no place for doubt. You either believed or you didn't. Proof wasn't required.

The vision had revealed this cathedral and the labyrinth to her; it had connected them to the man in her dreams. She would trust she'd find her answers inside. Even if the answers weren't to her liking.

Fortified, she clutched her purse under her arm and stepped forward, ascending the steps with ease. She pushed open the ancient door and strode inside. As she closed the door behind her, leaving the warm early evening outside, the temperature fell a few noticeable degrees, and darkness engulfed her. A shiver ran through her body, and she hugged herself, wishing she'd worn a light sweater instead of a scarf draped over her shoulders. Her dress had only three-quarter sleeves, and the thin material wasn't much for warmth.

She waited for her eyes to adjust to the absence of light. Shadows intersected with color from the hundred or so massive stained glass windows, filling the cathedral walls with an ethereal glow.

A group of visitors brushed past her. Claire quietly waited until they left. She'd chosen the late hour in the hopes of being alone in the church, wanting no witness to her search, not sure exactly what that would entail.

Before venturing farther, she made sure there was no one else around. She took in the impressive surroundings. The sheer height of the vaulted nave above her left her breathless. Goose bumps spread from her nape down her back as she silently stood witness to the blessed union of secular and sacred, spiritual and human, unimaginable and attainable, indelibly imprinted in every inspiring creation around her from pillars to statues to stained glass windows to stone floor.

On this site, even before the birth of Christ, people had worshipped, sought grace, offered sacrifices and gifts to their god. Faith floated in the air, crushing depths of despair and lifting it to the heights of hope.

How many souls had roamed through these walls? How many had come with a quest in their hearts? How many had found what they sought?

Would she?

From behind her, through the glorious rose window atop the western portal, the dying light from the setting sun filtered in, casting a mosaic of brilliant hues on the labyrinth on the floor.

The labyrinth of her vision! She instantly recognized it. Even the lit candles looked the same.

She had read much about the spiritual and emotional healing one could find in labyrinths. Chartres's labyrinth was re-created all over the world for people who couldn't make the trip to France. But she was here, with the real thing.

Heart thundering in her chest, Claire approached the circle of inlaid stones forming the labyrinth's pathway. Immediately she saw her ghost waiting inside, further proof she'd made the right decision in coming to France.

Relief washed over her. Claire waited for her ghost to approach her, expecting a repeat of the vision she had in her bathroom two weeks ago. Instead, the ghost turned her back to Claire and began moving down the tortuous path of the labyrinth.

Sure nothing would ever be commonplace again in regards to her relationship with her ghost, Claire eagerly followed her. As she stepped onto the first stone, a shiver careened down her body. Undaunted, she forged ahead. After only a few steps, the path veered sharply to the left, and then it veered to the right in a U-turn. The course continued in this meandering way until it reached the labyrinth's center.

Watching her every step—she didn't want to stray off the path—Claire continued on the journey countless other souls had made before her. In no time at all she neared the inner circle. Surprised, Claire glanced inside. An intense vibration emanated from the center, prickling her skin and causing the hairs on her arm to stand on end. She quickly looked for her ghost and found her still following the path a short distance away.

Obviously, the journey was far from over. As the path led her away from the center, Claire was tempted to take a shortcut and walk right in but reined in her impatience. She couldn't mess this up. It might be her only chance to find the answers she sought.

Fortunately, unlike a maze, the labyrinth had no obstacles to hinder the way, no frustrating dead ends, no wrong turns, no blinding walls or hedges. Only the certainty that, were she true to the meandering path, she'd eventually reach her destination.

Claire lowered her head again, inhaled and exhaled deeply a few times, and then resumed her trek. She forced herself to ignore the surrounding reality—the colors filtering through stained-glass windows, the sound of her sandals' heels clicking on the stone floor, the ghost slightly ahead of her. Emptying her mind of mundane preoccupations, she delved deep into her soul, seeking to awaken dormant memories of her nameless man and her past life.

A distant echo, like a thousand clamoring voices, reached her ears. Swept up in the melodious rhythm of centuries of prayers and chants, she quietly added her own to the chorus. Feeling almost weightless, she glided down the path.

Having lost conscious awareness of the passing of time, Claire wasn't sure how long it had taken her to reach the inner circle.

But then she was there. On the edge of her destiny.

The vibration from the center increased, reaching deep within her soul. The ghost beckoned. Claire breathed deeply and then took the last step into the six-petaled rose center of the ancient labyrinth.

And hopefully, to the truth she sought.

France
The Year of Our Lord 1202

The single spire of the *Cathédrale de Notre Dame de Chartres*, the highest point in town, could be seen from a great distance in the plains of Beauce, beckoning pilgrims from miles away. Keeping his gaze on it, Aiden approached the town proper. With the sun swiftly descending behind his back, he sought lodging for the night, divested himself from his hauberk—he wished to present himself to the Mother of God as a pilgrim, not a warrior—stabled his horse, and then made his way to the cathedral.

The open square enjoyed a flurry of activity, even this late in the day. People entrusted with the important task of rebuilding the shrine to the Blessed Mother went about their duty with diligent efficiency. Unsettled dust floated in the air, mingling with people and animals, but no one cared. An oxcart loaded with cut stones crossed his path, forcing him to halt momentarily. A man carrying dual pails of water on his shoulders sloshed little of the liquid as he avoided colliding with the cart and Aiden.

Two men carrying a huge piece of a stained-glass window walked before him in the same direction. The late afternoon sun pierced through the colored glass projecting a multihued prism on the dirty ground.

Aiden lagged behind, allowing the workmen to navigate the cathedral's steps. As he reached the huge open doors, a lord and his lady walked out.

"Aiden Delacroix," the man called.

Aiden immediately recognized the man as a close friend of Lady Marian's father, and, as such, a witness to Aiden's humiliating annulled marriage.

Forcing a smile to his lips, though he could do naught about the vexing heat of shame spreading up his neck, Aiden bowed respectfully, acknowledging Lord Clovis and his very young wife—his third wife, if Aiden counted correctly. The first had died trying to deliver Lord Clovis's longed-for heir, and the second had been set aside for her barrenness.

"I have wondrous tidings." Lord Clovis could barely contain his glee. "My lady is enceinte," he announced.

Aiden glanced at the petite lady's slightly rounded stomach, barely noticeable underneath her voluminous garment, and again forced himself to smile.

"May the Virgin Mary bestow her blessings on you and your child, my lady," Aiden said sincerely, bowing politely. He could not begrudge another man's fortune, however cruel a reminder it might be of his own woeful plight.

The lady shot him a sympathetic glance, and Aiden squared his shoulders in reaction. His predicament was widely known throughout Christendom—the main reason behind his difficulty to remedy it—and yet it still ached to be looked upon with pity.

"The Virgin has indeed blessed us," Lord Clovis chimed in, puffing up his chest, obviously well pleased, surely thinking himself most deserving of such grace. Aiden immediately regretted his unkind thoughts. He had no right to judge anyone. "Have you come to put your hope in her merciful hands?" Lord Clovis asked. "Lord knows it might be your only chance."

The man's voice held a hint of taunting that Aiden struggled to ignore. Before the sun set this day, the whole of Chartres, and possibly the near vicinity as well, would know of his presence here and his desperation. A cursed man was great fodder for gossip, notwithstanding however many good deeds that man might have performed in his life.

Gritting his teeth, Aiden forced himself to accept Lord Clovis's words as a gesture of goodwill and respond accordingly. "I pray she will be as merciful to me as she has been to you, my lord." Perchance Mary would find some redeeming value in his poor soul.

After a few more moments of boasting, Lord Clovis finally said his farewells. Relieved, Aiden ambled through the open doors beneath the magnificent portals of the cathedral. The smell of fresh mortar mingled with incense, and the darkness of the vault calmed Aiden. In awe, he admired the wondrous beauty of the stained glass windows bathed by the setting sun relieving darkness as no lit torch ever could. The unimaginable height of the nave reached to the heavens, as he hoped his prayer would.

Men labored in utter reverence. Though the stone structure of the cathedral had been miraculously completed in an astoundingly short time, there was still much construction yet to be done.

A few worshippers' chants resonated against the stone walls. Aiden unbuckled his sword belt and left it on the appropriate depository at the entrance. He bypassed the newly inlaid labyrinth surrounded by hundreds of flickering candles on the flagstone floor. Aiden would first pay his respects to the Queen of Heaven at the altar.

Emotion clogged his throat as he knelt before the sacred relic—the Virgin's Chemise—resting in the reliquary. Humbly he bowed his head.

He made the sign of the cross.

"Ave Maria, gratia plena, Dominus tecum . . . " He whispered the traditional prayer his mother had taught him. Then he lifted his gaze. *"Mère de Dieu!"* he prayed. "I beseech thee to find it in thy heart to look kindly upon this undeserving soul, and intercede with thy Holy Son, our Lord Jesus, on my behalf. In desperation, I come to thee to beg thy forgiveness for my many failings, thy mercy, and understanding. Queen of Heaven, watch over Jeanne, who suffered so undeservedly. In thy infinite compassion, have mercy on Cherise's soul. And if it is thy will, grant her rest in heaven and grant me the grace of a family so that I may worship thee all the days of my life."

He remained on his knees in silent prayer for a long time. Finally he rose, made the sign of cross once again, deposited his offering of silver in the donation chest, and respectfully backed out.

He approached the labyrinth feeling somewhat light-hearted. Petition given to the Holy Mother, he would continue on his quest for a family until he drew his last breath. Whether Mary would will it or not was out of his control.

As added penance, in the manner of a devoted pilgrim, he chose to follow the seemingly interminable path of the labyrinth, aptly named Chemin de Jerusalem, on his knees.

Head low, shoulders slumped with the enormity of his plight, Aiden labored down the path that at times brought him closer to its center, and at others took him farther away.

Corralling his thoughts in beseeching prayer, he shut out the presence of others around him. Ignoring the discomfort of his body, he thought of Christ's pain and loneliness on the way to the cross, his own paling in comparison.

When he reached the center of the labyrinth, the cathedral was immersed in shadows and quiet. The laborers and worshippers were gone. Alone, he remained on his knees and closed his eyes, seeking heavenly grace.

Abruptly, the overwhelming sweet scent of honey enveloped him, awakening memories and longings best left forgotten. Briefly, he savored the moment, surrendering his heart to the ephemeral joy of recalling a time in his life long gone when pleasure was still a part of his existence. Suddenly remembering where he was, Aiden opened his eyes, embarrassed at the inappropriateness of such thoughts.

Beseeching words of forgiveness died unspoken on his lips as his gaze fell on a woman of indescribable beauty who sprang from darkness into the inner circle, much like fairies were known to spring from the woods on the eve of Roodmas Day.

His heart stopped.

A torch on a nearby pillar cast light on her. In stunned silence, Aiden gawked at the exquisite dark curls cascading freely over her shoulders and down her back. A richly decorated, loosely tied veil, bright in colors of red and silver, inadequately covered her shoulders. The sleeves of her gown reached only to her elbows and the gown indecorously hugged her generous curves, slightly flaring at her hips and barely reaching her calves, looking more like a chemise than a gown. Her feet were encased in shoes of revealing thin leather straps from which peeked toenails painted vermilion!

Aiden shot to his feet.

Mère de Dieu! He had come looking for an angel of mercy. Had he found a fallen angel instead?

Whatever the answer, he knew his soul was as good as lost.

Chapter 4

CLAIRE stumbled into the inner circle of the ancient labyrinth, feeling as if she'd been unceremoniously lifted and dropped inside. Dizzy, she checked her balance and squinted against shadows broken only by the flickering lights of hundreds of candles.

Her heart drummed in her chest. Despite the darkness, her eyes had no trouble recognizing the man kneeling barely five feet away from her. Of her ghost, however, there was no sign.

Anticipation skittered down her spine as endless moments trickled by with hardly a change in the scene, frozen in one frame like a film in pause. No revelation appeared. No insight offered. No questions answered.

Disappointment clenched her insides. Would this be all she'd get?

And yet, several moments had gone by, and the vision remained.

The man knelt unmoving, unblinking, wordless . . .

And looking straight at her?

Claire shook her head. He couldn't, could he?

Shouldn't the vision work like a one-way mirror, where she would see him but he would be unaware of her presence? She was supposed to be on the outside looking in. There shouldn't be any interaction between them.

Suddenly the man shot to his feet. Startled, Claire stumbled back. She waited in silence for the vision to unfold. Nothing happened!

Impatient, she shifted in place. Desperation finally won over caution. Blood pulsing in her ears, she pushed her feet forward. A short step. When nothing changed, she dared to go farther. Another step. The clicking heels of her sandals echoed loudly and distinctly in the sepulchral silence of the cathedral, grating on her already frazzled nerves. The third and last step brought her to an arm's length of him.

This close, she easily took in his overgenerous mouth and slightly large nose—so French in appearance—with one sweeping glance. A lock of dark hair fell rakishly over his forehead, and the temptation to flip it back was difficult to resist.

She couldn't believe how real he looked.

So real that if she didn't know better she'd say she felt warmth emanating from his powerful body, that she breathed in his male scent.

Curiosity compelled her to lean closer. Would he feel as ethereal as her ghost?

Impulsively, she reached out and touched his face.

The soft prickles of a man's stubble and the warmth of live flesh seared her skin. With a choked cry, Claire jerked her hand away and stumbled back. Her vision obscured for a split second, then cleared promptly.

In that infinitesimal moment the touch had lasted, however, an image had popped up in Claire's mind, a brief glimpse of her past. A memory, not a vision: She had not seen herself locked in a tormented kiss with him behind the ancient village church; she had remembered being there, had seen him through her own eyes, had felt his mouth on hers. The moment, wrought with passion and sorrow, imprisoned her soul and shook the foundation of her very being.

God help her, but she'd swear she could still savor the taste of him, the feel of his lips over hers, his tongue in her mouth, and the sadness in her heart.

Her body shook with the power of the brief memory, her fingers tingled where their skin had touched, and her heart ached with the pain of some unnamed transgression of a past long gone.

Caught between wanting to slap the man for perceived past misdeeds and kiss him again, Claire stumbled back.

In one step, he engulfed the gap between them. Knowing she should retreat, she remained in place.

"Qui êtes-vous?" His deep voice reverberated in the empty walls of the cathedral as deeply as it resonated within her, as familiar as a childhood song long forgotten and quickly remembered.

Claire swallowed hard to dismiss the spell it already wove around her heart.

Her ghost had never uttered a word; the earlier vision of the man in her dreams had revealed only a muted scene; even the brief memory she'd had of their past together when she touched him had been devoid of sounds.

No stranger to bizarre occurrences, Claire had to accept the man standing before her was no vision, but a real person. Hadn't she felt flesh underneath her fingertips when she touched him a moment ago? Was he the reincarnation of the man in her dreams?

"Je suis Claire Peltier," she said. *"Et vous, Monsieur?"*

She didn't extend her hand for a handshake. Their brief touch had left her shaken; she wasn't ready for another dose so soon.

He squared his shoulders, looking so tightly strung he probably would snap if she did touch him again.

"Aiden Delacroix." His voice rang loud and clear, and just a tad defiant.

His name meant nothing to her, as hers seemed to mean nothing to him.

They measured each other for a few moments, one clearly expecting the other to take the next step. They were completely strangers, at least in this lifetime, and were understandably wary of each other. And yet something had drawn both of them to this place, at this time. Claire didn't believe in coincidences. They had come together for a purpose.

Whoever was most desperate would dare first exposure.

She knew how desperate she was.

What if she asked him—a man she'd just met—whether he remembered their past life together? Would he freak out like her father had when she'd told him she could see a ghost?

Claire wasn't too keen on being on the receiving end of a mocking, horrified, or worse, pitying look. And yet she couldn't miss the opportunity to find out about her past. It was just too important to her future.

She didn't have to hit him with everything at once, however. She could ease into the conversation.

"Are you here to meet someone?" she asked casually in French, since that was the language he'd first used with her. What she really wanted to ask was whether he was there looking for her. But that would come soon enough.

A reluctant nod was all she got as response.

Obviously, he was taking caution to new levels. Or maybe he was just being true to a taciturn nature.

"So am I," she offered.

His eyes narrowed with watchful interest. "Indeed? And pray tell me who do you seek?"

The odd pattern of his speech caught her attention. She wondered whether French was his native language. Foreign-born people tended to speak more formally than natives. She knew it; she worked with enough of them in her translating business.

A more direct approach might be more suitable, she decided. "I'm here looking for you," she said.

He looked disconcerted. Had she been too forward, too quickly?

"It is most unusual for a woman to speak so freely."

Claire eyed him guardedly. His antiquated thoughts and his odd choice of words raised a warning flag in her mind. Still, as a foreigner, his thoughts and notions would not always translate well. She eyed his clothing—a loose shirt over tight trousers and boots. Definitely a foreigner. "Being forthcoming might be the only way I have to find the answers I seek."

Was that wariness tightening the muscles in his jaw or only the flickering shadows?

"What answers do you seek?" he asked.

Here was her chance. "Answers to the past." She couldn't be more forthcoming without spelling it out. If Aiden had any inkling of what she was talking about, he'd give a little now.

Instead of opening up, however, his whole body tensed visibly. One hand shot through his hair until it clasped the back of his neck as if it pained him.

Definitely wariness, Claire decided.

He turned his face, and his gaze strayed beyond the confines of the labyrinth's inner circle. Hers followed.

Squinting against the shadows, Claire frowned. Weren't there pews and benches in that area of the cathedral earlier? And were those torches on the walls and pillars? The unfamiliar scent of incense and mortar made her uneasy.

"Would that I could forget the past!" Aiden's forlorn voice stole her attention and her gaze back to him.

Would that she could remember it!

Claire flinched at the thought of their opposing purposes. However, if he wanted to forget the past, that meant he did remember it. She must convince him to share what he knew. "The past has a way of haunting you unless you can put it to rest."

His bitter laughter echoed in the cavernous emptiness. "No one is more aware of that truth than I."

"Then you understand my need to know."

She could almost see his mind wrapping around the implications of opening up to a stranger. Claire had made that mistake a few times and hadn't liked the reaction she'd gotten. She'd quickly learned to know her audience before she opened her mouth.

"I understand," he said, offering no more.

Claire's heart quickened. "Then tell me what I need to know."

Aiden's breath caught in his throat.

Surely the woman's presence and her interest in the past meant she already knew about his predicament. Gossip often journeyed with the speed of an eagle, and though he had just arrived in Chartres, the town was certainly already aware of his presence and his mission. Lord Clovis undoubtedly saw to that. Aiden could almost see the man at the local inn, delighting the gossipmongers over a tankard of ale with the tales of Aiden's haunting, though he doubted there was a body alive that had not heard of it yet.

It was clear Claire sought either confirmation or denial of his plight.

He had yet to divine her purpose.

Her brazenness in touching him earlier, albeit briefly, the lack of decorum evident in her most scant attire, her boldness in questioning him proved Claire was no gentle born lady. She was neither a lord's wife nor servant. Her exquisite beauty, however, would assure her the role of a lord's paramour, regardless of the circumstances of her birth.

Perchance she was presently without protection and was looking to him for an offer. Given his predicament, she might even hope for a more advantageous arrangement than that of a leman.

Men would be more than eager to pay for her favors, to provide her with protection, but few would be willing to wed a wench who seemed to have little decorum and much brazenness. She looked to be more trouble than it was worth.

Mère de Dieu! Only he, in his desperate predicament, would seek such union.

Surely she was well aware of the fact. What desperate need drove her to risk her life, though? The violent nature of Cherise's haunting was well-known, thanks to Jasper's lies. No woman with her wits about her would chance a liaison with him.

And yet this woman had sought him out.

Aiden restrained the hope trying to unfurl in his heart. After so many disappointments, he was dubious of good fortune.

His gaze raked Claire's tempting body, and his own responded immediately, as it had at her brief touch earlier.

Not many wenches—and surely no lady—had favored him of late, and the humiliation of having to pay for physical relief had forced Aiden to disengage his heart when he occasionally took pleasure where it was offered.

And yet, despite his misfortune, he had not sought many such encounters, and he had definitely not lusted after every wench that had crossed his path, willing or nay. But from the time he first laid eyes on Claire, his heart thrummed with an excitement the likes of which he had not suffered in a long time.

Aiden locked his jaw, deliberately pushing the longing aside. He refused to dwell on the past. The future was all that mattered. His need for a bride could yield neither to mind, nor heart, nor body's desire. If Claire was willing, he would accept her without issue.

But first, he must know she was willing.

The wench was brazen enough. He would be equally bold. If perchance she was unaware of his plight, he must make her aware. As she had said, she had a need to know, and he the duty to tell.

Aware of the long pause since he last spoke, he decided to be brief and to the point. "I am haunted by a ghost." He held his breath and waited for her eyes to grow wide with abject horror and for her to flee in fright like all others had. Instead, she remained in place, enduring his stare with great fortitude.

That she had not yet fled was a good omen.

"So am I."

Aiden's mouth slacked open. He snapped his lips together. Did she mock him? "You are?" He heard himself asking like a witless fool. Had she not just said so? Perchance, he had not heard her well.

She nodded.

Her revelation stunned Aiden. He had thought his plight

singular, having never met another who shared it. Did she seek help with her ghost? Aiden almost groaned. This complicated matters considerably.

"I don't talk about this often," she said. "As you probably know, it can scare people away. So I do understand your reticence to speak about it."

The odd rhythm of her speech distracted him. There was more than a touch of foreignness about Claire.

None of that mattered. Claire was the first woman in all those long-suffering years to understand his plight, to share it in a twist of fate.

"It seems we have something in common," he said, "though I wish such fate on no one."

She shrugged. "It's not all that bad. My ghost is harmless, if inconvenient at times. In fact, she's been quite helpful lately. She's the one who led me to you."

Relief washed over Aiden. Claire's ghost was friendly. Then hope untied the knots in his innards. She had sought him out!

Mère de Dieu! Had he finally found his bride?

An uncommon bride under singular circumstances, no doubt.

Aye, Claire was no ordinary lady. It was plain she had led a life of ease. He had not missed the precious ring on her finger—gift or family treasure? She was not particularly young, but her face bore no marks, her hands no calluses, her hair, coifed carefully over her shoulders, shining like a full moon over water, her scanty gown seemed luxurious, different from any material he had ever seen. She looked hale and hearty, and surely capable of bearing children. His own mother had been of late age when she gave birth to him. His bride needed not to be of tender years.

Aiden caught himself. He was presuming much. They had yet to speak of marriage. But surely that was the reason she sought him out. He shrugged off the possibility her want might be of a different nature.

She *must* want what he wanted.

Honor, however, demanded he made certain she understood the true depth of his quandary—if she knew not already. He wished not to mislead her. But neither did he want to frighten her away. Had he any hope of an entente between them, he could not simply blurt out that his first wife had died in an accident believed to have been caused by the ghost of a former lover.

Caught in a dilemma, he hesitated. He would not purposefully put any woman in harm's way, but he was desperate for a bride, and Claire seemed to be quite capable of handling Cherise's ghost.

"I fear my experience differs greatly from yours," Aiden finally said. "My ghost bears no good will toward me or any female who dares approach me. As you can well imagine, that puts me in a rather difficult predicament."

She mulled over the meaning behind his carefully worded discourse for a brief moment before speaking. "That must create a terrible inconvenience for you."

"The matter is more dire than a mere inconvenience. It impedes me from having a wife, a family, since no woman would consider a haunted man for husband."

"I'm sorry," she said. "I understand the frustration of not having control over your life."

Was her life also out of control?

Perchance they could help each other.

Encouraged, Aiden thought it was time he made his need known. However, he suddenly found himself tongue-tied. In times past, he had presented his offer of marriage to his prospective brides' sires. It was unnerving to be forced to deal directly with the woman.

Particularly when he felt he was pleading more than offering.

He took a deep breath and let it out in a gush of air. "Claire," he said, her name gliding easily from his tongue. "As you must know, and I assume it is the reason of your presence here, I seek a bride. I am able to offer you my protection, my devotion, and my gratitude. Would you be willing to become my wife?"

Surely the incredulity on her face meant she was just overwhelmed by his offer. The shaking of her head belied that thought, though.

"I'm sorry, Aiden. Marriage is not at all what I'm looking for."

Disappointment sank like a stone in his gut.

"I have questions," she continued, "and I need answers. I was led to believe you could help me."

She was not willing.

Aiden swallowed down the knot forming in his throat. Once again, the burden of his quest to find a bride settled heavily on his shoulders.

"Can you help me?" he heard Claire ask through the haze of his discontent.

She had a need.

A need he might be able to fulfill. Could they possibly form an alliance? "What exactly is your need?"

She hesitated for the briefest of moments, then, shoulders squared, looked straight at him with what he thought was daring. "Do you remember me from your past life?"

She stood perfectly still. Her chest barely moved with her breathing, her brown, velvety eyes intent on him, her lips slightly apart. Her comely, strong-willed face, crowned with magnificent curls begging to be touched, was expressionless, but it was plain to see the worth of his answer to her. That she believed he knew her baffled him. Had their paths crossed in the past, he would never have forgotten such a woman.

His answer would surely displease her. Knowing he

would seal his fate, he nonetheless answered truthfully, "I have no memory of you."

Her crestfallen expression revealed her great disappointment. Aiden knew about disappointments. The past ten years had granted him a string of them. Their unrequited desires formed a kinship between them and he wished to offer her kind words of encouragement. Hard pressed to find any, he said simply, "Fate sometimes conspires against our hearts' desires."

She bit the corner of her lower lip. "Fate is not something I rely on. I'll find the answers I need, no matter the cost."

Admiration for her mettle filled him. That, too, they had in common—not giving up in the face of adversity. Despite being stripped of his birthright, he had never despaired of recovering it. Through his many failed attempts to find a bride, he had never ceased to pursue it.

Claire would also persevere on her quest.

"Would that I could help you," he said.

She was silent for a long moment, then a light of hope shone in her dark eyes. "Maybe you can."

Excitement crept in again. Swiftly he buried it, lest it take hold of him. "How?"

"May I touch you?" she asked.

Her request caught Aiden off guard, unlikely and inappropriate as it was. *Mère de Dieu!* Was that her need? A brief liaison in exchange for coins? Shame locked his jaw. Tempted as he was, he would not even consider it. He managed a glare of contempt at her, bitterly aware the feeling was directed at himself. At his desperate plight. At his shameful need.

Mustering his trampled pride, Aiden spat, "I have no need for the services you offer."

Comprehension swiftly dawned on her. He expected her to lower her head in shame; instead the impudent wench tilted her chin up. "That is *not* what I meant."

"What other reason is there for a woman to touch a man?"

Weariness shadowed her face. She shook her head as if trying to control her temper. She opened her mouth, closed it, and then finally said, "You misunderstand me—"

"I think not," Aiden interrupted, livid that she toyed with him, and with himself for wanting her even as he denied it.

Aye, he wanted Claire with the hunger of man who had not shared a woman's bed in a long time. But mostly, he wanted her because in the depths of his soul he sensed she could bring him the joie de vivre missing in his life.

And knowing that this lone opportunity escaped through his fingers like flowing water, he became angrier.

Mère de Dieu! He could not bear any more humbling.

He withdrew a silver coin from his coin pouch and offered it to her. "For your troubles."

Her gaze glided from his hand to his face. She looked angrier than he was. For a devastating moment, Aiden feared he had made a terrible mistake.

A fear soon confirmed.

"Shove it," she spat, sidestepping him and walking out of the labyrinth, the cathedral, and his life, leaving behind the sweet scent of honey and a knot in his throat.

Chapter 5

THE insufferable lout!

"I have no need for the services you offer," Claire mimicked as she dashed out of the cathedral. Indignation blinded her. If she'd stayed inside one more minute, she would've socked the bastard. A strong breeze slapped against her face, twirling her hair all over her eyes. She stopped and hunted for a hair clip inside her leather purse. Finding it, she gathered her curls and captured the unruly strands away from her face.

God, but it was dark outside! She flipped her gaze skyward. A cloud-shrouded moon and a starless night offered no light to guide her. The temperature had also dropped a few degrees, and there was a scent of fresh earth and rain floating in the air. A storm was approaching.

The weather should account for the unusual darkness,

but only a power outage could explain the absence of lights.

How appropriate, she thought without humor as she cautiously shifted her feet on the stone floor, seeking the steps she knew were there somewhere. Her hopes of finding out about her past life had also sunk into the black void of Aiden Delacroix's lack of answers and indignant response to her approach.

Finding the steps, she gingerly descended them; her hands sprawled ahead of her for balance and to avoid any possible obstacle.

She'd had every intention of explaining herself to Aiden. Even after he had unreasonably jumped to the wrong conclusion and accused her of prostitution. In a cathedral, of all places! But when he'd offered her that coin, as if to pay for the services he was refusing, she'd just lost it.

She stumbled on the last step, righted herself, and then slowly stomped her way through the open square. Her thoughts returned to Aiden. Damn him! Had he not been such a jerk, she wouldn't have jeopardized the only chance she might have to find out what happened in her past life.

Frustration stiffened her body. She inhaled deeply, willing herself to calm down. The smell of burning wood filled the air. Someone had lit a fire, she thought. In the distance she saw flickers of light—maybe candles?—sparsely sprinkling the darkness. She listened to the sounds in the night, oddly pastoral in quality—crickets, a dog howling, a horse whinnying.

Where were the cars? And people? The place looked deserted. Not that she could see a damn thing. Never in her life had she been in such pitch-darkness. It was unreal.

Something soft and furry brushed against her legs. Claire jumped, a scream lodged in her throat. The white furry ball disappeared in no time at all. She sure hoped it was a cat.

Her nerves beginning to unravel, she suddenly heard voices in the distance.

Thank God! People! She sharpened her attention, but couldn't discern the intermittent sounds drifting to her. She couldn't even tell from which direction they came. As the wind wavered, so did the sounds.

It was disorienting!

She swirled around, totally confused. Could she find her way back to her hotel? It was just a couple of blocks away. All she had to do was cross the open square in front of the cathedral, veer right, and follow the street beyond. If she held on to the buildings, she'd get there in no time at all. She'd better hurry up before the storm broke.

She resumed walking.

Surely she could do it, even if she couldn't see beyond her nose. She had only to keep her cool.

As she had not, earlier in the cathedral, she subtly reminded herself. She admitted Aiden wasn't the only one who had overreacted. She had, too. Why had she allowed him to rile her so? She'd acted as if he wasn't her only option to find her answers.

Of course, she wasn't herself lately. Her nerves, exacerbated by the stressful wait to come to France—the longest two weeks of her life—had her jumping out of her bones even before she ever got here. Since the day she'd decided to undertake this trip, she hadn't eaten well, hadn't slept well, and had worked overtime to clear her calendar. By the time she'd left New Orleans, she was already physically and emotionally exhausted. It was no surprise she couldn't think straight.

She'd tried to catch a nap this afternoon, soon after her arrival, but sleep had eluded her. Anticipation had tightened her guts to such a mess, and busied her mind with thoughts of the past, that she could only toss and turn on the soft bed.

She had gone through much to get here. And what had she gotten for her troubles?

Not the truth of her past in the form of a vision, but a man of flesh and blood—who rattled her cage like no other man had and who thought the worst of her but wanted to marry her.

Of course she overreacted and ran.

But *had* she stayed, her sensible side reminded her, she could've provoked another casual touch and confirmed whether the memory of that mind-blowing kiss was a fluke or the first of many to come.

Her mind and heart warred. One commanded her to return to the cathedral and face Aiden, damn the embarrassment and inappropriateness. Let him think whatever he wanted of her. She needed her answers, damn it!

The other warned her of the emotional overload on her already frazzled emotions. She couldn't forget how that brief memory had shaken her.

She glanced over her shoulder. The cathedral was a blurry mass in the darkness, but Claire remembered its magnificence.

So unlike the little church of her memory. The thought came unbidden.

Where was that place? What had her past self and Aiden's been doing behind that country church? Besides the obvious, that was. Was theirs an illicit affair gone wrong? Was that the reason behind the tremendous sorrow in her heart?

Was there a connection between that memory and Aiden's unrealistic marriage proposal? Had he had a memory as well as she had hers? If he had, he sure had kept it to himself. Besides, he had denied remembering her.

And yet he had proposed. How bizarre! But who was she to talk? Hadn't she come to France looking for answers to her past life? Compared to her quest, his desire for a wife wasn't all that odd. She understood that; she wanted a family, too.

It was the way he went about it that bothered her. Only a very desperate man would propose marriage to a stranger, but even in normal circumstances she'd be insane to consider the possibility. With all the emotional baggage she already carried, he would be the last man in the world she'd consider marrying.

Aiden was trouble; he—or better, his past incarnation—had caused her tremendous heartache, of that she was sure. She wanted nothing to do with him but to find out what happened in their past together.

And yet his disappointment at her refusal had been so evident as to be almost palpable.

A twinge of commiseration bit her.

She knew how it felt to be lonely. She wished that pain on no one. All her relationships had failed miserably on account of her unresolved feelings for a man who no longer existed. She thought of Scott with regret but knew she'd done the right thing by breaking off their engagement. Without her, he'd still have a chance to find true love.

As for her, she'd settle for finding peace.

Aiden, however, had not many options. With a less-than-friendly ghost chasing women away from him, not only was he a very lonely man, his life was even less under control than hers was.

She was sure he had tried every means possible to get rid of his ghost, as she had tried to learn about her past. No wonder he'd been reluctant to speak of his needs to her at first. Zeroed in on her own needs, she'd been less than sympathetic to his. She hadn't even given him a chance to explain why he had proposed. Had he been looking specifically for her? What or who had led him there?

Not a vision—he hadn't recognized her at all. If he looked exactly like his past self, it stood to reason she'd look like hers, too. Since she hadn't seen herself in her memory—she had remembered being there with him, had felt the emotions, and had savored his kiss—she couldn't know for sure.

Therefore, if a vision hadn't brought Aiden here, his ghost sure as hell hadn't. It was going out of its way to keep Aiden alone. Why? Were her and Aiden's ghost somewhat connected? They seemed diametrically opposed. His was interfering, hers, usually passive, was quite helpful of late.

Claire decided not to mull over this mystery. She had enough on her plate right now.

The irony of their similar situation didn't escape her, however. Happiness eluded both of them. And that was something she wanted to have in common with no one.

Stepping on a loose stone, she almost lost her balance. With a mild curse, she bent to dislodge the small rock from her sandal and to rub the sore arch of her foot. Her purse slid from her shoulder, and she fumbled to catch it, touching the rough ground. Puzzled, she stooped down and swept her hand over packed dirt. She scooped a handful of dry soil and pebbles.

She straightened herself up, rubbing the dust from her hands, and then placing her handbag firmly on her shoulder again.

Had she wandered in the wrong direction? Shouldn't she have bumped into something by now, a building, a light post, a garbage can, anything solid? Her eyes, barely adjusted to night vision, saw an indistinguishable outline of buildings in the distance. From that direction, several flickering lights moved her way. A group of people carrying candles or lanterns, she guessed. The memory of a religious procession she'd seen in her youth when she lived in France as an exchange student suddenly sprang to mind. That day had been Good Friday, though, which wasn't the case today. Who could they be honoring with a procession?

Claire wasn't up to date with saints' birthdays, but she knew May was traditionally celebrated as the month of the Virgin Mary in the Catholic Church. With Chartres being dedicated to the Mother of Jesus, it stood to reason the gathering could be a procession in her name.

Most likely the lights were people trying to find their way in the blackout, just like her.

Whatever the lights represented, though, she'd better get to them before they disappeared.

Thought springing to action, Claire moved her feet again. She'd taken only a couple of steps when she became aware that she was being followed. Uneasy, she stole a quick glimpse behind her shoulder. In the darkness all she saw was a shadow, an undefined silhouette of a person, possibly a man by his height and shape. Nervously, she moved faster.

All she needed was to be mugged in a foreign country.

Abruptly, strong hands caught her arm.

She jerked, gasping.

"Claire."

She heard Aiden's voice but couldn't respond. Dizziness overtook her. Darkness disappeared, sunlight shone in its place. She was again behind the little country church. This time it wasn't a moment of passion she remembered, but one of pain. The man in her past—an eerie twin to Aiden with the darkest blue eyes she'd ever seen—stood before her. While she waited for an answer to a question she didn't remember asking, and didn't hear a response, his handsome face turned into a mask of brittle determination, and her heart split into a thousand shards of sorrow.

Darkness engulfed her again. Claire found herself clutching Aiden's arms like a drowning person to rotten wood. Though their contact wasn't broken, the memory was gone. She felt sluggish; her head swam, as if she suffered from a hangover.

"Claire—" She heard Aiden call again as if from a great distance.

She inhaled deeply, gathering her strength. Steadying, she wrenched her hands away from him. The realization that not only had she to contend with the emotional pain from the memories but her body suffered as well, didn't sit well with her.

"It is me, Aiden. Are you ill?"

She had to fight the instincts telling her to run as fast as she could from him. However, putting distance between them would help her outrun her memories, but not her past, and surely not her pain.

"You scared the daylights out of me," she accused, stumbling back, irrationally wanting to lash out at him. She couldn't blame Aiden for a painful past he didn't even remember. But she couldn't separate him from that past either.

"I beg your forgiveness. It was not my intent to frighten you. You left the cathedral with such haste that I had no chance to apologize for my ill manner. Clearly I misunderstood your intentions."

Uncharitably, she refused to accept his apology. "You most certainly did."

"Perchance, as a way to make amends for my rudeness, would you allow me to escort you to your lodgings?"

Again, Aiden's odd French caught her ears. She had thought him a foreigner, but now she wasn't so sure. The peculiar rhythm of his speech and his odd choice of words almost reminded her of her medieval poems. Not that she would know how those ancient words would sound, but in her mind they would possess that same unusual quality.

She didn't have time to puzzle over the nuances of language. Her heart and mind were waging another battle. Why did everything concerning her past have to be so conflicted?

"It is unsafe for a woman to walk alone," he continued, still trying to convince her. "Particularly at night," he added, a little impatiently, maybe annoyed at her lack of response.

"I can take care of myself." Why was she so angry with Aiden? Apart from unwittingly scaring her, and for a temporary—she hoped—lapse in judgment in the cathedral, he had done nothing to harm her. He had nothing to do with the wrenching emotions battering her heart. He was the unknowing conduit to her memories. She couldn't fault him for that.

"Be that as it may, I insist you accept my protection."

"And who would protect me from you?" She snorted, still under the influence of the disagreeable emotions. There was a fine line between love and hatred, trust and fear. And she teetered on it like an equilibrist without a net.

"Had I wished to cause you harm," he spat, his patience clearly at its end, "I would not be debating with you whether you should accept my protection."

Claire recognized the merit in his words. In this darkness and with no one around, Aiden could overpower her without anyone even noticing. And yet, what did she know about him? He could be a murderer, a rapist, a lunatic.

Against all common sense, something told her she could trust him with her person.

Just not with her heart.

And hers was caught in a vise right now.

She rubbed her temples. "How do I know you're not sweet-talking me to lure me away for some nefarious intent?" Even to her ears the accusation sounded melodramatic and without foundation. Why did she insist? Her only explanation was that the memories had unbalanced her.

Silence fell heavily between them. Hearing her own labored breathing, she struggled to calm down. There was an almost imperceptible move from him, a shifting of shadows, and she tensed again. Had she needled him too far? Would he become violent? Suddenly she realized with perfect clarity what he was doing. His hand reached behind his neck, and he was rubbing the back of his head. A sign of annoyance, she thought. She'd seen him do it inside the cathedral.

"I have already revealed my intentions," he declared. "If you doubt my honor, then I shall vex you no longer with my presence. Good eve!" In a matter of seconds Aiden disappeared into the darkness.

Deflated, Claire stood rooted to the ground. Already regretting her rudeness, she considered calling him back. Stubbornness and pride held her tongue-tied. She knew her relationship with Aiden's past incarnation had been volatile. That fact, and the two brief memories she recovered, were coloring her strong reaction to him. There was also a very real fear lacing her action. She didn't like the fact that it appeared she had lost consciousness, even if for a very brief moment, while the memories came to her. She didn't like the thought of being vulnerable and at the mercy of a stranger. Particularly this stranger.

Still, he might be her only chance to find her answers. And she had sent him away.

She glanced over at the flickering lights, now looking even more distant—*they were moving away from her, not coming her way*—and panicked. She was in unfamiliar surroundings, in pitch darkness, with no one she knew, and she had sent away the only person who could help her.

She could slap herself silly. Instead, she rushed toward the general direction Aiden had taken. The motion forward dislodged her handbag again. She replaced it back on her shoulder and then remembered she wasn't as helpless as she'd first thought. She had means to call for help.

With a sigh of relief she slid her hand inside the bag. She carried only necessities, and a few Dove dark chocolates for emergencies. She decided to save the chocolate for later and grabbed her cell phone.

This afternoon, when she arrived in Chartres, she'd programmed her hotel telephone number on her cell. Congratulating herself on her presence of mind, she flipped the phone open. The lit screen incessantly looked for service.

Damn! Cell towers worked in a blackout. What was wrong with her phone? Just this afternoon she'd spoken with her brother, and it'd worked just fine. She moved a few steps in different directions, looking for better reception, but the phone failed to respond. She flipped it off, jammed it inside her purse, and extracted a chocolate square from it—now it was time for one. Popping it in her mouth, she decided what to do next.

It was too late to call Aiden back. Her only choice would be to find the lights and the people holding them.

STUBBORN WENCH!

"I can take care of myself," Aiden muttered as he stomped away from Claire. Did she think her haughty demeanor was protection against the evils lurking in the night?

Clutching a satchel to her—ridiculously too large for a coin pouch and impractically too small for a traveling satchel—as if it contained a treasure, and wearing a gown that revealed much and concealed naught, was certain to attract the unsavory characters she thought she could handle so well on her own.

It would serve her right to fall prey to the ruffians roaming the night in search of unsuspecting victims.

And she feared *him*? Bah!

His hand flew to his neck, and he pulled his own hair in frustration. He inhaled deeply and then let it go.

Mère de Dieu! What had him so vexed? That Claire was no damsel in distress eager for his rescue and protection? Or that she wanted naught to do with him?

He was used to women avoiding him. He utterly objected to it, but he understood their fear. Claire had no such excuse. She had rejected him for no reason other than . . .

Why had she rejected him? Was it dislike or indifference that motivated her? Aiden knew not which displeased him most.

And yet she had wanted to touch him. Why?

Not for lust—she had adamantly denied that. Not for need of coin—she had refused what he had offered. What possible reason would she have to wish to touch him? Then react as she did when he touched her?

He could not comprehend her. Claire kept him unbalanced, and he liked it not. One moment she was the hope to end his tribulation; the next the nail to seal his coffin. Salvation? Damnation? Which one would she be?

He would never know if he walked away from her.

The thought made him slow his pace.

Were she not the only woman he had ever met unafraid of a ghost, and were he not the desperate man that he was, he would not even consider such a disagreeable wench for a bride.

But she was, and so was he.

He had allowed her to rile him to such a pitch that he had forgotten she was possibly his last chance at a bride. If she disappeared into the night, he might never find her again.

Then what hope would he have?

Abruptly, Aiden changed directions. He hoped he could still find her. He hoped she had not fallen prey to the very ruffians a moment ago he so unkindly had wished upon her. The thought sat like spoiled venison in his belly. Urgency rushed his steps.

He wished he knew more about Claire. Who was she? Where did she hail from? What was her true quest? She had appeared out of nowhere, uncommon in beauty and dress and speech. Foreign born, he had thought. Perchance not even of this world.

A witch? A fairy? She was odd enough to be either.

He was desperate enough not to care. If she possessed any magical powers, he would beg her to use them on his behalf. He would pay whatever price she dictated. He would be willing to go to any lengths to garner her aid.

Reality soon sank in. Considering their two brief meetings, were she able, instead of saving him, Claire would surely turn him into a toad or some other slimy creature. Or steal him into the woods, as fairies were wont to do.

Nay, Claire was a mere woman, albeit a strange one, who wanted what he could not give her and refused to be what he so desperately needed.

Somehow he had to find a way to change that.

His eyes, accustomed to the darkness, gladly sighted her. She shone like a beacon in her creamy gown. Any half-blind man would see her. That was how he had found her earlier.

Excitement thrummed in his chest. It had swept him since he first laid eyes on her. For long, lonely years, the emotion had been absent from his life. Not since . . . He abruptly reined in the memory; he wanted to erase the past, not dwell upon it. He forced his thoughts back to Claire, his future.

Jaw tight, he approached her silently, unsure of how to proceed. Though she was in the wrong for sending him away, he needed to make peace with her.

Remembering how she had reacted to his touch earlier—a puzzle, since moments before she had sought it out—he refrained from handling her.

"Claire," he called out.

She spun around. "Aiden, I thought you were gone." Not only had her voice lost the hard edge of before, it now contained a clear note of relief.

She had obviously recovered her senses, Aiden thought, somewhat mollified and encouraged. "I believe we both acted in haste earlier." He gave her that much. No sense in antagonizing her outright. "But if you still wish me gone—"

"No!"

He exhaled quietly; relieved she had refused his half-hearted offer. He had chanced and won.

"No need to," she said. "I know you mean well and I . . . Well, I apologize for being so rude."

"It is prudent for a woman to be guarded, but I merely wished to see you safely to your destination."

"I know. And if you're still willing, I gladly accept your company now."

He would not gloat. He would not chastise her for sending him off, thus forcing him to come back after her. He would accept her apology and grant her his protection. It was what he had hoped when he had set out to seek her again.

"It will be my honor." He moved to stand on her right, freeing his sword hand in case of need. "Have you already procured a chamber in the inn?" he asked. "Or are you lodging with friends?"

"I have a room at the De la Poste," she said. "It's only a couple of streets down the road. If it weren't for this darkness, I'd find it with no trouble."

He had not heard the inn referred to by that name, but

he paid little attention to such matters. "Indeed, the inn is not far. We should reach it without delay."

"Good," she said, then rushed to follow him as he began to walk. He slowed his steps. The terrain began to slant down toward the banks of the River Eure. Claire stumbled—no wonder, considering her unusually flimsy shoes, if you could call what she wore shoes—and Aiden moved to catch her.

She quickly evaded his hands. He straightened and squared his shoulders, leaving her to manage on her own. *Stubborn wench!* Why had she the need to do all on her own? Or was his touch what she wished to avoid? Aiden despaired to understand Claire. One moment she clung to him as if her life depended on it, the next it was as if it pained her to be near him.

This conflicting reaction to him boded ill to their future together, did he, by a miracle, convince her to become his bride.

Aiden reined in his impatience. One step at a time. All he must do now is take her safely to the inn, thus proving his honor to her.

Once there . . .

Well, he would cross that bridge when he got to it.

Chapter 6

TAKING great care to remain close to Aiden, but not so close they'd touch—the last thing she needed was a debilitating memory while she stood in the darkness with a man she'd just met—Claire struggled to keep up with his pace. Aiden walked with the sure step of a man who either knew the terrain well or was using invisible night vision goggles.

Claire was impressed.

This ungodly darkness unsettled her. The wind had picked up strength since she'd left the cathedral. It howled like a wounded animal. The weather was taking a turn for the worse. She wished they'd hurry up and find the hotel. She didn't want to be caught outside in the dark and bad weather. Besides, even candlelight would help chase away the shadows clouding her mind.

"I understand Chartres is not your home," Aiden said over the wind. "Where do you hail from?"

"America. New Orleans," she said and stumbled again. If she weren't careful, she'd break an ankle in one of those holes she kept falling into every other step. Aiden stopped and waited for her to regain her balance. She noticed he didn't reach out to help her this time. Obviously, he took the hint she didn't want to be touched.

They fell into step again.

"Orléans," he said. "I had not thought you so near."

Claire gave a double take in his direction. Near? What was near about a city across the ocean? She must've misunderstood him. Or maybe *he* had misunderstood her. Could he have thought she'd said Orléans, France, and not New Orleans, United States of America? She thought she'd made it perfectly clear.

Claire frowned, unease creeping in.

Realizing she was wrinkling her forehead, she relaxed her face. There was no need to rush old age.

There wasn't much she could do about her doubts at this point. It was best if she disregarded the misunderstandings and kept the conversation going. Exchanging tidbits of information that didn't pertain to her past life wasn't essential, but it served the purpose of establishing a rapport between them.

"How about you, Aiden? Are you French? From Chartres, perhaps?"

"I am Norman by birth and English by fate. Delacroix is my home."

So he was French, after all. She tried to remember if she'd ever heard of a town called Delacroix. She didn't, but then she couldn't account for all the small towns in France.

"Are you in town on business?" she asked and immediately bit her tongue. What if he was here with the sole pur-

pose of finding a wife, as she was to find her answers? She
didn't want to anger him by reminding him of her rejection
and break the tenuous understanding they had reached.

Fortunately, he ignored her question. Claire took it to
mean she was right in her assumption, and he didn't want
to talk about it right now. Good! She quickly changed the
subject. She pointed at the flickering lights in the distance.
"I was going to ask someone in that group to help me back
to the hotel before you reappeared, but I never caught up
with them. Do you know where they are headed?"

He glanced quickly in the direction she'd pointed. "To
the woods, I suppose," Aiden said.

"What for?"

He crooked his head toward her. She couldn't see his
expression, couldn't know what he was thinking. Why did
it take him so long to answer her?

"It is Roodmas Eve." The tone of his voice indicated he
thought she should know that.

Claire recognized the term, but only because she was
fascinated with medieval history. Roodmas was the medieval Christian Church's chosen name for Beltane, the pagan Celtic celebration of the beginning of summer, or May
Day as it was commonly known now. In those days,
Beltane was a time of unashamed celebration of human
sexuality and fertility. Young men and women spent the
night in the woods, celebrating love and life and the rejuve-
nating power of nature. Since such escapades usually led to
rushed weddings and unexpected births, the medieval
Church naturally frowned on the ritual. Hence, its attempt
to associate Beltane with the rood—the cross—and the
name change.

How odd that Aiden had chosen that particular term.
And that he thought she would know it.

Again that weird feeling of something not being quite
right swept over her.

She glanced back at the moving lights.

As far as she knew, Beltane was still celebrated these days by Wiccans, much as it was in ancient times, with bonfires, dancing, and communing with Mother Nature. She didn't know about frolicking in the woods, though.

"Are you celebrating?" she asked.

He snorted. "My ghost would not allow me such pleasure."

Claire hadn't realized how insidious Aiden's ghost's interference in his life was.

They fell into silence again.

The rough and uncertain terrain slanted seriously downward beneath her feet. Her heels aided the darkness in keeping her unbalanced and hesitating. They slowed her progress. She didn't remember the streets being so rough when she traversed them earlier, but maybe Aiden had taken a shortcut she didn't know about.

"Earlier, in the cathedral—" His voice pulled her once again out of her thoughts. "You spoke of a need to know about the past."

Her heartbeat slowed to an almost stop.

"If you still wish to pursue your quest, I shall be glad to be of aid to you."

What was he offering her?

The only way he could help her was by allowing her to touch him. She wasn't sure he understood that. But as touching Aiden had turned out to be such an emotional and physical roller coaster, Claire wasn't sure she had the fortitude to try again so soon. Besides, the two brief memories she'd unearthed had elucidated little of her past, and with no guarantee there would be more memories or that they would be more revealing in nature, she was naturally reticent.

And yet, the alternative wasn't an option either.

If only there was another way. Maybe Aiden had some ideas of his own.

"What do you have in mind?" she asked.

"I assume you seek kin—a father, a brother, perchance? I can help you find them."

Aiden thought she was looking for her family? Where did he get that idea? Obviously he hadn't understood her question in the cathedral. "It's a little more complicated than that. When I spoke of seeking answers to my past, I didn't exactly mean the immediate past."

"Whatever your meaning, wherever your quest leads you, I shall take you. I know I can help you, Claire, if you but allow me."

Claire looked at him. His tall form was shapeless in the darkness, but the way he carried himself glowed with intensity. Aiden meant to help her. But would he still be willing when she explained she sought answers to her past life, which incidentally, was intimately linked to his?

And if, against all odds, she succeeded in gaining his cooperation, what would he ask in return?

Or need she wonder?

"All I ask—" he said, as if reading her mind.

She almost groaned. "Aiden, please . . ."

"All I ask," he repeated. "Is that you *consider* my proposal of marriage. You need not avow yourself now. Just promise to consider it. And if in the end, you still wish to decline . . . then so be it."

Claire sighed. How could she promise to consider a proposal she knew she'd never accept? Wouldn't she be deceiving him? Giving him hope when there was none?

Torn, Claire shifted in place. It was dark, it was getting colder, and her feet ached. She needed time to decide what to do. Naturally, she chose to dissemble. "Can we discuss this over a glass of wine?" A good glass of Merlot and a comfortable chair before a fireplace would do wonders to clear her mind.

He begrudgingly agreed. At least, she thought he did,

since he didn't actually answer her, but resumed the trek to the hotel. She hastily followed him.

In an attempt to distract her mind from the thoughts of Aiden and her past, her gaze scanned the area around her. A landscape of distorted and unrecognizable shapes took form—the rough outline of a building here and there, flickering lights that revealed nothing familiar. However little she knew of Chartres, in the darkness the city did not resemble what she remembered.

Again unease swelled inside her. She slowed her steps, trying to orient herself.

Between lulling intervals, the wind flapped against her face, freeing strands of her hair that promptly coiled before her eyes. Claire stopped, removed her hair clip, gathered her hair again, and securely fastened the strands back.

Suddenly lightning streaked the sky.

The split second of light was too fast to show any detail, but it was enough to shed doubts in Claire's mind of where she was going. The outcrop of buildings resembled nothing of the area around her hotel. The accompanying thunder roared in the distance. And then another lightning bolt.

Claire knew she was not where she was supposed to be.

Chartres was an old town with a famous historical district. Surely that was where they were headed, judging by buildings she'd glimpsed in the brief light. The problem was that her hotel was nowhere near that area.

Had Aiden misunderstood her, or was he willfully misleading her? With what purpose?

Thunder echoed the maddening beat of her heart.

She forced her breathing to ease, refusing to fall prey to unnecessary panic. She was sure there was a perfectly plausible explanation for this.

Why didn't she feel completely reassured?

Maybe because plausible was rarely part of her life?

She decided to speak up. "Aiden, I think there's been a mistake. This is not the way to my hotel."

"The inn is but steps away." He pointed to the direction of a torchlike luminaire, supposedly attached to a wall. She couldn't see the wall. The damn light could be floating in the air, for all she knew.

"Maybe so, but I'm sure that is not where I'm staying," she insisted.

"Where else would you be lodging? There is only one inn in Chartres. And you told me you had not sought shelter with a friend."

Only one inn? Was he insane? There were quite a few hotels in Chartres. His answer didn't make sense, and Claire couldn't go on dismissing their misunderstandings or blaming them on a language barrier. She had heard him loud and clear. His statement either made Aiden a liar, or . . .

Or what?

What the hell was going on? Who was Aiden, and what did he want with her? Where was he taking her? Where was she?

The panic she had so successfully kept at bay reared its ugly head. She could face bizarre. But this wasn't bizarre; this was frightening.

Her gaze darted in all directions, but pitch-darkness severely limited her choices. She could run back from where she came—if she could see her way—or she could seek help ahead.

Her gaze strayed to the beaconing light. She was close enough to the building she didn't need Aiden's guidance. She could reach it before him. He was bigger and stronger than her, but she was lighter, and hopefully faster. Surely there were other people inside. She could get help.

She didn't dwell on the urgency gnawing at her to put

some distance between her and Aiden. It was a visceral decision, a self-preservation instinct moths clearly lacked when they blindly sought the light.

Slowly, she bent over and casually removed her sandals. He said nothing, accustomed by now to her constant stops. Without warning, she straightened and dashed away. As she reached the shabby-looking building, illuminated not by a torchlike luminaire but a real torch spouting smoke, a foul smell, and little light, the rough hewn oak door blasted open, and a man walked out unsteadily.

Forced to step aside—she wasn't about to ask help of a drunk—Claire wrinkled her nose. The man reeked of sweat, beer, and some other unidentifiable and equally offensive odor.

Noticing her, he abruptly stopped, causing someone else to stumble behind him. The drunk pushed the man behind him and cursed vilely—a word Claire hadn't heard before and didn't care to know the meaning.

From inside the place a cacophony of sounds reached her—laughter, animated conversation, clinking of metal on wood. Muted light spilled out around the drunk and the other man behind him. Not enough to illuminate, just enough to cast yet more doubts in Claire's mind.

Finishing his short diatribe, the drunk returned his attention to her. He leaned against the doorjamb to better look at her, or to avoid falling to the ground in a drunken stupor, which she'd prefer, for then she'd just step over him. Instead, she endured his scrutiny, fully aware Aiden would catch up with her at any second, and she'd have to contend not only with a drunk but with a very angry man as well.

"What have we got here?" the man slurred. He, too, spoke the same odd French as Aiden. Claire didn't care at all for the lecherous glance he shot her. As he stood under the torch, she could see his face clearly enough to know he had his mind in the gutter. "Looking for company, wench?"

When he lifted his hand in the direction of her chest, she stepped back to evade his unwanted touch. At the same time, Aiden stepped between them, gripping the man's hand and pushing him back. "The lady is with me."

Surprised he'd still defend her after she'd left him without a word of explanation, Claire didn't dispute Aiden's claim. Particularly when two men—two very big, mean-looking men—stepped behind the drunk in the man's obvious support.

Claire fell farther back, peering worriedly from around Aiden's wide shoulders.

"Lady, heh?" The drunk stumbled forward, shoulders puffed, his face in Aiden's face. The intimidating posture wasn't entirely effective, since the man was at least six inches shorter than Aiden. However, he did have the two giants behind him to fall back on. Aiden seemed impervious to the latent danger.

The drunk squinted and then laughed. "Aiden!" he said, patting Aiden amicably on the shoulder. "I knew not it was you. I have no desire to fight you over a wench. Particularly when I know your need is surely greater than mine." Laughing, he fell back on his heels, relaxing his stance. On cue, his friends did the same.

The man's joke did nothing to ease Claire's mind, nor did the fact he and Aiden seemed to know each other.

"Lord Clovis. We meet again." Reassuringly, Aiden's cool voice indicated he didn't share the man's mirth.

"So, you finally found a wench to warm your bed," Lord Clovis said. "Well done! Well done!" he congratulated Aiden as if he had won a contest. "I have pitied the unnatural state you have been forced to live in. God deliver me from such fate." He crossed himself.

The man's words made Claire very uneasy. Aiden's lack of response didn't exactly ease her mind.

Lord Clovis leaned forward unsteadily. "In the name of fairness," he whispered. "Is she aware of your plight?"

"She is," Aiden said.

"Ah!" Lord Clovis stole a glance at Claire, then his gaze darted nervously around. After a moment, apparently reassured there was no one else about, he turned his attention to Aiden. "Knowing did naught to protect Lady Marian or your wife from the wrath of your ghost. Is she certain of the risks?"

Aiden was married? He couldn't be. He was looking for a wife. And what risks was Lord Clovis talking about? Aiden hadn't explained the nature of his ghost's haunting, but surely, to most people, merely being haunted by a ghost was frightening enough.

"I am but Lady Claire's escort," Aiden said in a tight tone, clearly unhappy with the discussion.

Why was Aiden referring to her as *lady*?

"Ah! Let us pray *she* understands the difference."

Claire was puzzled. Who was Lord Clovis referring to?

"It is kind of you to care," Aiden said, not seeming touched at all. "But Lady Claire's safety is my concern, not yours."

"Indeed. It is her life and your soul at peril. I merely wish to forewarn you both."

"Your warning is noted, my lord," Aiden said. "But the night grows late. Let me keep you no longer. I am certain your lady wife eagerly awaits your return."

Lord Clovis shrugged. "Indeed, it is a blessing to have a family, a wife, an heir on the way. A home to call my own and to know my name shall be carried through time by my offspring." He stared up at Aiden. "Not many of us are so blessed and so deserving."

Claire was puzzled at the hostile undertone of Lord Clo-vis's words. She watched as he sidestepped Aiden and then walked away, his friends falling into step behind him.

As they passed her, the sound of clinking metal drifted to her. Were they covered in metallic mesh? Lightning struck, illuminating their backs. Claire's eyes widened.

Armor and swords?

Thunder rolled. Her heart thumped madly in her chest.

Claire turned to face Aiden, who now stood under the torch, watching her. Slowly, her gaze swept over him. It was still dark, but she thought he, too, carried a sword, though he wore no metallic armor. Another flash of light confirmed her fears, robbing her of breath.

The uneasiness that had been etching at her since she'd first seen Aiden in the cathedral just carved deeper.

Mind clicking with sudden awareness, Claire recalled the changes she'd first noticed in the cathedral—the torches on the wall, the empty cavernous space where before there'd been pews and benches. In her eagerness to find her an-swers, she'd overlooked the inconsistencies, ignored their odd conversation, and dismissed their misunderstandings.

She'd followed Aiden blindly, and then mistaking the increasing unease taking hold of her, fled like a scalded cat afraid of cold water.

Everything was wrong!

Thunder rumbled again, the sound echoing closer. As the wind howled louder, lashing at her, a drop of rain fell on her face. Claire fought the crescendo of panic taking hold of her.

"Why did you take your leave of me with such haste?" Aiden demanded, oblivious to her shock. "What is the rea-son behind this erratic behavior? One moment you wish my company, the next you dismiss me summarily. I have done naught other than offer you my protection, my aid. I demand an explanation, Claire."

Claire listened to his rant, unable to form a coherent answer.

Lightning struck again. Then another flash. And another. All of a sudden, the sky resembled a flickering floodlight illuminating the world in intermittent intervals, adding another layer of eeriness to an already bizarre moment, confirming what her mind still fought to deny. What took her so long to see?

The ground shook with the force of the thunder that splintered the air as if the world was about to cave in beneath her feet.

No need for that. She was already free-falling.

Rain descended upon them. Big, fat, cold drops rushed down her body, chilling her soul. Her thin dress drenched immediately, molding itself to her legs and hips. Her curls lost their bounce and plastered heavily against her back and face.

"Answer me, Claire."

Aiden's voice reached her as if from a great distance. She couldn't speak if her life depended on it. Couldn't move. Couldn't think.

Her head spun wildly.

Oh, how she would welcome oblivion, should she faint!

No such luck. Consciousness clung to her like a curse while her whole body shook with the bizarre possibility that she was standing not before the reincarnation of the man in her past, as she'd first believed, but the man himself, in flesh and blood, and all that would entail.

How could that be? That man belonged to the past, a past long gone, forgotten, and never to return to her but in memories.

But Aiden was no memory. No vision. No dream.

He was real.

And that changed everything!

Claire closed her eyes. Aiden! The man who haunted her dreams, the missing puzzle of her past life, the man who held the answers to her past and her future in his hands.

She had sought self-discovery in Chartres Cathedral's ancient labyrinth's path. She had found herself on a journey to the outer limits of reality, instead.

Her past had finally caught up with her.

Chapter 7

FIGHTING the hysterics creeping up inside her, Claire couldn't deal with Aiden right now. She needed to figure out what the hell had happened. Where was she? What was this place?

Feeling trapped, she lashed out at him. "Let me pass, Aiden."

"What?"

"Let me go, please."

"Have you lost your wits?"

She must have!

Rain fell so hard she could hardly keep her eyes open, but Aiden didn't seem to be bothered. He barely blinked as he glared furiously at her, probably mentally debating whether to knock her unconscious or turn his back on her.

She hoped the latter.

He clenched his fists. She fisted her hands in response.

She was ready to risk a debilitating memory should the need to defend herself arise, even knowing she didn't possess the strength to budge him an inch.

And then, with a muffled curse, he stomped to the side.

Claire didn't hesitate. She rushed past him and into the inn.

Her heart stopped.

The place bore no resemblance to an ordinary inn. It looked more like a tavern in a seedy neighborhood, vaguely reminding her of a common English pub—dark, noisy, and teeming with people.

But there the comparison ended. Nothing was remotely modern about the huge wood-burning fireplace on the far wall, nor the rush-covered floor, nor the scarred wooden tables flanked by low benches, filled with rough-looking men.

Rooted to the floor, drops from her wet clinging dress sluicing down her legs to form a puddle beneath her bare feet, Claire forced herself to ignore the men's uncomfortable scrutiny of her. She brushed a wet curl from her face, wiped the water from her eyes, and pursed her lips tight to prevent her thundering heart from escaping through her mouth.

Either she had alighted in the Land of Oz or she had gone completely insane. Her gaze raked the place, looking for a hidden camera, a discordant note of modernism in this primitive environment.

Her gaze settled on a man at a nearby table, devouring the leg of some unfortunate animal with more gusto than it warranted. The way he looked back at her, as if he pictured her as his next meal, made Claire shudder with disgust. Swallowing the bile rising in her throat, she jerked her gaze away.

Another man gulped from a metal can as if the liquid it contained was a miracle potion that should be drained in large quantities and in record time. Yet another man, at a far end table, had his hands all over a poor waitress—a Hooters look-alike in the bosom department—obviously not with the intent of placing an order for food.

Claire cringed, feeling sorry for the woman, though thus occupied he was one of the few men who seemed uninterested in her. Others, however, kept their gazes locked on Claire. One in particular stood and ambled her way.

She tried to evade him, but the man cut her off, blocking her way, standing a little too close for comfort, clearly invading her space. Breathing through her mouth to avoid inhaling his putrid breath, Claire tilted her chin up and eyed him defiantly. Never show fear! Wasn't that people say to do when facing a ferocious dog?

"Pardon Monsieur," she said as she tried to circumvent him. The man ignored her polite request, blocking her way again, and continuing to leer at her.

"Looking for company, wench?" he asked.

Claire wanted to laugh in his face but found she couldn't muster the courage.

Behind her, a groan echoed. She flipped a glance over her shoulder. Not looking very amused, Aiden stood behind her. "The lady is with me," he spoke the familiar refrain.

Relief washed over her. Had she just tried to run away from him?

"She wears her assets for all to see," the man said. "And I have a mind to sample her wares."

In a move so fast it belied his inebriated state, the man grabbed Claire and pulled her to him. Shocked, she let out a muffled cry. But before her body even hit his chest, Aiden, with lightning speed, socked the lights out of her attacker with a well-placed fist in his face. Blood spurted from his broken nose. Cursing mightily, he stumbled back, letting go of her.

"Run to your chamber, Claire," Aiden commanded as he unsheathed his sword, preparing for battle. Bloody nose and all, her attacker was already on the move, equally armed. Horrified, Claire darted a gaze to all sides, looking for the chambers. Instead, she spotted two men, swords at hand, push away from the table they'd been sharing with her attacker, and rush to his defense.

Her breath caught in her throat. "Aiden," she cried in warning. To her relief, Aiden had already managed to disarm the first attacker, elbowing him in the face for good measure—Could a person have his nose broken twice in the same day?—as the other men reached him.

Aiden's sword sliced through air, parrying blows and inflicting bodily harm where sharp metal met flesh. By now, other men had joined the melee, randomly choosing sides with the obvious glee only men could feel about a fight.

The clash of metal against metal rang loud and unreal in Claire's ears. Her head began to spin as she numbly watched the surreal moment unfold before her eyes.

There was no sane explanation for what was happening.

"Go, Claire!" Aiden shouted amidst the chaos, shaking her out of her stupor and spurring her into action. Sighting a flight of stairs at the far corner of the room, she dashed in that direction.

Caught in the pandemonium that ensued, she was shoved from side to side as she attempted to forge ahead. Suddenly, her feet left the floor, and she found her back firmly imprisoned against an unknown wide chest, and her frightened cry drowned by the infernal noise of clashing metals, splintering wood, grunts, and curses in Old French.

Claire struggled to free herself from the arms that held her like iron manacles. She jerked from side to side, pulled every way she could, and still the hold remained.

Do something! her mind screamed, heart thundering painfully in her chest.

Understanding that strength wasn't on her side, she changed tactics, ceasing her struggle, and going limp, head slumped forward over her bent body. Dead weight, she slid down his body. To grip her better, the man slowed his progress and momentarily slacked his hold of her. Freeing one hand, she pushed forward, finding purchase on the floor, and swiftly shoved her foot back and up between his legs, delivering a well-placed heel to his balls.

He gasped, reflexively letting go of her to grab his damaged goods as he arched in pain, catching his breath. Momentum carried her forward. She stumbled but quickly recovered her balance.

She fought her way through the chaotic scene, battling grabby hands with her purse and sandals as she went. When she finally reached the stairs, she took them two steps at a time, moving up quickly. Before she lost sight of the room below, she stopped and glanced back, her gaze seeking Aiden. She spotted him. His dark, wet hair plastered against his face, and his hands gripped his immense sword. He fought with a grace that belied the bloodied reality of the moment.

This was no game. No sport of fencing where points were awarded for hits that had no blood spilled nor limb or life lost. This was real. As real as her mind could fathom.

Aiden could die!

And it would be her fault.

Time trickled with exasperating lethargy as the implication wrapped around her mind, refusing to let go.

This could not be happening!

She considered going back to help him but knew she'd be more of a hindrance than help.

A cup flew by, barely missing her head. The cup hit the wall with a thud and bounced in a shower of plaster to the floor of the landing.

Without waiting to see who had cast it her way, Claire dashed up the few steps that separated her from the top of the stairs. To her left, a semidark corridor led to the chambers. Or, at least, she thought so. For a moment, she hesitated, uncertain what lay in the shadows, but she couldn't afford to remain in plain view. Eventually someone would notice her and come after her.

Decision made, Claire scooped up the heavy pewter cup—maybe she'd need it as a weapon—and headed for the badly illuminated corridor. At the nearest door, she fumbled for a nonexistent doorknob. Giving up, she gently pushed the door with her shoulder. It opened with a squeaking of hinges in desperate need of oiling, the sound rivaling the cacophony downstairs and the thunder and rain outside.

Gripping the cup with one hand and her sandals with the other, she scanned the room. A little light shone in from the lit torch in the corridor, enough to reveal the shapes of a bed and table. Lightning streaked through the slits of a wooden shutter confirming no one was inside. With a sigh of relief, she opened the door wider and crossed the threshold, swiftly shutting the door behind her.

Utter darkness fell upon her.

She leaned back against the closed door, her body shaking with cold, fear, and regret.

Be careful what you wish for! The old adage never rang truer. Hadn't she sought her past? Well, it seemed her past had found her.

Not in a million years would she have predicted this bizarre turn of events. Good God! Had she really traveled back in time? Surely, there must be another explanation. But what?

Her mind went through the odd happenings of the last hour, and she couldn't account for what her eyes had seen. She had experienced, firsthand, many unexplainable things in her life, but time travel had never figured in her plans.

How could this be possible? What did she know? She wasn't a scientist; she knew nothing about the time-space continuum, quantum physics, or any such gibberish.

But she also knew that science wasn't the only answer to the unexplained. There were forces reigning in the world that were beyond comprehension.

Chartres Cathedral was built on the grounds of an old Druid church. The Druids were a mystical people whose knowledge had been lost with the passing of time. No one knew what magical forces capable of harnessing such power as to control time still resided in the ancient cathedral.

Could the labyrinth be the path between past and future? Was it how she'd ended up here? How long would she stay? Could she go back to her own time at will?

Claire had no answer to any of these questions. All she knew was that Aiden was the key to her quest for the truth about her past. Through him, she had already recovered two brief memories. Surely, more were still to come.

However, the fact that he didn't remember her suggested her past self had not met him yet. Then how had she recovered memories from a past that hadn't happened yet? Was she supposed to prevent the past from happening? Was fate giving her a second chance with Aiden? The thought horrified and enticed her at the same time. Even if she accepted the possibility of a second chance—and she didn't—she couldn't avoid making the same mistakes of the past when she didn't have a clue what had gone wrong between them in the first place.

Her head ached in bewilderment. She needed to stop overthinking, simplify her goals, and look at the past as a puzzle to be solved.

Now that she knew Aiden was the man in her past, the man who once stole her heart, scarred her soul, and messed up her future, she needed to distance herself emotionally from him.

Heavy footsteps in the corridor outside her door jerked her out of her reverie and back to reality. Quietly, as much as her thrumming heart would allow, she slid to the side, flattening her back against the wall, trying to disappear in the shadows. Cup raised high above her head, she waited for her assailant, prepared to fight for her life.

The door slammed open. Even though she expected it, she still jumped in reaction. Before she had a chance to lower the cup, the point of a sword prickled the hollow of her throat, robbing her of breath. As if knowing that at the slightest provocation the sword would sink deeper and end her life, her heart—that a moment ago wanted to breach her chest with its maddened beat—suddenly silenced.

"Drop it."

Aiden!

Claire almost cried with relief. She opened her fingers, and the useless weapon fell. Fearing any sudden move would have her skewered by mistake, she fought her knees from buckling under her. "Aiden," she whispered. "It's me, Claire."

"Mère de Dieu!" He dropped his sword. "Claire, are you harmed?"

Chest heaving, she gulped for air. "I'm fine," she lied, unable to keep the tremor from her voice, unable to push the thought aside that she could have died. At Aiden's hands no less.

Life was suddenly all the more precious.

"Damnation, woman! What were you thinking?"

He slammed the door shut with his heel and then marched across the room in two large steps. Claire remained where she was, using the wall for support. She didn't think she could move without her legs giving out.

Sparks flew, and the flame of a candle burst to life, casting light over Aiden's back. With the candle he lit a torch on the wall. His back still to her, he returned the candle to the table and then leaned over it, his hands tightly gripping the edges of it. He remained like this for a long time, the seconds ticking languorously in Claire's mind. Was he trying to control his temper or compose himself after the fight? Maybe both. Were she in his place, she'd be livid. And scared stiff about what could have happened.

Claire waited patiently until he was ready to talk. She used that time to gain some measure of control over her rubbery limbs.

Finally he pivoted, but instead of shouting at her as she'd expected, he simply glared at her in silence.

With what she thought was great fortitude, Claire withstood his stare, but after a while his silent condemnation began to grate on her nerves. She knew she was in the wrong. She knew she had unleashed a series of events that could have cost both of them dearly. Why didn't he just come out, berate her, and be done with it?

"I'm sorry about what happened," she finally said, unable to wait any longer. She winced at the defensive edge in her voice, even though she was truly sorry. Damn it! She had gone about it all wrong, but she hadn't meant for any of this to happen.

Still, he said nothing.

She sighed and infused a more remorseful tone into her voice. "I'm glad you aren't hurt." At least she didn't think he was. A quick glance revealed no telltale signs of serious injury. A little blood on his chin, dark splatters on his shirt that she sincerely hoped were someone else's blood. He seemed to be all right. Then again, internal injuries weren't visible to the naked eye. "You aren't hurt, are you?"

The tip of his tongued glided over his split lip.

The memory of that tongue in her mouth intruded suddenly, scattering her thoughts and filling her heart with longing. Good God! She didn't need to remember a French kiss now. How inappropriate that she'd think of it in a situation like this. Swallowing down the taste of him, she shooed the image away.

It still baffled her that she could have a memory of a moment that hadn't happened yet.

Abruptly, the true implication of that thought sank in. If the kiss hadn't happened yet, then it still loomed in a near future.

Somehow, the possibility scared her stiff and warmed her insides at the same time.

"I thank you for your concern." Aiden finally broke his silence, rescuing her from her never-ending mental questioning. "But I am quite capable of defending myself and what is mine."

"I don't doubt your ability," she said. She had witnessed his skill with the sword. A skill most probably learned in childhood, honed with daily practice, and perfected in war. Aiden was quite capable of defending himself.

Nor did she doubt he'd lay his life on the line for someone else. Hadn't he done so for her, a complete stranger?

However, under no circumstance, and especially the present one, she would consider herself his. They belonged to different times, different realities. There could be no ties between them but what had happened—or would still happen—in this time.

Ordinarily, she was quite capable of taking care of herself. She'd done it for most of her life. Even when her father was alive, she'd been pretty much on her own, watching out not only for herself but for her younger brother as well.

Except these were not ordinary times. She was out of her element here and ill prepared to deal with the realities of this time, as the recent events proved without a doubt. Much as she hated to admit it, she needed Aiden on two levels: for protection and for answers. Yet, she'd done nothing but antagonize him since the moment they'd met.

Shame for her apparent lack of gratitude colored her

red. Aiden had saved her life at the risk of his own. She owed him big.

"I'm sorry you had to risk your life on my account, especially after the way I treated you earlier," she said. "I cannot thank you enough for coming to my rescue."

Aiden came to stand before her, looming above her like a cloud ready to storm. In the depths of those dark eyes, she saw the flame of anger and frustration burning brightly. She braced herself for the tempest. She deserved every bit he'd dish out.

"Had you not fled from me like I was the devil trying to steal your soul, none of this would have happened," he quietly accused, not without reason.

"Had I known things would turn out the way they did, I wouldn't have left," she said, trying to appease him.

He exhaled heavily. His hand flew to the back of his head, his fingers forcibly kneading knots of obvious frustration. "I understand you not, Claire. You seek me out; you send me away. You accept my escort; you flee from me. It is beyond reason, even for a woman, to be so fickle."

She understood his frustration. Hell, she felt it as deeply. And so she let the fickle woman comment pass. But she had no answers for him. She herself didn't understand her perplexing ambivalence toward him, the push-and-pull forces that threatened to tear her apart. One moment she trusted him, the next, deep doubts filled her. She'd sought him out, but now that she'd found him, against all logic, she wanted him gone. She didn't trust herself with him.

It was enough to drive a person to lunacy.

"At the time I thought it was best if I left," she said simply. How else could she explain it?

"And now, what think you best? Or need I ask, since you are bound to change your mind yet again?"

She deserved his belligerent tone.

Reason blared in her mind to return to the cathedral immediately, and back to her own time—assuming she could go back at will. God knew what could happen to her heart if she remained with Aiden for any amount of time. She already looked at him differently, knowing he was the man from her past.

Her treacherous heart, which had everything to lose, however, tugged her in the opposite direction. This was her chance to find out what had happened between her and Aiden. To discover what pains had so scarred her soul that she made this fantastic journey through time.

Both paths had their consequences and rewards. It was up to her to choose which one to follow.

Damn free will! Nothing was more difficult than making a choice. And yet, wasn't that what she had been looking for all along? The right to live her life as she'd choose?

"It is time you made your decision," Aiden appropriately demanded. "If you wish to go, speak your mind now, and you are free to take your leave of me. I vow to abide by your wishes, but I shall not be wrenched around like a dog on a short leash."

Decide, damn it! Claire silently demanded of herself.

She looked at Aiden. His lips tightened in a thin line showing his displeasure. A frown traced a line on his forehead.

Like her, Aiden, too, had much at stake.

Claire sighed. She must be like a moth, after all, heading full flight for the flame knowing damn well she was going to get burned.

The air between them crackled with tension akin to the charged storm outside.

Knowing Claire held his fate in her hands, Aiden held his breath and waited for her answer. Fool that he was to want to strike a bargain with a woman whose mind had changed so often in so little time. And yet, he had not a slew of options.

He licked his split lip, tasting the metallic tang of blood. His muscles ached, his elbow throbbed, but he cherished the pain, glad for the release of frustration it granted. God knew Claire had vexed him to such a pitch, had trouble not found him, he would have gone looking for it himself.

At least now he could face her without the danger of unduly unleashing his displeasure on her.

"There are things about me that you don't know and couldn't possibly understand," she said. "Things I cannot and will not explain."

"That much I have already surmised," he muttered. Thus far she had explained naught and muddled much. Mystified by her behavior, he battled to keep in mind her worth to him. "Claire, keep your secrets if you must, but give me your pledge that you shall consider my proposal of marriage."

"What you want from me I can't give you. I can't marry you, Aiden. I won't be here long enough for any sort of relationship between us to develop."

The finality of her words sank like a knife through his heart. Why did he insist on his quest when it was clear fortune would never smile upon him? Defeated, he turned to the door and opened it ajar. "Then I shall trouble you no more."

"You offered to help me," she reminded him, taking a step in his direction.

"And you have rejected that offer, twice if I well recall."

"I didn't think I could be of help to you then."

"You have just again assured me you cannot."

"But I think I can."

That caught Aiden's attention. Was she tricking him again? How could he withstand another onslaught of hope? Still, he asked, "How?"

"What exactly does your ghost do that frightens women away from you?"

Why would that matter? And what could he say that would not send her on a mad dash away from him? But Claire would do what Claire would want, regardless of what he said, he reminded himself. That much he had learned about her in this short time he had known her. He shrugged. "Women are easily frightened."

"Not all women. I have a ghost of my own, remember?"

How could he forget? That was exactly what made her so special. Not her exotic curls, not her velvety eyes, and surely not her carnal lips that begged to be kissed.

Mère de Dieu! He must control his thoughts, for his thoughts controlled his body, and his body controlled his actions.

"If I stay with you for a while, maybe we can show this ghost of yours that I'm not easily frightened. When she—the ghost is a she, isn't it?" she asked. He nodded. "When she sees her tactics are useless, she will leave you alone. When the news you're no longer haunted spreads, you should have no difficulty finding a suitable wife."

Could the deceptively simple plan be successful? Priests had failed, alms given had no result, prayers had made no difference. Did Claire hold the power to send Cherise back to the realm of spirits, freeing him to live his life as it was meant to be?

"That's what you want, isn't it? A wife?"

He nodded. Aye. A wife, a family. Any woman should do. Then why did it sting so much that Claire refused to entertain the possibility of becoming his wife? Could it be the excitement gripping his heart when he delved into the depths of her eyes? The promise of joy that shook him when she touched him?

"And what exactly do you wish in return for this . . . gift?" Surely there was a price to it.

"Your protection while I remain with you. And your promise to let me go when I tell you I need to, even if I'm not successful in my attempt to help you."

She left naught to chance.

Reason told him to turn his back on this madwoman and continue on his hopeless quest for a bride on his own.

Reason also told him he would be a fool to turn his back on the best offer—nay, the only offer—he had received thus far.

"And what about your quest?" he asked. "What can I do to aid you?"

"My quest is personal, and I will pursue it on my own."

Not even his help she needed. It was an unmanning bargain he made. How far was he willing to go to keep Delacroix Castle in his family?

He nodded his agreement. Apparently, he was willing to go to any lengths.

Should they shake hands on it? Kiss to seal the deal? Toast it with sweet wine? He decided naught of the kind. They just stood there avoiding each other's eyes as if they both already regretted their vows.

"I will escort you to your chamber now," he said.

Claire remained where she was.

What else did she want? His blood? He had already given her that. "What is the matter now?"

"I don't have a chamber."

"But you said—" He shook his head. "Never mind. Perchance the landlady will find you a place."

"I also don't have money."

"No coin, no chamber. No belongings as well?"

She shook her head.

"No lady-in-waiting and no horse, I suppose."

She gave a little apologetic grin. "Definitely no horse."

Doubt filled him. "Where were you headed when I met you, Claire?"

"Right here."

"Where from?"

"A faraway place."

"And how did you get to Chartres?"

"I flew."

Aiden eyed Claire cautiously. She looked serious, but surely, she jested. By now, he was accustomed to her odd speech, but her manners yet defied explanation. At least her looks, though exotic, were quite easy on the eyes. Witch, fairy, the devil herself, or merely an odd woman, she was all he had right now.

Perchance it was his fortune she had not agreed to become his bride after all.

"Very well, Claire. You may stay here for the night," he said, as if it was a grave concession he made, when in truth, he wanted her close. He did not trust her not to flee while he slept.

"Thank you for your kindness and generosity," she said, pushing herself from the wall. "I know it all seems quite strange to you, but everything will work out fine in the end."

Though he seriously doubted that, he sincerely hoped she was right.

"I will see you in the morning, then," she said, clearly dismissing him.

"This is my bedchamber," he quietly pointed out. He had no intention of making his bed in the common room. To ascertain she understood her need of him, he added, "You caused a veritable ruckus earlier. Disgruntled men might seek you out of revenge. If I am to protect you, I must remain close."

A shadow fell on her face. He gained no pleasure in frightening her, but he needed reassurance she would not try to flee from him during the night.

She opened her mouth to gainsay him. Wisely, she changed her mind, though. She darted a doubting glance at the small bed. Truth be told, it would be hard-pressed to hold one person let alone two, but he did not expect to share it with her.

That would be beyond a dream come true.

"You may have the bed," he said. "I shall lie on the floor by the door."

She nodded in obvious relief. "Thank you."

Finally he had gained some measure of control over his dealings with her. He knew not how long it would last, but he had a mind to prolong it as long as he could.

Chapter 8

HAD she made a pact with the devil?

Claire watched Aiden close the door and then march across the room. Not amble, not walk, not saunter, but march with the grim determination of a man with no time to waste.

Aiden was desperate enough to accept her help without demanding she spill her guts about the true nature of her motivations or origin. Considering that her behavior had been less than enticing and that he surely couldn't have helped noticing how odd she must look, she was lucky he still struck a bargain with her.

On her side, she was also desperate enough to ignore the danger of remaining with a man who once had caused her enough pain to last her beyond a lifetime. Still, he'd been nothing but understanding and respectful since the moment they met. At least, she could trust he wouldn't slash her throat open with that sharp sword of his.

She wished she were as confident of her heart's fate.

Once she had loved and hated him; those emotions were still painfully raw today.

She didn't plan to stick around long enough to risk her heart, however. It shouldn't take more than a couple of days for her to show Aiden's ghost she wasn't scared of her and banish the haunting, gather a few memories along the way, and then whisk herself back to her own time.

A simple, quick and, she hoped, efficient plan.

She ignored the nagging voice reminding her nothing in her life had ever been simple.

Aiden fussed with a pile of belongings she hadn't noticed before in the corner of the room. A big leather bag lay on the floor as if it'd been thrown there with no thought of where it'd land. In contrast, a chain-mail shirt was neatly stretched alongside the bag. Above it, on the wall, a long, dark coat hung on a peg.

On top of the leather bag there was what looked like a rolled-up blanket. Aiden picked it up, extinguished the wall torch, leaving the lone candle burning on the table, and then returned to where she still stood, frozen on the spot.

The flickering candle cast a soft light over him, blurring the lines of his handsome face and shadowing his powerful body. "Have you changed your mind about the bed?"

Claire shot him a doubtful look. Was he joking or trying to weasel his way out of sleeping on the floor? Maybe she should offer to trade places with him. It would be the right thing to do, since this was his room and he'd been generous enough to share it with her.

She eyed the dirty floor and then shook her head. No way was she sleeping on that. Aiden didn't seem the kind of man who demanded luxury or who would put his comfort before someone else's. The status quo worked just fine for her right now. "If it's all the same to you, I would rather take the bed."

"My offer still stands; the bed is yours," he said, sounding not in the least upset.

So, he *was* joking earlier. Somehow that was not a trait she would have attributed to Aiden; he seemed overly serious all the time.

Aiden unbuckled his sword belt and laid it on the floor, then unrolled the blanket and spread it in front of the door. No one would get in this room without bumping into him. Claire guessed that was the idea.

Watching the back of his dark head while he arranged his sleeping spot, Claire pondered on the wisdom of provoking a touch and a memory now. Would he misinterpret her intentions? After all, they were alone in the room.

As Aiden rose, he whisked his wet shirt over his head, revealing broad shoulders and a wide, muscled chest generously sprinkled with dark hair. Heat crept up her neck. She couldn't help but drink in the sight of him.

No way would she touch him now.

Aiden was a powerfully built, immensely attractive man. She was in no way immune to his rugged charms. She hadn't expected to feel such a potent sexual attraction to him.

Hurriedly, she wrested her hungry gaze away from him and practically ran to the other side of the room, putting as much distance between them as it was possible in this little shoe box of a room.

With her back to him, she tried to block out the image of his naked chest, closing her ears to the sounds of his undressing. Would the man sleep in the buff as he shared the room with a stranger? The alternative would be for him to sleep in wet clothes, a problem she also faced. Didn't he have dry clothes in that bag of his? *She* didn't have a choice.

Bothered, Claire busied her eyes and mind on inspecting the bed. On the surface it seemed clean enough. She pulled the woolen cover down. The sheet didn't look pristine white, but there were no telltale stains. She lifted the pillow, fluffed it, and then returned it to the bed.

Despite its simplicity, it sure beat sleeping on the floor.

Had Aiden slept in this bed before? The thought came unbidden, bringing with it the memory of his naked chest. Chasing away such thoughts, Claire ambled to the table, refusing to steal a peek over her shoulders. "Are you set?" she asked.

"Aye."

She blew the flame out, and in the blessed darkness quickly removed her own wet clothes. The thought of both of them naked in this confining room wasn't too reassuring.

Hurriedly, she wrung her dress almost dry, and then stretched it, and the scarf, on the table. She found her way back to the bed, tucked her purse and sandals out of sight underneath it, her panties under her pillow, and removed the hair clip from her head. She ran her fingers through the damp curls, dreading to see how they'd look in the morning.

She lay down on the lumpy, straw-filled, thin mattress and pulled the cover over her body. Wild images of Aiden's naked body danced before her eyes in the darkness. To make matters worse, the memory of that powerful kiss replayed in her mind.

Get ahold of yourself! her mind screamed. She appreciated male beauty, she even occasionally used eye candy in moments of loneliness, but she wasn't in the habit of going weak-kneed at the sight of every handsome man she met. It was her damn past blurring the lines in her mind. Those buried memories colored her reaction to him.

Hot and bothered, she shifted in bed, trying to find a comfortable position. The rough blanket scraped against her naked nipples, adding fuel to the fire of her thoughts.

Giving up sleeping flat on her back, as she usually did, she turned on her side. Sleep eluded her as it clearly eluded Aiden. She could hear him tossing and turning on the floor.

Was he having the same troubling thoughts as she? He didn't seem particularly attracted to her. He hadn't made any moves in her direction, anyway, with the exception of wanting to marry her. But that was more of a need than a want. She couldn't fathom why the thought that he wasn't attracted to her bothered her so.

Again, she credited that to the remnants of old feelings.

Finally, after what seemed an eternity, he quieted down. Claire remained awake a while longer, listening to the rain falling outside and Aiden's even breathing.

The sounds eventually lulled her to sleep.

She thought she'd just closed her eyes when she felt a stab on her back. Startled, she jerked upright. With one hand flat against the mattress for balance, Claire reached her other hand to scratch her itching back. In a flash she remembered where she was. At the same time she felt something crawl on her hand.

With a muffled cry, she jumped out of bed, shaking her hands and skipping wildly on the floor.

In a split second, Aiden was by her side. She could feel his presence, though she couldn't quite see him in the darkness. "What is the matter?" he asked.

"There is something in my bed."

"What?"

"A bug, I think."

He sighed. What did he expect her to say? A monster was in her bed? Or one of those scruffy looking men that seemed to populate this time? "Bugs are everywhere,

Claire. In the air, on the floor, in the ceiling. It would be impossible to keep them from the bed."

Don't let the bedbugs bite. Now she knew where the saying originated. She just never thought she'd experience it firsthand.

There was no way she was returning to that bed until she was the only living thing in it. "Can you light the candle?" she asked, regretting not having been a girl scout in her youth. Without matchsticks, she didn't have a clue how to make fire.

With a sigh of resignation, he set to do what she asked. Before the flame came to life, Claire remembered they were both naked. She hastily snapped the cover from the bed, shaking it in the air for good measure, before wrapping it around her body. She tried not to stare at Aiden's buttocks, but, God, she had a thing for men's buns, and Aiden's were worth a longer look.

His body began to shift as he turned around, and Claire snapped her gaze away, turning her back to him. It took all of her willpower not to sneak a peek over her shoulder. If the rest of Aiden measured up to his gorgeous buns and upper body, she was in deep trouble.

She occupied herself in removing the sheet and flapping it in the air like a flag in a hurricane. Then she removed the thin mattress from the simple bed frame and smacked it with her hands until the thing was flat. A few unidentified bugs did fall from it, and Claire rushed to smash them with one of her sandals.

She knew how to deal with bugs. She was from New Orleans, after all, though she'd never had one in her bed before.

At least they weren't spiders. She detested spiders.

Through the gap in the bed frame she inspected the floor. She looked up at the open ceiling, but in the shadows, she couldn't see whether bugs gathered in the rafters. Satisfied she'd done all she could, she returned the mattress and sheet to the bed.

She ran a hand through her still-damp hair, ignoring Aiden's chuckle behind her. "You may blow out the candle now," she said, proud that she hadn't even chanced a backward glance.

AS ALWAYS, CLAIRE KEPT HER EYES CLOSED FOR A FEW moments when she awoke, languidly stretching until she eased her mind into full awareness. Her stiff body responded in crackling sounds never heard before, and her mind answered in screaming warnings. She jerked awake, flared her eyes open, fully alert, and sat up in bed.

The light of the blessed sun filtered through the cracks in the wood shutter. Underneath the window, yesterday's rain gathered in a puddle on the floor.

Claire's gaze raked the room, falling on the floor by the door. Aiden wasn't there. She looked at the corner of the room. His belongings weren't there, either. Had he abandoned her?

The thought sat like a badly digested meal in her stomach. The frightening moments she'd been through since she left the cathedral yesterday had made her keenly aware of her precarious situation, and without Aiden's protection, she was pretty much on her own to deal with the unsavory characters that seemed to populate this time and place. But worse than that, she'd be without her answers.

If Aiden had had a change of heart, she hoped he hadn't gotten too far, for she was going after him. She'd be damned if she got nothing for her troubles.

She jumped out of the bed. On the table she found a bowl, a carafe of water, and a dish containing what she assumed was soft soap. She smelled it and wrinkled her nose.

Bypassing the malodorous goo, she splashed her face with cold water, dried it with a square of cloth neatly folded by the bowl, and then hurriedly dressed herself with her still-damp clothes. She raked her hair clip through her curls, lacking the special wide-bristle brush she normally used, and hoped her hair didn't look like a spiderweb.

She was dabbing a drop of honey-scented cologne between her breasts when a knock on the door startled her. She almost dropped the small bottle to the floor, and then quickly hid it in her purse. Had Aiden returned? "Come in," she called, and then almost bit her tongue. What if it was one of her attackers? The ridiculous thought that any of those men would knock on her door asking permission to enter calmed her down.

The door opened slowly, and a petite woman, almost entirely covered by the bundle of clothing she carried in her arms, entered the room.

"May I help you?" Claire asked, sure this place couldn't possibly offer maid service.

"Ah, my lady, I be the one helping you. I be called Mari." She lifted a black eye to Claire. Had she been injured in the fight last night? A pang of guilt jabbed at Claire as she tried to remember if she'd seen the young woman before.

"My father relayed to me the tale Lord Aiden told him of your ordeal," Mari said, dropping the bundle she carried on the bed, revealing she was a serious candidate for breast reduction.

Ah! Claire's memory was suddenly jogged. *The waitress.*

"Marauders set upon my lady stealing all your belongings, leaving you in your undergarments, and killing your escort and lady maid. You must have been frightened out of your wits!"

What the hell was she talking about?

" 'Tis a wonder you survived," Mari continued without a

pause. " 'Tis a blessing indeed that aid happened upon you. Howbeit, a mixed blessing, I say, as it was Lord Aiden who rescued you. 'Tis understandable my lady would not wish to be alone after such an ordeal, and I am certain naught unseemly happened in this chamber last eve. Lord Aiden, being a lord of the realm and a knight, surely spent the eve in vigil guarding my lady's life and honor. Still, my lady's reputation might suffer. Tongues wag without reason, you know."

While Mari talked, her gaze took in every inch of Claire. Maybe making mental notes so she could wag some tongue of her own later on, Claire decided, somewhat amused. When her gaze settled on the ruby ring Claire wore on her middle finger—a gift her father had given her on her sixteenth birthday—Mari gasped. "My lady, what a wondrous ring! I never saw the likes of it, so bright and shiny, worthy of a princess. 'Tis mighty fortunate indeed you hid it from your attackers. It must be worth a king's ransom."

Resisting the urge to hide her hand, Claire continued to listen to Mari's monologue. "If I was in my lady's shoes, I would offer the ring as just reward for Lord Aiden's coming to my rescue, and be done with it. And if my lady permits me to be so frank—" As if she had been anything but, Claire thought, unable to put a word in edgewise.

"However overly grateful you might be to Lord Aiden, methinks 'tis a grievous mistake to put your life in the hands of a haunted man." She lowered her voice. " 'Tis rumored his ghost is insanely jealous and spares no woman who dares approach him." She crossed herself. "Naught under heaven could ever convince me to spend a moment alone with a haunted man, not even a man as handsome as Lord Aiden. Consider yourself fortunate indeed, my lady, that no harm has befallen you thus far. And though 'tis mighty brave of you to allow him to escort you, surely you will not entertain any further dalliances with such man.". She raised her black eye to Claire. "Mayhap my lady is even unawares of his plight?"

The sudden pause caught Claire by surprise. After words being spat at her like a machine gun, the silence rang loudly in her ears. Mari's accent was much stronger than Aiden's, and it took Claire a moment longer to wholly grasp her speech. Claire shook her head. It still baffled her she could understand Old French at all.

With relief, Claire surmised from Mari's hurried report that Aiden hadn't fled as she'd feared. In fact, he'd been quite busy concocting an extraordinary story to explain her presence and their meeting. As for her reputation being tainted, that was not something she worried about. She didn't belong to this time, she didn't prescribe to these old-fashioned rules, and she surely didn't care what people thought of her. She was here for a very limited time with only one purpose in mind: to unveil her past.

Somehow, though, she couldn't quite ignore the slight tightening of her heart. How ridiculous! She wanted nothing to do with Aiden but to know what had gone so horribly wrong in the past between them.

Realizing she had left Mari hanging for an answer, she decided to corroborate Aiden's story and further their cause. "I'm well aware of the ghost's existence, and I'm not afraid."

"Ah!" Mari breathed. The single word carried a wealth of meaning. Was she disappointed or surprised? Expecting Mari to fire off a series of questions, Claire was surprised when she changed her tune. "I see my lady already wears her undergarment." She lifted two dresses for Claire's inspection. "Which one would my lady fancy?"

Befuddled, Claire stared at the dresses.

Having done her job in warning Claire of the ghost, maybe Mari felt justified in turning her attention to more mundane matters. And then she droned on about how she had gotten her hands on the gowns, of how fine Claire's undergarment was—by which of course, she meant Claire's dress—and what a wondrous veil, such rich colors and silky fabric.

Claire tuned her out. Brown or green sage? She hesitated. Neither color did much for her complexion. Made of velvet, the gowns were too heavy for spring, and a little small for her 140-pound body.

Claire reined in her disapproval. She wasn't in a fashion show. And she couldn't refuse to wear the dress. She had already gained enough unwanted attention in the dark hours of night. How conspicuous would she look in broad daylight?

When in Rome . . . , she decided philosophically.

Choosing the green sage dress, she shifted her scarf off her shoulders and tied it around her neck, letting it fall on her chest, and then dropped the dress over her head, rearranging the scarf over it. She considered removing her own dress but decided against it. She didn't want to have to lug it about. Mari busied herself tying the lacings on the back of Claire's dress, tightening the fit.

Mari stepped back to inspect Claire and seemed content with the results. Her gaze lowered. "'Tis a bit short, but there is no hem to let out—" She stopped abruptly, her eyes widening in surprise. "Oh!"

Claire's gaze shifted down, looking for the source of Mari's astonishment. Her red polished toenails peeked from under the dress. Claire curled her toes, trying to hide them, but it was impossible. Seeing a pair of flat, low-cut, raw leather shoes on the bed—part of her ensemble, no doubt—Claire quickly put them on. They fit quite tightly, but as long as she didn't have to wear them for long stretches of time, they would do just fine. And they covered her red toenails.

The good news was that the sight of her polished toe-nails had effectively silenced Mari. If only she had thought of that earlier. Claire chuckled quietly, amazed she could be amused in such a stressful time.

"My lady, the hose." Mari regained her voice.

Claire eyed the pair of woolen stockings more appropriate for winter than the spring day outside and shook her head. "It's all right, Mari. I have no need for those at this time."

It was obvious Mari didn't agree, but at least she didn't argue. By now she probably thought that if Claire was crazy enough to get entangled with a haunted man, being a weird dresser wasn't too far off.

No matter. She had no time to pacify a stranger she probably would never see again. What mattered was finding Aiden to figure out how their plan had changed.

"Thank you for all your help." She wished she had some money to give to the woman. She hoped Aiden had already paid her for her services. Fitting her purse's short handle on her shoulder, and picking up her sandals, Claire headed for the door.

"My lady, your hair," Mari called again, still trying to do her job. She waved a little comb in her hand that would only ensnare her curls.

"My hair is fine as it is. I'm pressed for time, Mari. I don't want to keep Lord Aiden waiting."

"Not even a ribbon?" Mari insisted, clearly disappointed at Claire's lack of desire for hair adornment.

Claire shook her head. "Thanks." And then she left the room. She didn't dwell on her eagerness to see Aiden again.

AIDEN'S HEART FLIPPED WILDLY THE MOMENT HE sighted Claire descending the stairs. He rose and watched as she ambled his way, her curls bouncing on her shoulders and her skirt swaying with the gentle movement of her hips. There was something innately beautiful about the way a woman moved, Aiden thought. Mesmerized, he followed Claire's approach.

A moment too late, he realized he was gaping at her. Hastily, he averted his gaze and shifted back down the bench, leaving room for her to sit by him.

"Good morning," she said, alighting by his side.

Her sweet honey scent enveloped him. Aiden inhaled deeply, relishing the moment. It had been a long time since a woman shared a meal with him. Memories of moments past filled him. Quickly, he ignored them. The past was an anchor he wished to be free of.

"Good morn." He finally found his voice. "I trust you slept well."

"Well enough. Bugs and all."

The memory of Claire killing the creepy-crawlies with her odd shoes made him grin all over again. She had gone about it with such zeal, as if it was her God-given duty to rid the chamber of the pests.

Catching her looking oddly at him, he suppressed his grin, lest she think he mocked her. He was uncertain how to act around her, fearing he would set her off with a wrong word.

Mercifully, the serving wench appeared, bringing mead, cheese, and bread for Claire and another tankard of ale for him. The wench reached across from Claire to give him his drink, all the while eyeing him suspiciously.

He should be used to such response from women; he understood they feared his ghost and not necessarily him. Still, it never failed to vex him.

He took a good swig of his ale while Claire thanked the wench, and seeming unsure of her drink, as if she'd never had mead before in her life, sniffed it suspiciously. Apparently the sweet smell convinced her to give it a try, and she took a tentative sip. She nodded approvingly, and took a larger sip. "By the way," she said. "Thank you for the dress."

"It is not deserving of your beauty." At one time in his life, such words had flown easily from his lips. These days they were rarely spoken. It felt odd to be paying compliments to a woman, even when he truly believed in the truth of his words. Such niceties had long ago been stripped from his everyday life.

Aiden's gaze caressed Claire. A ray of sunshine found its way through the lone open window, falling on her head as a halo, revealing hints of red in her dark curls. There was fire in her, and the mere thought sent a shot of awareness through his body. He cleared his throat. "I shall have finer gowns made for you soon."

"I think this one will do just fine. There's no need to go to any more trouble than you have already."

"It was no trouble."

Her subtle reminder that she did not intend to remain by his side was not lost on Aiden. Though his heart rebelled against it, his mind warned that Claire was not meant for him.

The truth soured the ale in his belly.

He must get Claire to Delacroix without delay. The longer it took him to get her there, the more chances for her to have a change of heart.

"I was told of my misfortune and your daring rescue," she said.

It took a moment for Aiden to understand what she was referring to. Then he remembered.

Would she scold him for his tall tale? Not knowing why Claire was so oddly dressed, without an escort or maid, appearing out of nowhere and with apparently nowhere to go, he had spun the tale to explain her presence and their association.

Had he transgressed? Was she vexed with him?

Damnation! It was her doing. Had she trusted him with whatever secrets she so zealously guarded in her heart, he would not have had to lie on her behalf. Still, why should she trust him? She knew naught about him, and what she knew was not too enticing.

Perchance she was fleeing from her kin. Her safety might depend on anonymity. Even not knowing, he was prepared to defend and protect her.

"Was it not how it happened?" he chanced, eyeing her closely.

She took her time to answer. With not so much a flinch, she finally agreed. "It is exactly how it happened."

And right then, Aiden knew. The secrets Claire held in her heart were of immense importance to her. And grave enough for her to go along with the falsehood he had created. He vowed to eventually destroy the barrier she had erected between them and learn all that there was to know about Claire.

Her hand brushed back a stray curl from her face. Her costly ring, with the stone so unusually bright and clear, reminded Aiden again that Claire was no lowborn wench. And thus a very possible prey to intrigue.

"I was also told—" Her voice snapped his attention back to their conversation. "That you kindly agreed to be my escort. I assume you meant around town, right?"

"It is to Delacroix, my home, that we journey," he said. "And the sooner the better."

"I don't remember agreeing to travel anywhere with you."

Aiden cocked his head and shot her a fulminating look. *Mère de Dieu!* Had she another change of heart? "Are you already reneging on our bargain?" he asked quietly. If he lost control of his temper now, he would never regain it.

"I agreed to help you with your ghost. I don't see why I can't do that right here."

"The ghost lives at Delacroix," he explained, realizing that Claire knew little about the matter. Could that be the reason for her lack of fear? Aiden refused to dwell on the implications, were that true.

She scooted down on the bench and turned to him. "You mean to tell me your ghost doesn't follow you around?"

Her astonishment compounded Aiden's unease. "She need not," he said. "My fate is well-known in all Christendom. No woman, anywhere, would come near me. Did you fail to notice how the serving wench would not even approach me with my ale?" The mere speaking of it utterly vexed him.

She nodded. "Still, I'm confused, Aiden. If your ghost doesn't follow you around, and she lives at your home, then what prevents you from moving elsewhere?"

"Bah!" Aiden's fingers shot to the back of his neck. "Leave my home behind?" he sputtered. "I was born in Delacroix, and there I shall die. Never will I leave it, ever." The mere thought was abhorrent to him. For ten years, he had had no other purpose but to make Delacroix once again his, and for the rest of his life he would fight to keep it in his family. And now Claire wished for him to pack and leave without so much as a thought? The woman had lost her wits.

"All right, all right," Claire said. "It's not my place to tell you where to live, but I hadn't counted on leaving Chartres. How am I going to return home if I need to leave on short notice?"

"Why would you have to leave in a hurry?"

"You agreed not to ask questions," she reminded him.

Indeed, he had. Claire had his hands tied behind his

back. He blew out a breath. If he failed to convince her to follow him to Delacroix, all would be lost to him. He must reassure her any which way he could. "I vow to take you anywhere you wish to go, Claire. Anytime you wish to go." He could not be more accommodating. It was unmanning to make so many concessions, when she had made none of her own.

She took another sip of her mead, nibbled on the cheese, obviously pondering her next move. "How far is Delacroix?"

Aiden suppressed a sigh of relief. "It is not far, two, three days' ride."

"Not far!" She harrumphed. "And I bet we will be riding horses, right?"

He nodded. What else would they ride? Oxen? Perchance she expected a litter, Aiden thought. Where on earth would he find one on such short notice?

Obviously pondering what to do next, Claire took another sip of mead, nibbled on the cheese. Finally, she pushed the cup away and rested her hand on the table so close to his, his fingers itched to touch it.

She stared at their hands for the longest time, and then, without warning, pressed her warm hand on top of his. Awareness shot straight to his heart. Aiden sucked in a breath, his gaze darting from their hands to her face. Her eyes glazed over. She seemed caught in rapture, almost in pain. The slight trembling coursing through him surely emanated from her.

Fearing for Claire, he was about to withdraw from the contact, when in the next moment, she tumbled forward and he found himself shoring her limp body against his chest.

Chapter 9

IN *a flash, Claire was back behind the old country church. Bells pealed in the air, a cool late morning breeze blew in her face, voices clamored in the background, though there was no one within sight.*

The festive atmosphere contrasted sharply with her somber mood. Her heart was so heavy she could barely breathe as she stared at a luxuriously dressed Aiden standing before her. Then, as if in slow motion, the palm of her hand made contact with the hard planes of his face. His head slammed to the side with the force of her blow, then sprang back to stare at her with troubled eyes.

Sucked out from the time vacuum of yet another memory, Claire found herself in Aiden's arms. Quickly, she disentangled herself from the web of his embrace. Blood pounded in her ears, making it difficult for her to focus.

Sweat coated her forehead. She wiped it with a trembling, tingling hand.

"Claire, are you ill?" Aiden's voice was laden with concern.

She couldn't even look at him; her eyes clouded with residual anger from the moment she'd just recalled. She scooted away from him until her right hip almost fell off the bench. "Just give me a moment, please."

Gripping the table, she inhaled deeply, steadying her palpitating heart. What had Aiden done in the past to provoke such a violent reaction on her part? There was no doubt that that moment in time had set up a chain of events that haunted her into her next life.

The puzzle of her past life was beginning to take shape in the form of one repeating scene behind an old church. She needed a lot more pieces to have the whole picture, though.

Could she continue to withstand the debilitating memories? Would the effect on her body and heart continue to escalate? She thought she had lost consciousness for a brief moment while she was in the throes of the flashback. What would happen to her next time they touched?

And she was supposed to be alone on the road with this man?

Aiden pushed the cup of mead in her direction. "Take a sip. It might help."

She did, if only to gain time to compose herself.

The moment stretched indefinitely. Aiden finally broke the silence. "If you do not feel well enough to travel this morning, we can delay our journey till the morrow," he offered. "But no later. I have many obligations waiting for me at Delacroix."

Claire knew how desperate Aiden was to return home. That he offered to delay the trip on her account warmed her heart.

However, what would be the point of postponing the

trip? It could only serve to lengthen her stay in this time. She couldn't remain here indefinitely. She, too, had a life waiting for her at home—a business, a brother who would worry sick when he didn't hear from her in the next few days. Her heart tightened at the thought of causing Nick distress.

She wished time—past and present—didn't run in tandem. That the future would be exactly where she left when she returned, and Nick wouldn't even notice her absence.

She could wish, but time was out of her control. What she controlled were her decisions. She had promised to help Aiden with his ghost, and if his ghost lived at Delacroix, then there was where Claire should go.

Besides, who knew what kind of secrets Delacroix held for her? Maybe the old country church was within the property. Maybe seeing it would bring Claire a complete memory of what had happened between her and Aiden. Maybe meeting Aiden's ghost would be the catalyst to the answers to her past.

"I feel well enough to travel," she said and skidded off the bench. Maybe she had moved too fast, maybe she was still under the influence of the aftereffects of her flashback, but her head swam, and she swayed on her feet.

Aiden reached to steady her. Claire moved out of his reach. "Please don't." She didn't need to compound her weakness with another memory just yet.

His hands fell alongside his body. His face grew ominous. He understood nothing.

And she could explain nothing to him.

CLAIRE LIFTED HER HAND, SHADING HER EYES FROM the bright daylight as she stepped out of the dark inn. Puddles—the remains of last night's storm—spotted the unpaved roads where most of the muddy surface was already drying.

Warm air feathered against her face, redolent with the scent of flowers, greenery, and after rain. A tremor of awareness skittered down her spine as she surveyed her surroundings, taking in what her soul had sensed last night but her eyes had failed to confirm. Narrow streets, flanked by shabby-looking buildings, wound up the hill and down to the river. Her gaze glossed over them, absorbing the details of a hillock or bridge in the distance, until it rested on the cathedral at the top of the hill.

Her heart skipped a beat.

One of the cathedral's famous spires was missing. Chartres cathedral's twin spires were built in different centuries—one in the early 1100s, the other about four hundred years later. That meant her present time fell between those years.

Good God! There was no denying she had traveled back in time.

A shudder ran through her. She was really in the past, a part of unfolding history in a time long gone. Hardly easy to accept, yet impossible to deny. She had either to accept it or know she had gone insane. And she wasn't ready to admit to the latter just yet.

Maybe at the end of this adventure she would have lost her mind entirely.

Or maybe she would have finally found herself.

Either way, she couldn't waste time and energy dwelling on how she had breached the walls of time. This extraordinary journey was the answer to her quest; she must keep going.

Explained was her fascination with medieval life. She had lived in this time; vestiges of it had clung to her soul. Wishing she could explore the area, and especially the cathedral, in more depth, she glanced at Aiden, but he was already marching in the opposite direction. Meanwhile, a group of colorfully dressed women decked in flowers and accompanied by eager-looking men ambled past.

She turned her back on them and followed Aiden to the stable by the inn. While he went inside to arrange transportation, she waited outside. People continued to walk past her in a joyful parade, all heading to the top of the hill. She wondered what the celebration was. Flute music, animated conversation, and laughter drifted to her.

The atmosphere was charged with excitement, inviting and contagious. Claire shifted on her feet, curiosity making her antsy. One smiling young woman broke from her group and approached her. She placed a crown of wildflowers on Claire's head. "Come a-Maying with us," she invited with a big smile.

Claire accepted the crown but politely declined the invitation. *May Day!* Aiden had told her about the festivities last night, but she'd completely forgotten it, maybe because he had referred to it as Roodmas Day.

That puzzle solved, she found a tree stump and sat on it, preparing for a long wait. It would surely take a while for Aiden to hire and saddle horses, she thought. Meanwhile, she would distract herself with the sights. Before long, however, Aiden marched out of the stables, trailed by two horses and a boy carrying a stool. Surprised, Claire rose. Such efficiency meant Aiden had made arrangements earlier.

It annoyed her he'd taken for granted that she would follow him. Then again, he was just being practical. If she had refused him, he could always cancel his plans. Otherwise, he would be prepared.

Claire shook her head. Why must she debate every detail about Aiden, assigning motives she was far from knowing to be true? Because he raised in her a bewildering dichotomy of emotions, an odd mix of familiarity and strangeness, of attraction and repulsion.

She watched his purposeful stride toward her. Her heart fluttered. When he stopped before her, the sunlight shone on him, and Claire discovered Aiden's eyes were the deepest shade of blue she'd ever seen. Just like in her memories of him. Why had she thought they were dark?

With one enormous beast on his right, another smaller, but no less imposing, on his left, Aiden pinned her down with a wide grin and an admiring gaze. Was that a glint of male interest in his eyes? Until now, he had seemed less than charmed by her—though she must admit, he had reason. She'd been quite belligerent toward him.

He asked you to marry him! The thought intruded. But his marriage proposal had sprung from need not desire.

He bowed. "Hail to the queen."

Remembering her crown of flowers, she motioned to remove it, flushing with mild embarrassment. She'd mistaken mirth for interest. He was just joking with her.

"Nay," he cried, stalling her hand in midmotion. "Your beauty warrants such title. May Day could not have a more deserving queen."

Claire narrowed her eyes at Aiden. There was no amusement in his gaze but a keen male interest. He *was* flirting with her.

Pleased—maybe a little too much—she finally admitted her attraction to Aiden wasn't merely a reflection of the past. And, therefore, all the more dangerous.

Still, she couldn't help but admire his strong, handsome body. Surely he, too, found something attractive in her. Though not a stunning beauty, she had some pleasing features: her hair, her height, her curves. She wasn't obsessed with being overly thin, though she worked out to keep her weight under control. Men were appreciative of female curves.

In interest of keeping the mood light, she asked, "Is there a king of May?"

"No king. The queen rules supreme this day."

Wouldn't that be nice! "Well, if there was a king, you would fit the role quite nicely."

He seemed pleased with her compliment, which in turn pleased her again. She could get used to this.

She shouldn't get used to this.

"I beg your forgiveness for making you miss the festivities." He pointed at the people passing them by. "But we must be on our way."

Claire shot a wistful look in the direction of the cathedral. Torn between witnessing firsthand a medieval celebration she'd only read about and realizing she must be on her way, she agreed with him.

Aiden stepped back and with a wave of his hand, set the boy to motion. The boy placed the stool on the ground by the beautiful chestnut mare that was to be her mount, then quickly sprang back, giving Claire a wide berth as if she had some contagious disease. His nervous glance darted from Claire to Aiden.

What was that about? She wasn't underdressed as before. Did she look different than the other women of this time? Shrugging it off, she walked to the stool, expecting Aiden to help her mount. He remained where he was, holding both horses' reins and making no move to help her.

She thought medieval men were supposed to be gallant and chivalrous. So much for her royal status!

Disconcerted, she looked at the boy, who seemed to shrink back even farther.

All right! She didn't need their help. Peeved, she discreetly reached underneath her medieval gown and bunched up her tight-skirted underdress. The gown was wide enough to accommodate horseback riding; her dress was not. That problem resolved, she stepped on the stool, and holding on to the pommel, hoisted herself onto her mount with some difficulty. She teetered in the air for a brief moment, fighting not to go over the saddle and not to over-compensate and fall back. Thankfully, she finally settled safely atop the horse. The mare was one of the biggest horses she'd ever ridden. She hoped she wouldn't have trouble controlling her.

She rearranged her dress, leaned forward, and rubbed the mare's neck, making soothing sounds, giving herself time to familiarize herself with the feel of having a giant animal beneath her, and the mare, the same chance to get accustomed to her. It was fortunate she had riding experience, but she wasn't too thrilled at the thought of spending hours, or according to Aiden, days, on the back of a horse.

She almost groaned. Settling back, she took the reins from Aiden's gloved hands, taking great care not to touch him, and watched as he swung his big body onto his greater mount with considerably more grace than she.

From atop his stallion, he tossed a coin to the boy, who caught it while it still flipped in the air, and then with what she considered unnecessary care not to get too close, the boy removed the stool from under her foot. As he dashed away, he flipped another worrisome glance at her.

"What's up with him?" Claire asked.

Aiden shot her a confused glance.

"The boy seemed afraid of me," she rephrased. "Do you know why?"

"He was just being mindful. I warned him not to touch you," he said.

Comprehension swiftly dawned on her. Aiden had noticed her reaction to his touch and probably assumed she was abhorrent to physical contact. He couldn't know he was the only one who affected her adversely.

She decided to leave him in blissful ignorance. At least for now.

"That was nice of you. Thank you."

He nodded and pushed his mount forward.

WITH THE EXCEPTION OF A COUPLE OF BATHROOM stops and the concession of a much slower pace than he was obviously accustomed to, they rode almost without rest for most of the day. Aiden seemed to be inordinately preoccupied with reaching his home in record time. Claire was uncertain whether he was anxious for her to do her miracle work and get rid of his ghost, or if something else drove him to hurry.

Frankly, she didn't much care at this point. She was so tired and sore from the day's ride, all she wanted was a nice warm bath and a soft bed.

She got a cold stream and hard ground, instead.

But she did get wine. And for that she was immeasurably thankful. She sat on a blanket Aiden had spread on the ground for her, across from a fire he had built, consuming the meal he had provided—cheese and bread, both hard but surprisingly tasty. Or maybe it was her hunger speaking. She had no right to complain about the simple fare, since the thought of gathering provisions for the trip had never even crossed her mind before they left Chartres.

If her buttocks weren't so sore from riding, she'd probably kick herself for being so clueless.

Fortunately, Aiden had packed enough food for both of them. Not only that, but he also made fire with flint and kindling, and promised to hunt and roast a rabbit for tomorrow's meal.

A woman had to appreciate a man with such talents.

Now, if she could only get used to the idea of being transported back in time, in the presence of the man from her past, fighting to forget the memory of a passionate kiss and to understand the sorrow of a lovers' quarrel, she'd be in good shape.

Aiden offered her more wine. She accepted it. Through the canopy of trees she could see a few stars in the darkening sky. Fortunately, the weather wasn't anything like yesterday's rain and wind. Cloudless sky, mildly breezy, with a full moon bathing everything in silvery light, made for a very nice night.

Perfect for a romantic rendezvous.

Claire shook her head. That was not at all what she was looking for. "Tell me a little about your ghost," she asked. The subject ought to cool her dangerous thoughts.

Sitting by her, knees drawn up, Aiden extended one foot and pushed a piece of wood into the fire with the tip of his boot. Claire admired the muscles on his long leg, the sheer strength of him. Her thoughts fell into the dangerous zone again.

"She is the ghost of a woman I once knew." The stilted words came out like pulled teeth.

Why wasn't she surprised? Perversely, she pressed on. "Intimately?"

He shot her a what-the-hell-does-that-have-to-do-with-anything look.

She ignored it. "I'm just trying to understand the ghost's motivation." Though the reason was true, she was also morbidly curious about the woman in Aiden's past.

He inhaled deeply, took a good swallow from his cup. "She was my paramour."

His mistress? How cliché! It made perfect sense, however. A scorned woman took revenge on her cheating lover by returning from the dead and making his life miserable and lonely. And she was succeeding exceedingly. Of course, that was only her assumption. There could be myriad reasons for her to haunt Aiden.

"How long has she been haunting you?"

"Ten long years."

No wonder Aiden was at wit's end about it. Had he been alone all this time? As if lost in memories of times long gone, he stared at the fire. Claire took the opportunity to take another good look at him. A dark shadow covered his strong jaw, even though he had shaved that morning. As always, there was a lock of unruly hair falling over his forehead. It didn't seem to bother him. At least she'd never seen him move it away. It was almost as if he was too busy with other more important things to be bothered by such a small nuisance. He seemed to be in his early thirties. Maybe even younger. Life in these times couldn't be too easy, which would surely take its toll on a person's appearance. That meant his affair with this woman had happened when he was in his early twenties. At that young age it was easy to make mistakes, especially concerning affairs of the heart.

"Does the ghost come to you often?" Claire asked.

His gaze returned to her. Midnight blue eyes, she now knew. "She comes to me naught at all."

"What do you mean?"

"She appears only to the women in my life."

"So how do you know she truly exists?"

He snorted. "She exists. Too many people have seen her around the castle; too many lives have been affected by her haunting. Believe it, she exists."

Claire tried to relate that information to her experience with her own ghost. She never really thought herself haunted, though. Her ghost was just there at times, and at others she was not. Her appearances were so brief and without much significance—with the exception of the last two times—Claire had grown accustomed to her and usually tried to ignore her.

Though the ghost didn't appear directly to Aiden, the woman had wreaked such havoc in his life, he couldn't possibly ignore her or get used to her antics.

Claire thought of the similarities between them. Aiden haunted by his ghost, and she haunted by dreams of him.

"What does your ghost do to the women in your life?" she asked. She must do more than just appear to them.

There was a noticeable pause before he answered, "Frightens them witless."

That much goes without saying.

Obviously, he either didn't know exactly what went on with the women and his ghost or he didn't want to reveal what he knew. Regardless, she was getting nowhere with her questions. Maybe if she changed the subject from ghost to victim? "Lord Clovis mentioned you had a wife."

Aiden nodded. "Jeanne. She died soon after Cherise."

"Cherise, being your paramour," she clarified.

He nodded.

"Did they know each other?"

"Briefly."

What a wealth of information that curt response hid.

The wife and the mistress. Were they part of Aiden's life at the same time? Although in medieval times it was an accepted practice for a married man to have a mistress, Claire couldn't stomach the thought. Maybe his wife hadn't either. She itched to learn the details, but *that* would be prying. Besides, if she insisted, he might turn the table on her and demand that *she* explain herself for a change.

"Is there a connection between Jeanne's death and Cherise's ghost?" She remembered Lord Clovis's veiled accusation.

Aiden flipped his cup over the fire. The wine spilled out, hissing like a striking snake. He bolted to his feet. "Despite common belief, Cherise had naught to do with Jeanne's death."

Claire was taken back by Aiden's fury. How could he so adamantly defend a woman who was the cause of all his troubles? Bristling, her sympathies clearly with Jeanne, the cuckolded wife, Claire rose to face him. "Lord Clovis seems to think otherwise."

"Lord Clovis relies on gossips for his opinions."

"How did Jeanne die?" she demanded.

He sighed. "She fell down the staircase."

"And Cherise was nowhere in sight?" Why was she being sarcastic?

"It was said she was there," he admitted.

"Apparently she was there, and she spooked your wife to death," Claire felt compelled to point out. Why couldn't he accept that? Why did he feel the need to excuse Cherise's unacceptable behavior?

"Although Jeanne was a good woman and deserved a better fate, her death was an accident," he insisted, further riling Claire.

Good God! He had cared more for his mistress than his own wife! The realization took Claire's breath away. Blinded by a jealousy she'd never experienced in her life, she walked away from Aiden.

After a few calming breaths, she was able to face him and speak again. She had to let go of the subject of Cherise. Just the mention of the woman's name had her emotions all in tatters.

"How about Lady Marian?" Claire asked. "Was she also your wife? Is she dead as well?"

"Lady Marian fled on the eve of our wedding. Our marriage was annulled, and she is in a nunnery now, alive and well, as far as I know."

At least this one wasn't dead! "Any other casualties I should be aware of?" How many wives had Aiden had?

"Since then, and apart from you, no other woman has dared approach me."

"Can you blame them for being afraid?" Claire snorted. Cherise was more than troublesome; she was out to get Aiden, and pity whoever got in her way.

"I do not blame them, but I grow weary of my plight. That is why I am in desperate need of your help, Claire. Perchance you should apprise me of your plan."

Her plan? She wished she had one.

She'd first thought that by showing no fear, the ghost would realize she had found her match and eventually leave Aiden alone. She hadn't counted on a very determined ghost, or an evil one. She had no experience with those. And no matter what Aiden chose to believe, Cherise wasn't an innocent bystander. She was deliberately driving women to their death and seclusion and God knew what else.

Claire had no desire to be her next victim.

A sudden thought struck her like a thunderbolt. Good God! What if she was wrong in her assumption that her past with Aiden hadn't happened yet? When Aiden had failed to recognize her, she had jumped to the conclusion they had just met. The truth, however, was that she didn't know what she looked like in the past; therefore, she could've been anyone.

Aiden's mistress, his wife, or his almost bride.

Of the three, she could easily dismiss two. Lady Marian was still alive, therefore she couldn't be her. Cherise, the ghost, could also be eliminated. A soul was indivisible and couldn't exist in two different places at the same time.

That left Jeanne, the wife. Being betrayed by her husband and driven to her death by his mistress would surely scar any soul and explain Claire's ambivalent feelings toward Aiden: love and hatred, trust and mistrust.

Claire didn't want to be consumed with revenge. Needing to keep a sane perspective about this whole affair, she reminded herself her purpose in this time was to uncover the truth, not punish anyone for past misdeeds.

But a little settling of accounts between the two women wouldn't be out of place, either.

"My plan is simple, Aiden. I intend to stand up to Cherise. No ghost will send me running, tumbling down stairs, or hiding in a nunnery. In the end, Cherise will be gone, you will be free, and so will I."

It was time for her to do some serious butt kicking.

Chapter 10

THE past four days had been a test in fortitude for Aiden. Between dodging Claire's constant questioning, forcing his horse to a crawl to accommodate her slower pace, thus sorely testing destrier and chevalier's patience, and fighting to control his body's reaction to such close proximity to a more than desirable woman—a challenge he had not faced in years—his nerves were as thin as a hairbreadth.

Thus it was with great relief that he sighted the towers of his home piercing the blue sky. He halted, twisted on his saddle, and waited for Claire to catch up with him. He pointed to the towers through the break of trees. "Delacroix."

With a renewed surge of energy, clear by the way her slumped shoulders straightened, Claire leaned forward for a better look. "Wow! It looks quite imposing."

Pride swelled in his heart. Nestled on the top of a hill, surrounded by a massive stone curtain wall and double baileys, Delacroix was indeed quite imposing. "It has been in my family for generations," he said. "I cannot fathom living anywhere else."

She sat back. "Let's hope you won't have to."

His sentiments, exactly. "Shall we proceed?"

"Just give me a moment." She removed the curious hair clasp—it was not made of ivory, bone, or wood, but of a shiny black material he had never seen before—from her dark curls and raked it through the strands like a hair comb. The movement released the scent of sweet honey entrapped in her hair, stirring in him old memories and new desires. Heart beating harder in his chest, he fought both useless emotions in equal measures.

After days on the road together, Claire's sweet scent was beyond tempting. He had never witnessed anyone perform her daily ablutions with such diligence. At her request he had scurried for water sources in the places they had stopped for the night, so she could bathe. He suspected her sweet fragrance sprang not only from a clean body but also from perfumed oils and whatever other wonders she carried inside her little satchel.

Enthralled, he watched as she twisted her hair in an odd lump on the back of her head and pinned it in place with the unusual clasp, leaving most of her soft curls to undulate over her back and shoulders, and only a few wisps to crown her face in a charming and uncommon coiffure.

He liked that she wore no head coverings. It would be a sacrilege to hide such a glorious mane. He only wished he could feel its silky texture between his fingertips.

While his hands tightened around the reins of his horse, hers smoothed down her skirts. She turned her gaze on him. "I am ready to see your home."

And she looked ready, indeed, though she needed not

have troubled herself much. Claire was beautiful whether covered in mud and rags or decked in furs and jewels. She was not dainty and petite nor fair nor coy. She was a voluptuous, self-assured woman who would strike desire in any man's heart. A little too disagreeable at times, but life with Claire would never lack luster.

That she desired to look presentable as they reached his home pleased him, though he was acutely aware her behavior had little to do with pleasing him.

And that thought brought another to mind. How was he to introduce Claire to his people? He wished he could call her his wife, even if for a short time. Somehow he knew she would disagree. The close proximity such a guise required would give him the opportunity to woo her and possibly make the arrangement permanent. He did not relish the thought of going bride hunting again did Claire succeed in sending Cherise's ghost away.

"There is the matter of explaining your presence at Delacroix," he said. "I believe I should introduce you as my wife."

"I don't think that's a good idea."

Her prompt response, though expected, vexed him. "Are you not concerned with your reputation?" Traveling alone with him, arriving unescorted at his castle, spending unsupervised time with him would greatly affect her reputation.

"Not at all."

Her reply further vexed him. It was most unusual for a woman to be so dismissive of the power of gossipmongers.

But Claire was an unusual woman.

Still, though no one at Delacroix would learn—at least not from him—she had already spent the night with him, albeit innocently, in his bedchamber at the inn in Chartres, they would not so easily dismiss her presence alone with him in his castle. And he had every intention of spending as much time with her as he could.

People tended to fear or disrespect what was different. Claire, with her odd manners and speech, would give enough fodder for gossip and possible adverse reactions. Her disregard for the consequences of her behavior would clearly compound the problem. Particularly, did he succeed in wooing her into marriage.

"Be that as it may," he said. "A woman at my side at Delacroix has been an unseen sight for many years. People will wish to know about you, and if they get no answers, they will make up their own. It is best if I tell them you are my wife. That would entitle you to their respect and obedience."

"And what would they say when I leave?" she retorted. "And I will leave, Aiden. Make no mistake about that. They will think I fled like the others. And that would not help convince other women you are ghost-free."

Feeling a headache coming, Aiden rubbed the back of his neck. He could not fault her reasoning. Damnation! But he could not allow her to dictate her wishes on this. She had already taken too much upon herself. He must gain some measure of control over her.

He inhaled deeply, calling to mind peaceful thoughts that insisted on eluding him. After so many years without womanly companionship, the first woman who dared brave his company had to challenge him every step of the way.

It vexed him. It excited him. Claire made his blood pump harder in his veins. *Alive!* That was how he felt with her.

"Tell them I'm a ghost hunter," she suggested. "That would precisely explain my presence here."

Oh, nay! He would not let her erect another insurmountable wall between them. "That would not do at all. There is no such a thing as ghost hunter. You would be ridiculed by all, or worse, be thought a witch. You do not wish for them to fear you. Besides, let me worry about my fate after you take your leave from my life." As far as he was concerned, that was not a foregone conclusion, anyway. "Thus, I would rather introduce you as my wife, my bride-to-be, or my paramour. Make your choice. Anything else would complicate matters, and I am not willing to be so bothered."

She pursed her lips together, clearly unhappy with his challenge. He stood his ground. He would not back down now. He knew he was chancing much. Claire could spin around at this very moment and leave him alone with no future whatsoever. He held his breath, waiting for her verdict.

"If those are my only choices, then I shall be your beloved bride-to-be." There was no mistaking the sarcasm in her voice.

"Then, beloved bride," he returned in kind. "Follow me to your new home."

"Temporary home."

Aiden allowed her to have the last word. He had won this battle, and was relieved beyond words.

He led her down the dirt path that would take them through the village and eventually into his castle walls. With each step their horses took, Claire snapped her gaze in one direction or the other, taking in every detail with wide eyes, as if she had never seen a village before.

Aiden knew not what to make of Claire. There was so much about her that defied definition. Shrouded in mystery, she seemed at the same time approachable and unreachable. She had the poise of a lady and the brazenness of a lowborn wench; the naiveté of a damsel and the sensuality of a courtesan. She intrigued him and vexed him in equal measures.

He knew not whether to pray for her to change her mind and wed him or to accept that she would quickly depart from his life. After all, such a disagreeable wench could only mean trouble for any man.

Then why did the thought of Claire's departure displease him so?

Despite the odds against a union between them, particularly her intolerance of being touched—a sure preclusion to a true marriage—Aiden refused to discard the possibility. Had she been sorely used in the past? Was that the reason she shied from his touch? he wondered. The thought infuriated him. He would gladly kill any man who had dared hurt Claire.

Did she allow him, he would take matters into his own hands and avenge any wrongdoings done to her. But she had not given him leave, had not even confided in him, had not appointed him her champion. In sooth, she had asked naught of him in return for her aid in the matter of his ghost.

Their relationship was one of inequality. And he liked it not at all. Perchance he could find a way to balance the scale.

They passed the gawking villagers and reached the outer bailey iron-shod gates of his home. He waited for the guards to open the gates for him and ignored the same look of surprise on their faces he had seen on the villagers.

He knew what they were all thinking. Wondering how he had found himself a woman brave enough to follow him to his haunted castle, and when the next tragedy would occur.

Incredibly, the tidings of his arrival preceded him so rapidly people began appearing from every corner of the bailey, gathering on each side of Aiden's and Claire's horses, like a royal guard waiting for inspection.

He sensed Claire's edginess, obviously ill at ease with the spectacle. He pulled his horse closer. "Be not afraid. I shall remain by your side."

"I'm not," she said, clearly lying. "I will be all right."

He nodded.

By the time they crossed the inner bailey's gates, a multitude had already gathered there waiting for them: servants, villagers, men-at-arms, knights, and among them, Jasper.

Damnation! He had hoped—futilely it seemed—that in his absence, Jasper would have left Delacroix. At least the king had not yet arrived.

Aiden halted his horse and dismounted, eager to reach Claire before anyone else did. Jasper was quicker, dashing to Claire's side and offering her his hand.

"Allow me, my lady."

"Jasper, nay," Aiden called in warning, but Claire had already given him her consent. His hands braced her waist and brought her safely to the ground.

Mouth agape, Aiden watched as Claire bore Jasper's touch with no sign of distress whatsoever.

Mère de Dieu! It was *his* touch alone she abhorred!

Anger, frustration, and humiliation twisted Aiden's innards. In two large steps, he reached them in time to hear Jasper say, "Welcome to Delacroix. I am Jasper." Aiden bristled. Jasper had no right to welcome anyone to his home.

"I am Claire."

"Lady Claire," Jasper whispered. "What a sweet name."

Aiden's patience evaporated. He glared down at Jasper. "I see you have met my bride."

Oh what pleasure it was to see the smile disappear from Jasper's face.

His mood slightly ameliorated, Aiden turned to Claire. "You must be exhausted. Let us seek our rest in the great hall."

He did not offer her his arm, fearing she would refuse and thus humiliate him in front of every breathing body in his castle, but waited for her agreement.

CLAIRE'S GAZE RESTED ON THE THREE-STORY HIGH, rectangular fortification that seemed to pierce the cloudless sky, and she suppressed a gasp of awe mingled with dread.

She had already accepted the fact that she had traveled centuries to the past, but emotionally, she could hardly cope with the reality of it.

Taking a deep breath, she willed her feet to move. Immediately, pain shot through her chafing thighs, raw after the long ride. Her quivering legs, much like those of a seaman stepping on solid ground after months at sea, couldn't quite find the right balance for walking.

Four days on horseback, riding through a roller coaster of hills and meandering paths, through woods so thick she had to duck not to be hit in the face by tree branches, was no easy task for a woman who didn't even like camping.

It was no wonder that when medieval people traveled, they carried their servants, bathtub, bed, and all with them in an attempt to make the journey bearable.

As Claire slowly gained ground, she felt Aiden's eyes, and a hundred others, watching her closely. Were Jasper's among them? She stole a glance over her shoulder, but Aiden's great body blocked her view.

Having taken an instant liking to Jasper, Claire was profoundly curious about him. Who was he? Had they met in her past life? He had welcomed her to Delacroix with the authority of a proprietor. Was he related to Aiden? Maybe a younger brother or cousin. They looked nothing alike, with the exception of their height, but then again, she and her brother looked quite dissimilar as well.

Family or not, she didn't miss the undercurrent of antagonism between him and Aiden. She might have exacerbated it when, in her eagerness to get down from her horse before she fell off it in utter exhaustion, she had allowed Jasper to help her down, forgetting Aiden believed she could bear no one's touch.

Well, now he knew it was his touch alone that affected her so.

She stole a glance at Aiden. He didn't look too pleased. She hoped his anger wouldn't interfere with her quest for answers. Fearing an escalation to her flashbacks and that she would give him the wrong idea, she had avoided his touch during the trip. However, as soon as an appropriate moment arose she would seek his touch and his answers again.

With that in mind, she had better pacify him in some way. Besides, Aiden deserved an explanation. She had much to thank him for.

She wouldn't have survived this grueling trip without Aiden. Noticing she was no great equestrian, he had slowed the pace on her account and had helped her care for her horse. He had acquiesced, without loud grumbling, to her frequent requests of water and privacy for bathing, and had fed and protected her.

In her defense, she had done the best she could in a very inhospitable environment. She hadn't cooked but had washed the dishes, gathered wood for fire, and berries from the woods—though some of those Aiden had thrown away for being poisonous. She had refrained from complaining about the long hours on horseback, or the hard ground, or the bland food, and she had ignored the loud, unidentifiable animal noises coming from the woods.

Under her probing, Aiden had broken the monotony of the trip with stories of his fighting in the Crusade, his travels, and the wonderful things he had seen. He even spoke of his dreams of breeding horses, and his plans for Delacroix Castle, once the curse was lifted, but he had balked at speaking further of the women in his past.

At one point, obviously annoyed at her insistence, he had simply stated that he had told her all she needed to know about his past.

How wrong he was! She had barely scratched the surface, and she had no intention of stopping there.

Aiden might be a candidate for the award of most stubborn man in the world, an honor previously belonging to her brother, but she could be as obstinate.

She might have given in to his bride-to-be ruse, despite her misgivings, simply because she'd been too tired to think of a better excuse at the time. She winced at the thought of *ghost hunter*. Even as she'd suggested it, she'd known that wouldn't wash with medieval people.

However, she had seen right through his ruse. Apparently, Aiden had not given up the notion of making her his wife. If her suspicions that she was once married to him and had died because of his betrayal turned out to be true, the role of his wife was one she would never assume again. In any time period. Despite her obvious attraction to him.

Once was enough to have her heart broken for eternity.

She would give him no second chance.

Something soft brushed against her leg, startling Claire. She jumped, catching sight of a white fur ball, a cat perhaps, disappearing behind the crowd watching her. Aiden barely had time to break his stride, slide to her side at the last moment, and avoid bumping into her back.

Claire let out a sigh of relief, thankful for his thoughtfulness. Weakened as she was, she didn't think she could handle a debilitating memory right now. Besides, it wouldn't look too good if she fainted before everyone upon her arrival.

"Sorry," she said.

"Are you well?" Aiden asked.

"Yes, but I'm very tired."

He pointed to an arched doorway on the side of the building. "We are but a few steps from rest."

She nodded. "Lead the way."

She followed Aiden through the doorway and up a narrow, steep stairway that led to the entrance of the great hall on the second floor.

As she walked in, her feet disturbed the rushes covering the stone floor, and a faint smell of sweet fennel rose, overpowering for a fleeting moment the scent of burning wood coming from the sprawling fireplace splitting the opposite wall.

She stopped to take in the massive room with long window slits that offered little illumination and brought in a draft of cool air. Torches on wall brackets flickered warm light on the rich, colorful tapestries hanging on the walls.

Claire had to make an effort not to gape, but it was hard to appear nonchalant when she knew this was a real castle and not a movie set or a dream.

Aiden nudged her forward with an inquiring gaze. It was then that she realized, after a quick glance behind her shoulder, that a multitude, including Jasper, had lined up behind her when she'd stopped. As soon as she moved, people quickly filed past her in the direction of linen-covered tables set perpendicular to yet another table on top of a platform against the back wall.

Aiden headed in that direction, and Claire followed. At the table, a priest—if his dark robe hadn't given him away, the big wooden cross prominently hanging around his neck would have—stood, apparently waiting for them.

The priest lifted his hand, Aiden kissed it. "What need brings you to my table, Father Aubert? It has been long since you last graced my hall."

There was an edge to Aiden's voice that surprised Claire. Was he mad at the entire world?

"I heard of your return and thought it my duty to welcome back the lord of Delacroix." He crooked his head and shot a glance in her direction.

Aiden moved aside, exposing Claire to the priest's

scrutiny. "Then, Father, you may also be so kind as to welcome Lady Claire, my bride-to-be."

The priest hid his shock well, with the exception of a twitch on his upper lip. He lifted his hand to Claire. Tempted to shake it, she kissed it as Aiden had done, though her lips barely touched the wrinkled skin. As tall as she, they stood at eye level, which clearly didn't impress him well. He inched his chin up, giving him the height advantage. Claire let him. No need to make unnecessary waves with a man of the cloth.

He was wiry as a toothpick, not the caricatured image of the rotund medieval priest. His full head of snow-white hair contrasted sharply with the dark of his robe, and his eyes shone with what Claire thought was disapproval. Didn't he want Aiden to find a wife?

"Father," she said to break the interminable silence.

He looked her over really well and then demanded, "I shall hear your confession as soon as possible, my lady."

I think not!

She smiled agreeably. She didn't even want to think what a medieval priest would say if she confessed to being a time traveler from the future.

And that she believed she had lived in this century before.

And that she had been married to the very man to whom she was supposed to be a bride-to-be now.

No, she didn't want to think what the priest would say.

The word *heresy* flashed crimson before her eyes along with burning flames.

She continued to smile agreeably and followed Aiden around the table. He took his place at an intricately carved armless chair, pointing to a simpler chair by his side.

Claire took her seat, flanked by Aiden and Father Aubert. Jasper's bright blue eyes bore into her as he, too, found his place by Aiden. He seemed itching to tell her something and looked clearly annoyed by the seating arrangement.

Caught between a rock and a hard place, with the deep blue sea blocking her escape, Claire knew it was only a matter of time before the devil in the form of Cherise made an appearance.

Apparently, everyone else was wondering the same.

Uneasy gazes pierced her from every direction as an eerie silence filled the hall. Was the distrust and fear she saw in their eyes solely a result of Cherise's pernicious haunting? Or was their distrust aimed at her, a stranger in their midst?

A young boy carrying a bowl of rosemary-scented water placed it on the table before Aiden, distracting her from her disturbing thoughts.

"My lady first," Aiden commanded, and the boy obeyed. As he was also carrying a piece of cloth in his hand, Claire assumed this was a washbowl.

She washed her hands, dried them with the cloth, folded it neatly, and returned it to the boy with a word of thanks. The boy moved the bowl to Aiden, who went through the same motions, then the bowl was moved once again to the priest, and finally to Jasper.

Claire wondered what would be the pecking order had Aiden not offered the bowl to her first.

Father Aubert rose abruptly. For a moment, Claire thought he would demand her confession right then and there. Or worse, condemn her before even hearing her. Realizing everyone else had also risen, she belatedly sprang to her feet.

"Mensae caelestis participes faciat nos, Rex aeternae. Gloriae. Amen." The ancient priest's surprisingly strong voice filled the hall.

"Amen!" Everyone responded in unison, including her.

It suddenly dawned on her she had instantly understood the priest's prayer of thanksgiving said in Latin. She knew a little Latin, but not enough for such quick assimilation. Obviously, the same power that enabled her to understand Old French was at work here. Claire shook her head. She didn't pretend to understand any of what was happening to her.

As they settled back on their seats, a young man filled the pewter cup before her and Aiden. She understood the medieval custom of sharing drink and food. She waited until Aiden offered the cup to her, and then took a good, fortifying swallow. The wine was tastier than what they had on their trip, though not the quality of the wine she was accustomed to drinking in her own time. She returned the cup to the table, expecting Aiden to turn the rim to an unused spot before drinking from it. Instead, he placed his lips precisely where hers had been before, clearly savoring her discomfort as he drew a swig.

He offered her the cup back, his gaze holding hers captive, challenging her.

Should she show defiance by drinking from another spot? Or should she return his challenge by touching where his lips had tasted?

Claire took the cup from him, taking care not to touch his fingers, and brought it to her lips, her gaze sustaining his. Her lips touched where his had been, and the memory of the passionate kiss of the past flashed before her eyes.

Warmth rose to her face, her breath quickened. Realizing she had licked her own lips while staring at Aiden's mouth, she quickly looked away.

And found all eyes dead on her.

Chapter II

AIDEN'S hunger for food vanished the moment Claire had licked her lips while looking at him. A hunger of a different kind devoured him. The thought of those lips closing over his made him tremble with a need the likes of which he had not felt in a long time.

Out of necessity, he had learned to curb his lustful nature, lest he go insane. Since meeting Claire, however, he could think of naught else but to feel the softness of her skin under his fingertips, to taste the sweetness of her tongue, to bury himself inside her so deep, he would forget all those lonely, empty years.

Aiden groaned. And realized he had done so out loud. If he was not mindful, he would disgrace himself at his table, before Claire and his entire castle.

Would that not be the crowning moment of his humiliation!

Aiden forced his gaze away from Claire and onto his seldom-filled hall. All eyes were on the high table. Aiden could well imagine their thoughts. Few of the knights, men-at-arms, and women knew him from earlier years. Most were retainers of Jasper's late father. When Aiden recovered the castle ten years ago, he had much hope of bringing old and new together. He had vowed not to blame them for their lord's greed.

It might have worked out well had the haunting not begun and the ill tidings spread so quickly. Soon, visitors became few and far between, until no one came anymore. Peddlers refused to make their usual stops at the castle to sell their wares, and even the nearby villages became reluctant to offer any trade with Delacroix's people. Whoever could, left; others, who had no choice, remained.

With the passing of the years and his continuing failure to bring a wife and normalcy to Delacroix, people grew even more distrustful and resentful. Every ill begotten on them was blamed on Cherise's ghost, and consequently on him.

He could not fathom living the remainder of his life under such a dark cloud if Claire failed to drive Cherise's ghost away. He must wed again! Not only for his own needs but also for the needs of his people. Delacroix must thrive once again.

With a flip of his hand, he motioned for a page to fill his cup. Claire did not wait for him to serve her but picked at the food at random. She even smelled the meat before tasting, not a sign of good manners.

Once again, Aiden was not certain what to make of her.

"I have tidings from the king." Jasper spoke, intruding on his thoughts.

Aiden inhaled deeply. He had known the truce would not last. "And what has our sovereign to say?"

"He has postponed his visit indefinitely."

Murmurs of disappointment filled the hall. Could Jasper not keep his voice down?

"I was looking forward to seeing the king," Father Aubert said. "It would be the first visit from our monarch to Delacroix."

Aiden did not miss the priest's accusatory tone. He had no doubt on whose side Father Aubert's loyalty lay, since he had inherited the priest from Jasper's family.

"The king was supposed to come here?" Claire asked, looking impressed.

"Aye," Jasper answered in Aiden's stead. "A courageous man, the king is. Not many have braved a visit to Delacroix in many years."

"Why?" Claire asked, and seemed to want to bite her tongue. Aiden wondered if she'd realized the reason as soon as she asked the question.

Silence blanketed the hall. No one wanted to miss a word spoken at the high table.

"My lady," Father Aubert said. "Surely you are aware of Lord Aiden's plight."

"Do you speak of him being haunted by a ghost?" she asked.

The priest crossed himself.

"I am well aware of Aiden's predicament. And I have no fear."

Aiden heard the collective gasp, saw their horrified gazes sweep over Claire. Even Jasper seemed to have lost his voice in shock.

Mère de Dieu! How he admired Claire's mettle at this moment.

"My lady is courageous," Jasper said. "But surely you do not fully comprehend the danger you place yourself in by merely being here."

"It is just a ghost," Claire insisted.

"It is an evil spirit," Father Aubert spat.

"You cannot possibly be Aiden's bride," Jasper added.

"Claire is not your concern, Jasper."

"A lady's safety is every knight's concern."

"This lady's safety is mine alone."

"As was my sister's?"

The accusation hung heavily in the air.

What could he say that he had not said a thousand times before? Everyone present here knew he believed Jeanne's death was an accident. He had already made that clear to Claire. To pursue the matter would be to give fodder to doubts in her mind. And that, Aiden did not need.

"It has been an arduous journey," Aiden said. "Perchance my lady would like to seek her rest."

Claire said nothing.

A small grin spread on Jasper's face.

Would Claire gainsay him before everyone? Aiden wondered.

His gaze strayed from her to the tables below the dais. No one was eating. All eyes were on them. All ears attuned to every whisper.

Finally, Claire leaned toward him, so close he thought she would touch him. His breath quickened with the possibility.

"I would like to hear what Jasper has to say," she whispered near his ear. "If you wish this conversation to be private, then arrange for a place where the three of us can talk out of reach of prying ears. Otherwise, you leave me no choice but to defy you before everyone here. I will not face Cherise blindfolded, Aiden. You owe me this much."

She smiled in a beseeching manner, giving the impression she was begging his indulgence on some frivolous matter.

Aiden hoped he was equally successful in hiding his emotions. Keeping his brittle smile from turning into a frown, he took a moment to compose himself. Knowing

Claire, she would do exactly as she said. He had no choice. And he resented the hell out of that.

"Perchance my lady would enjoy a little fresh air before you seek your rest," he said loud enough for everyone to hear.

"Oh! What a splendid idea, Aiden."

Jasper chimed in. "May I join you, my lady?"

"If my Lord Aiden has no objection," Claire said, giving him an innocent look.

As if he had a choice!

Jasper shot him one of his annoyingly mocking grins. Had he heard Claire's whispered words?

"You know where the garden is located," Aiden said. He rose and led Claire out of the great hall.

THE SUN SLOWLY MADE ITS WAY DOWN THE WESTERN horizon, casting long, reaching shadows before Claire, Aiden, and Jasper, as they stepped out of the stairway into the bailey of Delacroix Castle.

Aiden turned left, then left again, rounding up the corner, heading for the back of the castle, obviously with a clear idea of where they were going. Claire followed in silence. Jasper didn't fall too far behind. This was not a stroll in the park. There was purpose to their trek.

The sweet scent of honeysuckle and roses suddenly reached her. The wind must have turned, she thought. She hadn't noticed the fragrant air earlier.

At the back of the castle, a six-foot tall trellised wall of thick, twining honeysuckle vines thriving with fragrant flowers enclosed a secluded garden, offering great privacy from prying eyes. The wall ran for about thirty feet, ending where the terrain suddenly sloped down. A stepping-stone stair, embedded on the slanted ground, led down to an orchard in the meadow below.

But Aiden didn't go in that direction. Instead, he found a

man-made gap in the trellised wall and ducked underneath
it. Curious, Claire followed him in.

A carpet of green grass and wildflowers covered the
ground, looking amazingly undisturbed, since there was no
discernible path for walking. Not wanting to crush the pretty,
vibrant flowers, she trod with care to a hedge seat in the middle of the garden, some fifteen feet from the entrance.

Unfortunately, nature didn't fare as well under Aiden's
and Jasper's big boots, as they mindlessly trampled their
way to her side.

Claire circled in place, taking in the panoramic beauty
surrounding her. Along the trellised wall and the castle's
wall, separated by neat rows of stones, flowers and herbs
grew in abundance on a raised plot that extended three feet
from the wall. Every so often, a small ornamental tree—
evergreens, Claire thought—broke the pattern.

Surprising, however, was the absence of rosebushes.
She could distinctively detect their heady scent. Weren't all
medieval gardens filled with them? Following her nose,
she ambled around the hedge seat, finally locating its
source. A lone rosebush partially obscured by honeysuckle
vines brimmed with pale rosebuds, some in full bloom,
others just opening their silky petals.

The potent perfume the lone bush exuded, matched,
mingled, and at times, overpowered the sweet scent of the
more abundant honeysuckle in a battle of senses that had
no loser.

"In my sister's time, this garden was filled with roses,"
Jasper said, startling Claire out of her thoughts.

Jasper's sister, Jeanne! Claire had surmised that much
from the conversation at the hall. A strong emotion filled
her, a tightening in her heart. If she believed she was
Jeanne in the past, then Jasper would be her brother. Maybe
even Nick's past incarnation.

No wonder she had instantly liked him.

He broke one honeysuckle vine entwined around the rosebush. "There wasn't a *chèvrefeuille* in sight then. In verity, I once caught Jeanne tearing at a lone vine with such ferocity so at odds with her gentle nature."

If Jeanne didn't like honeysuckle, how did Claire become so fond of the sweet-smelling flower? Then again, surely there were things in her future that had no relation to her past life.

"Did you ask her why?" Claire asked.

He dropped the broken vine on the ground. "She called them leeches. Said they soaked the life from others. I was just a boy then, I did not question her further. Now I wonder whether her words were meant as an analogy for people and not plants. She died days later."

The pain in Jasper's voice tore at her. "You must miss her terribly."

"Indeed, I do. Jeanne was more than a sister to me. She took me under her loving care when our mother died at my birth, even though she was little more than a child herself. And when my father remarried soon after, she protected me from his new wife's wrath. God saw fit not to allow the witch to birth children of her own, and thus she saw fit to make our lives miserable."

So much of that story reminded Claire of her own relationship with Nick. She, too, had taken her brother under her wing when their mother had suddenly died. But unlike Jeanne and Jasper, she and Nick were fortunate enough to grow to adulthood together.

Claire considered a life without Nick, and a hole burned in her gut.

"Jeanne was a gentle, loving woman and undeserving of her fate," Jasper said, shooting a glare of pure hatred at Aiden. "Were it not for you and your paramour," he accused, "my sister would still be here amongst us."

A muscle twitched on Aiden's cheek, but he said nothing. Claire had a feeling they had rehashed that subject many times before.

Jasper returned his attention to her. "I know you not, my lady, and neither do I pretend to understand the reason behind your liaison with this man, but I beg you, heed my words: If you wish no evil to befall you, as it befell my sister, you—"

"Jasper—" Aiden grunted.

Defiantly, Jasper ignored the threat in Aiden's voice. "—You must depart immediately from Delacroix. This is a dangerous place for a woman."

Doubt spread quickly in Claire's mind. Was Jasper's overdramatic plea a result of his sorrow, or was there more to Jeanne's death than Aiden had let on?

"I understand your bitterness," Claire said. "But how can you be sure the ghost of Cherise had anything to do with Jeanne's death? Maybe it was an accident."

"My belief exactly," Aiden interjected.

Aiden would believe that, wouldn't he? Claire thought with some bitterness. But wasn't she defending Cherise as well? She wasn't defending her, Claire justified herself. She was just trying to get to the bottom of this story.

"There was no accident, Jeanne was murdered," Jasper declared with absolute certainty. "She did not fall down the staircase on her own; she was pushed down by Cherise's ghost."

"A ghost is a spirit," Aiden retorted. "It does not have solid hands to push people around."

"Somehow Cherise did just that," Jasper replied.

Claire tuned them out. A frisson of unease iced her heart. Could it be possible? Could Cherise have pushed Jeanne down the stairs? Claire remembered the ethereal nature of her own ghost in the future—she clearly remembered her hand going through her ghost when she'd attempted contact with her.

And yet, hadn't her ghost also moved a magazine—a solid object—from the rack in her bathroom and dropped it at her feet?

Good God! Jeanne's death could have been the direct result of an intentional assault on Cherise's part.

Claire felt the blood drain from her face. Had she been too nonchalant about this whole ghost thing? Again the thought that her ghost and Cherise was one and the same assailed her. Before, she had dismissed it quickly. The very nature of Cherise's haunting precluded her from uniting Claire with Aiden. But now she wondered . . .

Had Cherise lured her centuries into the past to punish her once again? Was she destined to die twice at the hands of her past enemy?

But if that was her intention, why hadn't Cherise harmed Claire in the future? Why bring her to the past?

It made no sense. Vaguely, she caught the end of Aiden's rebuttal. "—It is cruel of you to frighten her so."

"I mean not to frighten her but save her life."

"By spreading falsehoods?"

"I saw it with my own eyes." Jasper punctuated each word with a jabbing finger in Aiden's direction. "Cherise pushed my sister down the staircase. You believe whatever your black heart tells you, but I know the truth."

"You would not know the truth, did it bite you in the face."

An irrational anger shook Claire. *Damn Aiden!* His wife had died because of Cherise. *She* could be in danger, and he still defended his former mistress? Had he loved the woman that much?

"Why can't you admit that Cherise's ghost is no angel?" Claire asked Aiden. "She has haunted you for ten years now, has made your life miserable, and was the cause of your wife's death, whether she actually pushed Jeanne down the stairs or merely caused her to stumble down in fright."

Silence greeted her words, which irritated her even more. It was impossible to have a good fight with a man who kept his mouth shut.

"Face the facts, Aiden. If it weren't for your former mistress, you wouldn't be in the situation you are right now. Why do you doubt Jasper? What has he to gain by lying? Don't forget he has lost his sister."

"And I have lost my wife."

"You don't seem too heartbroken about that."

"How can you say that?" Hands balled into fists, Aiden turned a furious glare at Claire. "You know naught about the past. Jeanne was a gentlewoman, and I cared for her."

"Obviously not enough, since you dishonored her by betraying her with another woman."

"My liaison with Cherise preceded my marriage to Jeanne."

"Oh, so that's supposed to justify your behavior."

"I see no need to rehash the painful past," he said.

He wouldn't, would he? Claire thought bitterly.

"Both women are dead. What you need to know is that Jasper has much to gain by spreading such lies."

"Such as?"

"Delacroix. My birthright—"

"Which is also mine," Jasper interrupted.

"I don't understand," Claire said.

"It is a long tale, but I will give you the short of it. Years ago, Jasper's father stole Delacroix from my father—"

"Your father dishonored himself and lost his castle on his own."

"Now that Delacroix has returned to its rightful owner, Jasper thinks he can use the same underhanded tactics as his sire to recover it."

"There is no need for underhanded tactics. Delacroix is mine, and it shall—"

"Stop it! Both of you," Claire cried, before the word match between them turned into fist fighting. They eyed each other defiantly, breathing heavily like two fighting bulls, unwilling to give an inch.

Unbelievable! "One of you lost a sister, the other, a wife, and you bicker over who will inherit this pile of stones?"

Two heads spun in her direction. Jasper looked chastised; Aiden paled. Had she hit a nerve with both men?

Intellectually, she understood their motivation. Land ownership was the ultimate goal for the medieval man. But emotionally, she wanted to sock them until she drew blood.

Wasn't this castle big enough for the both of them? Couldn't they unite in their loss? Claire breathed deeply to calm herself. Who would inherit Delacroix was none of her business. She had enough to deal with right now.

"Jasper, I appreciate your concern, and your candor, but if you don't mind, I would like to speak with Aiden in private."

"I am not certain it is prudent for you to be alone with him. The ghost might appear at any time."

According to Aiden, Cherise did not appear to him; therefore, for all accounts, she was safer with Aiden than alone. However, she didn't share her thoughts with either man.

"You have no right to dictate Claire's actions," Aiden said.

"I am perfectly capable of deciding my own actions," she interrupted.

Another moment of silence fell upon them.

Then Jasper bowed respectfully. "I shall abide by your wishes, my lady. Do you need me; I am at your service." He shot Aiden a fulminating glare, then pivoted and left.

Claire waited a few moments after Jasper had left the garden, and then turned her attention back to Aiden.

"Why did you fail to warn me of Cherise's true menace?" she asked.

"I told you she haunts the women in my life."

"You didn't tell me she had caused the death of your wife."

"That is Jasper's understanding, not mine. Besides, I would never allow any harm to befall you."

"How can you expect to protect me from Cherise's wrath when you failed to protect Jeanne?" Claire wouldn't even consider that Aiden might have wanted to get rid of his wife. If she believed that, even for a moment, she'd be certifiably insane to remain in his presence.

In a clear sign of exasperation, Aiden's hand flew to the back of his head, and he kneaded it forcefully, as she'd seen him do several times before. "Jeanne never spoke of being haunted. Never told me she was in danger. How was I to know? Her death was the first report of the ghost's appearance. And it was Jasper who spread the rumor."

She heard the anguish in his voice, saw it in his face. "But now you do know. And yet, you still defend Cherise."

"I have done Cherise wrong, Claire. I wish her to find her peace, as I wish to find my own."

"You have done your *wife* wrong," Claire corrected, miffed.

"I have done both wrong," he finally admitted. His shoulders slumped. With the weight of his guilt or with the hopelessness of his situation? Maybe both. Maybe neither.

Claire didn't know. And therein lay her problem. She couldn't accept Aiden's defense of Cherise, but neither could she entirely condemn him for doing so.

Her anger lost its edge, and an overwhelming tiredness weighed her down.

Every truth she uncovered about her past revealed yet another layer of secrets. There wouldn't be one simple answer to her quest, as she'd hoped.

Her gaze rested on Aiden's face. There was pain there, a deep, ingrained pain. For Cherise? For Jeanne? For himself? Incredibly, it didn't matter. Her heart hurt for him, and she wanted to pull him closer, run her hands through his thick, dark hair, and comfort him.

Claire rebelled against the temptation. She didn't want to feel anything for Aiden. Not pity, not love, not desire. He had wronged her. She would be damned if she let him wrong her again.

Chapter 12

THE moment Claire stepped back into the shadows of the great hall, a chill ran through her body. Unsure whether it was the cold seeping from the dark stone walls or some presaging of doom that made her tremble, she vainly rubbed her arms to make the sensation go away.

What had she gotten herself into?

It was a little too late for regrets, she reminded herself. She had put herself into this predicament; it was up to her to see it to the end.

Unable to match Aiden's long steps, she shuffled after him through the nearly empty hall until they reached a flight of narrow stone steps hugging a tall wall, half hidden in an obscure corner.

Claire was so tired it was a tremendous effort to lift her feet high enough to clear the steps. When they reached the landing, her heart was pumping hard. She stopped to catch her breath and stole a glance back to the darkened staircase. Had Jeanne found her death down those steps? Instinctively, Claire moved away from the ledge.

Aiden waited for her beside an open door. Claire moved through the opening and into what looked like a huge walk-in closet. There was no window, but two large torches offered adequate illumination. Two very big wooden chests lined the wall facing the door. To their left, another more elaborately carved trunk lay by a sitting stool, and on the opposite wall, several wooden pegs, some empty, some in use, flanked an arched doorway. Some of Aiden's belongings were already there: his traveling leather bag, his coat hanging on the peg.

Aiden crossed the open archway, and Claire followed him into the bedroom. Her breath caught in her throat. It was magnificent. Almost as large as the hall below, its walls were decorated with rich, colorful tapestries. Several strategically placed torches chased shadows into obscure corners.

Warmth and the earthy scent of burning wood radiated from a cavernous fireplace with a carved mantel, giving the room a homey feeling. Before the fireplace, a cloth-padded wooden bathtub filled with steaming, fragrant water beckoned invitingly.

Claire almost moaned at the thought of a hot, scented bath.

Reluctantly she pulled her gaze away and over to the solid wooden table, big enough to seat at least eight people, flanked by two benches and an armless chair, by the far wall.

Two arching windows, with a pillow-lined alcove underneath them, graced the wall between the table and a massive, canopied bed set on a raised platform in the middle of the room. The bed's linen curtains hung open, revealing silky pillows in deep burgundy and a woolen coverlet lined with white fur.

Claire's stomach suddenly knotted.

Had Aiden shared it with Jeanne?

Considering she believed she'd been Jeanne in her past life, she could hardly understand the stab of jealousy prickling her.

Claire swung her gaze away from the bed. She was just tired. It had been five very long days since she'd stepped inside Chartres Cathedral and her life had turned inside out.

"Does it meet with your approval?" Aiden asked, leaning a shoulder against the wall.

"It is quite an impressive room." Were she to live here, she'd change nothing but replace the rushes on the floor with thick rugs.

Catching herself, she quickly dismissed the thought.

She had no intention of living here. Ever again.

"The bed and the table were carved for my father for the occasion of his wedding to my mother," Aiden said.

"They are beautiful." Her gaze fell on a beautifully carved trunk near him. "Did that belong to your parents as well?"

Aiden's gaze fell, and he pushed away from the wall as if he'd seen a snake. "Nay. It belonged to Jeanne."

Claire realized that the memory of Jeanne affected Aiden. She just wasn't sure exactly how.

"You might find a suitable gown in there," he said.

It was creepy to wear a dead woman's clothes, even if she'd been that woman in a past life. However, she didn't think she could continue to wear the same dress she'd had on for four days now. She'd washed it a couple of days ago, but she was sure, once she undressed, the thing would probably walk around by itself.

Claire nodded. "I will."

"I believe you shall be quite comfortable here. It is very unlike the small chamber we shared in Chartres."

That got Claire's juices flowing again. Did Aiden mean

to share this room with her as well? She could do without that one temptation. "Any place is fine with me. I don't want to inconvenience you."

"It is no inconvenience."

Was he joking? Hadn't he been as bothered by her naked presence as she'd been by his?

"Naturally, I shall sleep in the antechamber," he added, probably in answer to her horror-stricken expression.

Managing to swallow her relief, Claire eyed the smaller room through the open archway. Even that was too close for comfort. "Wouldn't that scandalize the whole castle?" she asked.

"I thought you cared naught for your reputation."

Touché!

"It is *your* reputation I worry about. The more permanent you let people believe our relationship is, the more you will have to explain when I leave. I think you are digging your own grave."

A shadow crossed over his eyes. "I am a man who refuses to die without a fight."

"That is your prerogative. I'm just warning you."

"Besides, how can I protect you if I am far away?"

"Do you realize there are no boundaries for a ghost? Cherise can go through walls or appear anyplace. Your being a few feet away offers me little protection."

"My being far offers you none," he countered. "Besides, you must not believe everything Jasper says."

"I know enough about ghosts to know that what Jasper claims is possible. I don't know enough about your former mistress, however, to know whether she wishes merely to chase me away or kill me straight up."

A frown marred his forehead. "I would never allow harm to befall you. Trust me in that."

Trust him! Wasn't that the whole issue between them?

"Your secrecy about the past doesn't exactly lend itself to trust."

He arched one eyebrow. "If I follow your reasoning, then I must think the same of you. Secrecy shrouds you, Claire. You have never explained your willingness to help me, particularly when you ask naught in return. For all that I know, you could be in cahoots with Jasper with the intent of ruining me."

"That's ridiculous!"

"Is it?"

"All right. You made your point. I should trust you as you trust me, right?"

In two large steps, he reached her. Claire tilted her chin up at him. His blue eyes darkened, and he held her gaze unflinchingly. "If you truly believe I would put you in harm's way for my own benefit, I shall have the horses saddled and ready to depart at your command. I shall take you back to Chartres if you ask, Claire."

The moment of truth. "You would take me back now, if I asked, after all the trouble you went through to bring me here?"

"I would. I shall." There was no hesitation in him.

Was he bluffing? Should she call him on it? Should she give him the benefit of the doubt? There wasn't a single reason she could think of to explain Aiden wanting to harm her. He'd had plenty of opportunities to do so these past days.

Now, Cherise was another matter.

Claire shook her head. She'd been wasting her energy fighting Aiden. She needed to stop that. She'd come here to find out about her past, and her past was intimately tied to both Aiden and Cherise. Besides, she might be blowing things out of proportion. Jasper could be wrong about Cherise; he was only a boy at the time of his sister's death.

Maybe Jeanne had been so scared at the sight of a ghost she'd missed her step and fallen to her death on her own.

That wouldn't exonerate Cherise, but it would give some perspective on her power.

Claire wasn't easily scared. She'd seen a ghost before, and she was prepared to be spooked. Even if Cherise had the power to handle solid objects, Claire wasn't powerless. She could fight back. Forewarned of the possibility, she was ready to defend herself. Cherise would not get the best of her. Not this time around.

"I offered you my help with your ghost, Aiden. And I don't intend to go back on my word. Now, if you'll excuse me, I'm exhausted, and I would like to rest."

There was no denying the relief stamped on Aiden's face. He lifted his hand toward her, his fingers so close he almost touched her hair. Her stomach quivered—she wanted his touch that bad. Catching the sway of her body forward, she flinched back, out of his reach. She wasn't afraid of a flash-back now, she was afraid of her need for him.

She rushed to the bathtub, practically tripping on her feet. "Is this water for me?"

He nodded. "I shall order help for you." He marched to the door.

"Don't bother." She really wanted to be alone.

He pivoted. "You shall have a lady-in-waiting. No one would dare disobey me on this."

Realizing no one would want to be near her as long as Cherise was still around, Claire didn't want Aiden to force a poor, scared woman to serve her.

"I can take care of my needs, Aiden, and I would really rather be alone, anyway."

"Ah, Claire," Aiden whispered. "Clearly you have never been truly alone. I shall be in the antechamber, should you need me."

Heart caught in a fist, Claire watched him leave. She felt his loneliness in the depth of her soul.

AIDEN DOUSED THE OIL LAMPS IN THE ANTECHAMBER and sat on the floor, head and back against the cold wall, staring at the glimmer of light shining through the archway. Night replaced dusk outside, and he wished to rest, tired from the long journey and sleepless nights.

In silence, he listened to the sounds of Claire in the bedchamber: her gown whisked over her head, her shoes falling on the floor, her bare feet disturbing the rushes. Water splashed when she entered the bathing tub, conjuring up sensual images of her naked body.

He could almost see the warm, fragrant water lapping against her breasts, the contrasting cool air hardening her nipples. He envisioned her hands, slick with soap, sliding over her breasts, down her belly, her soft thighs, the dark triangle below. . . .

His loins tightened painfully. Aiden gritted his teeth and shifted uncomfortably on the floor, grudgingly resigned to endure the torment he had suffered since he had met Claire. It was difficult enough to control his raging desires with no woman around to tempt him. Having Claire so close, and yet unreachable, made it all the more agonizing.

Perchance he should seek another bedchamber for himself, put some distance between them, but he did not want to leave Claire alone. He should just step outside. He would still hear her, did she need him.

He did not move. He sat there, punishing himself, wishing for what he could not have.

The longing to hold a woman in his arms, to run his hands over her soft skin, to taste the sweetness of her mouth was so strong, Aiden locked his jaw not to groan out loud.

And for some unfathomable reason, he wanted that woman to be Claire.

For even when she vexed him, he wanted her nearby. When she mistrusted him, he strived to prove his worthiness to her. When she flinched from his touch, he despaired to make her want him.

Had he ever felt this way about a woman? His thoughts turned to the past, to the passionate Cherise who had made him burn; to the kind and gentle Jeanne who had made him care; to Lady Marian who had inspired no great emotion in him but shame.

Claire, on the other hand, inspired more emotions in him than he could possibly name. Jeanne's determination to prevail even when life accorded her defeat was present in Claire. As was Cherise's willfulness and passionate nature.

Ah! Passion. Aiden had glimpsed it in her eyes moments ago. Stunned, he had almost dared to touch her then. It had taken all of his willpower not to pull her into his arms, even knowing she would flinch from his touch. As she had.

It puzzled and vexed him that he affected her thus. He would give much to understand the reason behind her adverse reaction.

Claire was a mystery to him. He had always known what Jeanne and Cherise wanted from him. Claire, on the other hand, asked for naught. She neither bent to his will, as Jeanne had, nor rebelled against it, like Cherise.

She simply disregarded him with impunity.

As she disregarded the importance of his castle to him.

Pile of stones!

The familiar words hurled at him by two different women at two different times. Perchance a woman was simply incapable of grasping the importance of a man's birthright.

He listened as Claire finished her bath and then finally

settled down in his soft bed. She tossed for a few moments seeking a comfortable position, and then quieted.

Barely breathing, Aiden waited a long time for a sign she was no longer awake. Silence reigned in the bedchamber.

She slept!

Aiden wished he, too, could find his rest, but his unsatisfied body held him captive, clamoring for release. Fatigued as he was, slumber eluded him.

He closed his eyes, and his mind filled with thoughts of Claire's naked body—the fleeting image he had glimpsed of her body at the inn in Chartres, multiplied and enhanced by his imagination—her glorious hair spilling over his chest, his mouth on her breasts, himself inside her. Sweet release came swiftly. Aiden groaned, aloud this time, and clasped his lips, hoping Claire had not heard him.

There was no sound from the bedchamber. Heart still thundering in his chest, he reached for a rag and cleansed himself. Finally, body satiated but heart empty, exhaustion overtook him, and he dozed off.

When he opened his eyes again, he was uncertain of how much time had passed. He rose stiffly, stretched the kinks in his back, and then strode to the archway, stealing a glance inside the bedchamber. All the lamps still burned brightly, and through the open bed hangings, he saw that Claire slept in wild abandon.

He marched inside the bedchamber and silently doused all but one lamp. Honeysuckle fragrance spilled in through the unshuttered windows. Aiden distinctly remembered them being shut last night. Had Claire opened the windows in the middle of the night? Surely after he had fallen asleep; otherwise, he would have heard her. Usually, he was a light sleeper, but he had slept longer and heavier than he normally would. He looked through the window. Dawn was upon them. He must prepare for the day ahead.

He found a bucket of cold water by the bathing tub

and the soap container, and picked them up to use for his ablutions.

Instead of walking out, however, his feet brought him closer to the bed. The sweet scent of honey Claire favored wafted up to him. She lay on her back, arms thrown back alongside her head, face turned to the side, lips slightly parted, moist, inviting. The fur-lined bedcover rested over her chest, covering her breasts but tantalizing him with a peek of naked flesh. Her dark curls spilled over the pillows and her face, contrasting sharply with her pale skin. She could not know the effect her glorious hair had on him. Unable to resist, he leaned over and captured a curl between his fingers. The feel of the silky texture against his rough thumb sent a shot of pure pleasure through him.

Claire moaned and tossed her head to the side, pulling the strand of hair from his hand. Aiden stepped back. Even in her sleep, she rejected him.

Still, he should not be here, should not touch her while she was unaware of his presence. He wanted her awake. He wanted her willing. He wanted her to want him.

Mère de Dieu! He must have her at all costs.

Aiden spun around and crossed into the antechamber before he did something he would sorely regret.

Chapter 13

CLAIRE awoke slowly. Still immersed in the sensual dream, she kept her eyes closed, seeking to prolong the wonderful sensations thrumming through her. She could still feel the weight of a man's body over hers, his mouth slanted over hers, his deep thrust bringing her to the peak of pleasure. She sighed, stretching in the soft mattress, riding the last vestiges of the incredible orgasm.

Languidly, she rolled her head to the side. The sweet scent of honeysuckle burst into full fragrance. Mind still dulled by the dream, she opened her eyes, slowly focusing on the swaying bed hangings and the room beyond the white screen. A lone lamp burned on the far wall, and the weak gray light of dawn filtered through the open windows, casting more shadow than light in the room. Yet it was enough for awareness to hit her like a bucket of cold water, drawing shivers from her heated body.

In a flash, remembering where she was, she jackknifed in bed.

Had she been dreaming of Aiden, or was the erotic encounter a memory from their past together? But how could it be when she hadn't touched him? Either way, she'd had a glimpse of the passion she'd been missing in her life. For a moment, she wished she had in fact shared her bed with him. Quickly she dismissed the thought. Not only was that impossible, given that she couldn't even touch the man without spinning out of control physically and emotionally, but also it was a complication she couldn't afford. She had no intention of creating new memories with Aiden. The old ones had kept her captive long enough.

She crawled out of the bed. Her gaze fell on the open windows, and she ambled in that direction. The scent of honeysuckle was stronger now, floating in the air with the gentle breeze coming from outside.

Kneeling on the pillowed seat underneath the window, she stared at the cloudless, pewter-colored sky, still sprinkled with stars. Chased away by the looming sun, the full moon hung low in the fleeting night, fighting not to renounce its place as daybreak slowly approached from the east.

Claire inhaled deeply, trying to remember the last time she had greeted the birthing of a new day. Crouching down on the soft pillows, she rested her elbows on the windowsill and her eyes on the horizon.

A wisp of white on the ground below caught her attention. Curious, she leaned forward, realizing the garden was right under her window. No wonder the scent of honeysuckle was so strong. In the early hours of dawn, shadows still shrouded the secluded area, and Claire couldn't see the grounds clearly. After a few moments of scrutiny, she gave up.

About to relax back on the pillows, again she caught the

sway of gauzy white material with the corner of her eye. She sprang up immediately. The distinctive form of a woman seemed to materialize out of nowhere into the middle of the garden.

A shiver ran through Claire's body. *Cherise!*

Claire didn't dare move, afraid she'd lose sight of Cherise or give the impression she was afraid of her. This was their first encounter; time to establish the rules of the game. The ghost seemed to understand. She remained in place for what seemed an eternity, giving Claire plenty of time to see her. Then, unhurriedly, she reached up and unveiled her head, revealing wavy, red-sprinkled golden hair past her waist. She crooked her head up and looked at Claire.

Claire inhaled sharply. Despite the distance, and in the gray light of dawn, she recognized Cherise as her ghost in the future.

Gazes locked, Claire watched Cherise bring her fisted hand forward with controlled movements. A stick jutted out of her hand. She unfurled her fingers as if in an offering, and the stick—a deflowered stem, Claire belatedly realized—plunged to the ground. The petals floated in the breeze like small pale butterflies.

There was no misunderstanding the gesture. She had thrown a gauntlet at Claire.

Did Cherise think a crushed flower would scare her? Claire smiled down at the ghost, and taunted, "Bring it on."

"Claire!" Aiden called from the next room. Claire jumped. Remembering she was naked, she hauled a pillow in front of her to cover her body.

"Don't come in," she cried. "I'm not dressed."

"Are you well?"

"I'm fine. Just give me a moment." She spun around, glanced through the window, but Cherise was no longer in the garden.

Damn!

Claire dashed to Jeanne's trunk, jerked the heavy lid open, then pulled out the first dress she saw: a burgundy gown with embroidered sleeves. She dropped it over her head and pulled it down her naked body. She hurriedly laced it up, picked up her leather shoes, and dashed to the doorway.

She skidded to a stop. "Are you dressed, Aiden?" she belatedly remembered to ask. All she needed was to see him naked. The mere thought brought wild scenes of her dream back to mind. She shook her head to dispel the allure.

"I am dressed."

Relieved and a little disappointed, Claire crossed the archway. Aiden had changed clothes. His finger-combed damp hair and the faint scent of pine suggested he had bathed and shaved as well.

"Good morn," he said while he fastened his sword belt around his narrow hips. Hips that her thighs had eagerly embraced in her dream.

Gulping down a dry swallow, she leaned back against the wall. "Good morning." She dragged her gaze away as she put her sensible shoes on. They were ugly, and they didn't fit her well, but they were all she had. She didn't dare wear her own sandals. It would draw the wrong kind of attention.

"You rose early." His gaze raked over her. Self-consciously, Claire ran a hand through her hair, smoothing the curls in place. She must be a sight, hair unbrushed, face unwashed, dress unlaced. Aiden, on the other hand, looked freshly groomed and good enough to eat.

"I saw Cherise," she said to break the dangerous mood she was falling into again.

"Where?" he demanded as he pushed past her and into the bedroom.

"Down in the garden. I saw her through the window, and I'm going down to see if she's still there."

He spun around and in two large steps overtook her and blocked her way to the door. "You go nowhere. I will look into it."

"I don't think so. Did you forget the reason I came here? I need to show Cherise I'm not afraid of her. Besides, wasn't it you who thought she could do no wrong?" Did her words sound as brittle to him as they did to her own ears? *Damn, irrational jealousy!*

"I am not willing to take a chance with your life."

Foolishly pleased with his response, her brain ceased to function for a moment. Only a brief moment, mercifully. Her facing Cherise wasn't for Aiden's benefit only; it was largely for her own. "Thank you for your concern, but I'm going down to the garden, anyway."

He expelled an exasperated breath, then, resigned, opened the door wide. "Then we shall go together."

"Fine with me."

Claire crossed the threshold before Aiden. Though sunlight slowly crept inside her bedchamber, the windowless corridors were quite dark. She allowed him to go ahead of her. He knew the castle's layout better than she did. Single file, they descended the stone staircase. To prevent tripping on her gown—Jeanne must have been taller than she was—Claire gathered the skirts in one hand. With the other, she held on to the cold stone wall for balance. By the time she reached the landing, her hand was icy cold, and shivers ran through her body.

Aiden waited for her to reach his side, and then together they crossed a hall that was beginning to stir for breakfast. Servants were still setting trestle tables, but a few men were already consuming their morning meals. They acknowledged Aiden's presence with a respectful nod and watched her with undisguised curiosity.

Were they surprised she was still alive? Or were they shocked at her state of dishabille?

For the second time this morning, Claire wished she had paid more attention to her appearance. She wasn't worried about impressing these strangers, but she didn't want to look too conspicuous, either.

Plastering a smile on her face, she drew closer to Aiden. His lips curled into a small grin. What had him so pleased? she wondered.

Outside, the sun peeked behind the trees, streaking the sky with a blushing light. She managed to keep up with Aiden's pace, but the moment they entered the garden, she overcame him, going straight to the spot where she'd seen Cherise. She looked behind bushes, under the hedge seat, and thoroughly inspected the ground.

All she found was a single defaced rose.

She picked up the deflowered stem and showed it to Aiden. "Not exactly a welcoming gesture."

"What exactly did you see?" he asked.

Claire described the ghost and the circumstances of her appearance.

"It is Cherise," Aiden agreed. "Did she see you?"

Claire nodded. "I think she knew I was there all along, and this whole crushing of the flower is a symbolic warning to scare me off. It also proves she is very capable of moving and destroying solid objects."

Aiden rubbed the back of his neck. "Claire . . . Perchance it was a mistake bringing you here. It would be best did I take you back to Chartres."

Was Aiden starting to believe Cherise was a real threat? The thought was encouraging and sobering at the same time. However, despite the danger, she wouldn't turn her back on the truth now. "I'm not going."

"Think not of your vow to me. I release you of that."

"It's not only that. I will not leave until I get the answers I came for." The moment the words came out of her mouth, she knew she'd said too much.

Aiden's eyebrows furrowed. "What has your quest to do with Cherise?"

What could she say? Surely, the truth was out of the question. Aiden believed in ghosts, but the concept of reincarnation might be a tad too much for him to accept. Especially if she revealed she was his deceased wife.

Knowing that lies had a way of catching up with you, Claire decided to stick as close to the truth as possible. "Cherise has done me wrong in the past, and I want to settle this account with her once and for all."

"You knew Cherise?" He looked baffled.

"She stole the heart of a man I once loved." More truthful than this, she couldn't be.

Aiden frowned. "Sir Guillaume?"

Who the hell was Sir Guillaume? She didn't agree nor contradict him.

He took her silence as confirmation. "He never mentioned your name when we served together in the holy war, though when I met him, he was already wedded to Cherise."

The triangle had just become a quartet. "So Cherise betrayed her husband with you, and you betrayed your wife and friend with her. Charming couple you two made."

Aiden bristled at the obvious contempt in her voice. "Guillaume was already dead when I met Cherise. And Cherise and I were never together after my wedding to Jeanne."

His clipped words of excuse had little calming effect on Claire. Anger and jealousy churned inside her. Struggling to control her temper, she clapped her hands in mock praise. "Congratulations on your self-control."

Aiden's face flushed red. "Why do you condemn me so readily? You know naught of how it was for me back then."

"You're right. I don't know anything about what happened, so why don't you elucidate?"

"Why would you care?"

With stunning clarity, Claire realized she did care, and a lot. She cared enough to wish Aiden would deny his love for Cherise and would give her a perfectly reasonable explanation for his behavior.

Good God! She didn't seek the truth; she wanted to forgive Aiden. Cowardly, she refused to probe too deeply into her motivation.

Still, it would do her no good to keep goading him. She tapered down her animosity. "I'm sorry if I seem judgmental. It's just that I know how much it hurts to be betrayed."

"I suppose you have never hurt anyone unwittingly."

There he went again, defending Cherise. Before Claire could spout an angry retort, her former fiancé's face flashed before her eyes. She had hurt Scott deeply, even though she'd never meant to cause him any pain. Was she using one set of standards for herself and another for Aiden and Cherise?

She blushed with shame. She didn't know what had happened between Cherise, Jeanne, and Aiden. Could Jeanne's jealousy have been unreasonable? Could she trust Aiden's assertion that he and Cherise were not lovers after his marriage to Jeanne, even though it would be an acceptable practice in these times?

While her mind raced with unending possibilities, the silence grew ominous between them.

"I will take you back to Chartres," Aiden declared.

She shook her head. "I'm not going."

"I cannot allow you to risk your life for my sake," he said. "And it is foolish of you to do so for the sake of a man who left you for another woman."

Claire almost choked at the irony of his words. "I need to confront Cherise for my own sake, Aiden."

"What can you possibly gain by it?"

"Satisfaction."

"Is not your life too high a price for such small reward? This must end now, Claire. There has been enough tragedy at Delacroix. Forget the past. I have no doubt there are many men eager to win your heart and make you forget a man who was undeserving of you."

Hypnotized, Claire watched Aiden's hand reach for her.

"Were I free, I would be eager to make you forget him," he said. The moment he touched her, it was as if a lightning bolt had struck her. Her breath caught in her throat, her vision blackened, her knees buckled, and a memory overtook her mind.

She was back behind the old church with Aiden.

"Why must you fight me in this?" he asked. *"You have my heart, is that not enough?"*

"I would rather die than see you with another. I cannot accept it, Aiden."

"You have no say in the matter. Do not make demands of me that I cannot fulfill."

"Even after what I have just revealed to you?"

His gaze softened. He sighed. "That changes naught, and you know it."

Tears stung her eyes. Her chest compressed with pain. She could not breathe. Heart wrenched with sorrow, she allowed anger to overtake her.

"Bastard," she cried, and slapped him so hard, his face slammed to the side. As it sprang back, he stared at her with troubled, saddened eyes.

From a distance, Claire heard Aiden calling her name. She blinked.

"Claire, are you ill?" Aiden asked.

Dazed, she realized she was back in the garden, and Aiden bore her dead weight in his arms. Still holding her, he dragged her to the bench. They slumped down on the hard surface. By experience, she knew no other memory would come to her now that the first touch had passed.

Still, raw with the emotions from her flashback, she reached two trembling hands and rested them against Aiden's chest with the intent of pushing him away.

The warmth of his skin burned through the fabric of his shirt and seared the palms of her hands. Emotions that had nothing to do with remembrance flooded her.

Her mind screamed that Aiden had wronged her in the past. That though Jeanne had clearly asked him to give up Cherise, he had been unwilling to sacrifice his mistress for the sake of his wife.

Then why would he tell Jeanne that she held his heart? There must be another explanation for his betrayal. Had Cherise held some terrible secret over his head? Did Jeanne know what it was? Was that what she had told Aiden? Then why had Aiden reacted the way he did?

Nothing jibed. Claire just didn't know enough to connect the dots. Oh, why couldn't she remember everything at once? Why bits and pieces and not the full picture?

Her gaze settled on Aiden's face. The man in her past, the man she had loved, the man who had betrayed her. So familiar, and yet a stranger. She should know everything about him, but she knew nothing.

There was such loneliness in his gaze, her heart tightened. The need to comfort him made her lean closer. Awareness prickled down her body, tightening her breasts and flooding her insides with desire. Passion. Wasn't that what she had chased after her whole life? Hadn't she hungered for it?

She saw passion reflected in Aiden's eyes.

As much as she denied it, she felt the hunger, too. She wanted passion; she wanted to experience it even if for a moment. She slid her hands up his hard chest, trailed her fingers up his recently shaved neck, and burrowed them underneath his still-damp hair.

His intake of breath mirrored hers. For a long moment,

she thought he'd forgotten to breathe, and then she felt his warm, mint-scented breath on her face.

She wanted him to kiss her, and she knew he wanted to kiss her, too. And yet he made no move to lower his head closer. Was he waiting for her to make the first move?

Mère de Dieu! If Claire moved away now, Aiden would surely die. He knew he gripped her arms too harshly, but he feared that if he slacked his hold, she would simply disappear, for surely he dreamed. Her hands could not be on the back of his neck, her fingernails slowly tracing circles on his nape.

Slowly, he slid his hands to her back, under her glorious hair. Through the cloth of her gown, he felt her heat. He wanted to close his eyes, savor the moment, but he did not dare. He kept his gaze on her, memorizing every nuance on her beautiful face: her velvety brown eyes, her rosy cheeks, her slightly parted lips, and the pulsing beat at her throat.

He swallowed hard, not daring to pull her closer into his embrace for fear that if their bodies touched he would surely disgrace himself before her.

He leaned down, his lips barely touching hers. She didn't move away. Encouraged, he got closer. Openmouthed, he breathed her sweet breath, tasted her sweet nectar, drowned in the pleasure of it. He slanted his head, closed his lips over hers, and touched her tongue with the tip of his. The pleasure nearly killed him.

"Forgive the interruption. I thought no one would be here so early in the morning."

Claire jumped back, clearly flustered.

Aiden groaned.

This time he would kill Jasper.

Chapter 14

FACE flaming, Claire jumped to her feet, wavered, and almost fell before she righted herself again. She licked her tingling lips, ran a hand down her dress, rearranging it, though there was nothing out of place. Caught between wanting to curse at Jasper and thank him for the interruption, she did neither.

What was she thinking? Getting entangled with Aiden was the worst thing she could possibly do to herself. Why torture herself by having a taste of what she couldn't keep? Besides, she shouldn't encourage him to think she could change her mind and become his wife. The best she could do for Aiden was rid him of his haunting ghost. The best she could do for herself was to keep him at arm's length. A tall order, since she needed to touch him to get her answers.

Spell broken and reason returned, she avoid looking at

both men. "If you'll excuse me," she said, "I'll be returning to my room."

She hurried out of the garden, leaving them behind and not caring if they tore out each other's throats. Morning was blooming now, and by the time she found the entrance to the castle, the bailey was already teeming with life.

As was the great hall.

Ignoring the prying eyes locked on her, she crossed the hall looking neither left nor right, heading straight for the back stairs and her bedroom.

As soon as she entered her bedroom, she noticed someone had been there during her short absence. The bathtub was empty and the bed made. Remembering her personal belongings hidden underneath the mattress, she rushed to it. Her dress, panties, sandals, and purse seemed undisturbed. She checked inside the purse and was relieved that nothing was missing. But maybe she should find another place for them. After all, if someone had changed the bed linens they would have found her belongings. What would a medieval person think of such puzzling personal effects?

Aiden had reacted pretty well to her nylon/spandex dress, open-toed shoes, and leather purse. Surely, he had thought them odd, but he had made no comment. Would he be as nonchalant if he saw her wearing her lacy panties?

She didn't think so. The image of his blue eyes smoked with desire earlier in the garden swam before her; her nipples responded by hardening. Immediately, she chased the picture away. What was wrong with her? At this rate, she would soon be inviting the man to share her bed. At that thought, more pictures sprang to mind.

Claire groaned. She hadn't realized before that she was so visual. Since she'd awakened from her erotic dream with Aiden, she'd been in a constant state of arousal. In fact, since the night they'd shared a room in the small inn in Chartres she'd been battling her attraction to him. Their forced proximity during the long trip to Delacroix hadn't helped much, either. Furthermore, being naked underneath her gown was an added stimulus she could do without.

With that in mind, Claire picked up her panties. They smelled of mildew. She had washed them last night, and they obviously hadn't dried well. Damn! She would have to forgo wearing them today.

Clutching her belongings in her hands, she walked to the table where she found fresh water, soap, and a towel, along with food and drink.

Her stomach grumbled with hunger. She debated whether to wash first, but decided to eat instead. She was a breakfast type of person. If she didn't eat in the morning, she'd feel weak all day.

Sitting alone at the immense table, she devoured an apple, bread, and cheese, washing everything down with two cups of spiced wine. Warmth spread through her limbs, and satiated, she rose.

She walked to the anteroom, set a stool behind the closed door so no one, particularly Aiden, would surprise her as she washed, and then returned to the bedroom. She quickly undressed, bathed, and washed her panties again. She left them by the fireplace to dry quickly.

A dab of her own perfume between her breasts and behind her ears helped ground her back into her present self. She'd been delving so much in the past she feared she'd get lost in the process. For good measure, she popped a dark chocolate in her mouth.

If a medieval person tasted chocolate, history would surely change in some dramatic way, she mused.

Savoring the divine confection, she picked up her belongings and strolled to Jeanne's garment trunk. Normally, she wouldn't dream of going through another person's be-

longings, and sure as hell she wouldn't avail herself of a
dead woman's clothing, but Aiden had given her permission, and these clothes had belonged to her once.

Besides, maybe something here would provoke a flashback and provide her with a better picture of her past life as
Jeanne.

As she moved the garments, dried petals encrusted in
their folds released a strong rose scent. Jeanne's scent.
Pleasing, but nothing Claire would have chosen herself.

For a long moment, she admired the beautifully embroidered gowns, the delicate linen undergarments, head-
dresses, soft woolen hose, and a pair of embroidered
leather shoes a little too big for her feet. Jeanne must indeed have been a tall woman.

Choosing a soft linen chemise with tight long sleeves
that resembled the dress she came wearing from the future,
Claire dropped it over her head. She wondered what Aiden
had thought seeing her wearing "underwear" when he first
saw her. And in a cathedral, of all places. He must have
been shocked. It was a wonder he had said nothing. Maybe
he didn't want to embarrass her.

She dropped the burgundy dress she wore earlier over
her head, and then put on her leather shoes. Fully dressed,
she sat on the floor and returned her attention to the trunk.

A small, beautifully decorated wooden box with a simple metal clasp lay at the bottom of the trunk. Claire lifted
the box and set it on the floor before her. She opened it and
found an ivory comb, a silver mirror, and several colorful
ribbons inside. There was also a velvet bag with draw-
strings. She pulled the strings open and spilled the contents
on her lap. A heavy ring with an unpolished red stone—
ruby, she guessed—a gold bracelet with an elaborate
chevron pattern, a couple of gold circlets, and several silver brooches with stones of different colors encrusted in
them.

She examined the pieces one by one. Though beautiful, none of them elicited any emotion or memory in her. It puzzled Claire that nothing so far—not the castle, not the garden, not this room, not even Jeanne's personal belongings—had brought forth a memory. It seemed only Aiden's touch triggered them.

With a sigh, she returned the jewelry to the bag and the bag to the box. She had no use for these items, though they sure would fetch a fortune at an auction in the future. Not that she intended to take anything but answers back with her when she returned home.

She replaced the box where she found it. Deciding the trunk would be a good place to hide her belongings—no one would need to mess with it when they cleaned the room—Claire put them at the bottom of the trunk and closed the lid. She rose. Maybe too abruptly. Her head spun for a moment, and she had to hold on to the wall for balance. Was the mulled wine stronger than she thought? She was used to drinking wine, though usually not sweet wine, and surely not for breakfast.

She waited a little, but the dizziness didn't pass. Stumbling to the bed, she fell across it. She closed her eyes for a few moments and then opened them again. Something on the bed caught her eye. Claire's heart skipped a beat, and she lifted her head slightly. A deflowered rose with its bruised petals artistically arranged around the stem lay on her pillow.

Adrenaline rushed through her veins, chasing away the sluggishness. She jerked up, and the room spun around her for a dizzying second. She took deep, cleansing breaths, her gaze flitting around.

Was Cherise in here?

"All right, Cherise, show yourself." The sooner there was a confrontation between them, the sooner they would resolve the issue.

There was neither answer nor sign of Cherise.

Was she down in the garden? Claire circled the bed, her mind clearing with every passing moment. She headed for the window, but a loud noise coming from the anteroom made her stop. Changing directions, she rushed across the room. The stool she'd set against the door lay horizontally on the floor, the door ajar. Claire jerked the door wide open and stepped outside.

At the end of the dark corridor, Claire caught a movement, but with no windows and only one lit torch on the wall, the shadows could be playing a trick on her eyes.

Something soft and furry scraped against her ankles, and Claire jumped, her heart quickening. A white-furred ball scampered down the corridor. A cat! The same animal she'd seen when she first arrived at Delacroix?

As if to give Claire a chance to confirm her thoughts, the cat stopped midway in her mad dash and darted a green glance back at Claire.

A flash of recognition struck Claire. The cat eerily resembled Coco, her stray cat in her own time. Did animals reincarnate? Some thought they did; Claire hadn't come to a conclusion about that yet.

Whoever the cat was, it looked as if it wished for Claire to follow it.

And why not? Hadn't she traveled back in time, met the man of her past, and intended to confront a ghost? What harm would it do to follow a cat down a corridor?

The cat awaited her decision, not moving until she did, and then very slowly, as if to give Claire time to follow it.

Before Claire could catch up with it, however, the cat stopped again, glanced back at her, and then jumped, apparently disappearing through the wall.

Claire blinked. Was she having delusions now? Or had the sweet wine mulled her mind?

She rushed to the spot where she'd last seen the cat.

Where she thought there was a wall, a narrow, tunnel-like staircase—not the one she used earlier, but one for the servants' use maybe?—led to the floor below. Again, she thought she caught a movement, but only a weak light seemed to wait for her on the other side of the staircase.

Claire took a step down and suddenly stopped. Had Cherise used the cat to lure her out of her bedroom so she could push her down the stairs to her death as she had done to Jeanne?

Heart stammering in her chest, Claire flattened her back against the wall and darted a glance down the corridor.

There was no one there.

She inhaled deeply and exhaled slowly. She was sure Cherise had been in her bedroom earlier—who else would set a defaced rose on her pillow?—but since walls were no barrier for ghosts, Cherise could be anywhere by now.

Would she be falling into a trap if she went down this stairway? Claire wondered. She would not allow Cherise to intimidate her. As long as she was aware of a trap, there'd be no surprises.

They had to meet again; sooner would be better than later.

Awareness prickling her body, Claire crept down the cold and gloomy staircase. As she slowly made her way, disembodied voices and banging sounds echoed to her in waves. She flicked her gaze from her darkened back to the weak light in front of her, feeling as if she was descending into the bowels of hell.

It was with relief that she stepped off the stairs and into an empty room. The voices were stronger now, and the tantalizing scent of cooking meat and baking bread permeated the air.

Surely, hell wouldn't smell this good.

She quickly inspected the room before she followed her nose. Walls lined with shelves filled with cups, flasks, jars, linen, and serving trays clearly revealed that the small room functioned as a pantry. The kitchen shouldn't be too far.

Standing at the foot of the staircase, Claire eyed a door across the room. She was ready to go investigate it when the cat whisked by her feet going in the opposite direction. Once again the cat seemed to disappear into nothingness.

This was getting weirder, Claire thought. The cat was leading her somewhere. Cautiously, Claire stepped into the opening on the stone floor, resembling an open basement door. A staircase led to the ground floor. At the end of it, Claire saw the distinct shape of a woman dressed in black from head to toe disappear around the corner at the end of the stairs.

"Wait," Claire called, but the woman didn't stop.

Without hesitation, Claire took to the stairs. The farther down she got, the stronger the scents and the louder and clearer the sounds of animated conversation, giving no doubt of where she was going. She stopped a couple of steps from the landing, still hidden from prying eyes, and braced herself for the imminent scrutiny of strangers.

A small boy, arms full of firewood, saw her first. His big, dark eyes, too big for his small face, grew enormous, but he said not a word.

"Boy, daydreaming again?" A big woman stepped up to where the boy stood and thumped him on the head. The boy wavered on his feet but didn't drop the firewood nor did he steal his gaze away from Claire. "I swear, one day—" Noticing the boy's stare, the woman turned a curious gaze to Claire.

Resisting the urge to thump the woman on her head, Claire stepped into the huge, bright, and overly warm kitchen. One by one, heads turned to her, voices silenced, and rosy cheeks paled. Frozen in place, as in a game of musical chairs, waiting for the music to start again, they all stared at Claire. The woman with her hands immersed in a huge trough of water; the two young girls at a scarred table, knives in hand, cutting vegetables; the old woman watching as hens roasted on spits, while another stirred a huge black cauldron; the boy with the firewood, and the big woman. Of the mystery woman in black, there was no sign.

"Good morning," Claire said.

After a momentary silence, she took their untranslatable grumbling and bobbing heads as a response. Their reserved welcome canceled the heat emanating from the cooking fires. Never had Claire felt so out of place.

She had expected such a welcome from Cherise but not from the castle's people. Why were they so cold toward her? Didn't they want their lord to find a wife?

The fear in their eyes was real enough, though. Whether they feared for their own sake or for hers remained to be seen.

Sure they would remain frozen in their stationary positions unless she left, and therefore, no one would have dinner tonight. Claire made her way through the kitchen toward the outside door.

As she stepped into a small courtyard, she took a long, deep breath. Her thoughts strayed to Aiden. Since her arrival, she had noticed people's coldness toward him. Having just had a taste of their lack of warmth, she felt deeply for him, particularly when he suffered such treatment in his own home. Yet he didn't even consider moving elsewhere. Obviously, Delacroix meant a great deal to him. Much more than she could ever understand.

Would things improve for Aiden once Cherise's ghost was gone?

Of course she was taking for granted that she would be able to get rid of Cherise, though she had no idea how she would accomplish that.

The bright sunlight outside chased away some of Claire's

gloom. Maybe she should take a closer look at the old church, see if anything would elicit a memory in her.

She looked around to see which direction she had to go, catching sight of the cat standing by the woman in black. At least she thought it was the same woman, as she was as drably dressed. She crouched by a small patch of cultivated dirt—a vegetable/herb garden, Claire guessed—picking a bunch of unidentifiable leaves.

Maybe the cat belonged to her, Claire thought.

"Are you a witch?"

Claire's heart almost jumped out of her throat. She pivoted. The firewood boy stared at her with his big, haunting eyes.

"You almost gave me a heart attack," she said, hand pressing against her chest. "You shouldn't sneak up on people like this."

"You speak oddly. Surely you are a witch."

Was that what they all thought she was? She'd better dispel that notion fast. She didn't want Father Aubert hearing such a tale and getting on her case. "No, I'm not a witch. And it's not very nice to be calling people names."

"Then why do you have a familiar?"

Claire followed the boy's gaze to her feet where the cat now rested. It moved fast!

"The cat is not mine," she said. "It must belong to that lady over there." She pointed to the woman in black, who now stood looking in their direction. A dark veil in the Muslim fashion covered all of her head and most of her face.

"The ghost's sister? The cat is not hers."

Cherise's sister? Aiden had made no mention of a sister. Claire snapped her mouth closed and gazed back at the boy. He seemed serious. "Maybe I'll ask her later whether the cat is hers or not," Claire said.

"No need. She cannot speak."

Damn! Claire stole a glance over her shoulder, but the woman was already gone.

"Cats are agents of evil," the boy continued, drawing Claire's attention back to him. "No one but a witch would keep company with one."

"You must not believe everything you hear."

"I hear you are Lord Aiden's bride. Is that false?"

An untruth she couldn't rebuke. "That is true."

"Then you must be a witch, for only a witch would dare face an evil ghost."

"Well, I'm not a witch, but I believe if you show no fear, a ghost can do nothing against you." She wasn't exactly sure of that, but it did sound good.

"You are a witch!" His eyes grew even bigger.

Claire gave up convincing him otherwise. She could deny it until the end of time, and the boy would still believe what he wanted to believe. "I'm Claire. Do you have a name?"

"I am Giles."

"A handsome name for a handsome boy."

Hurt flickered in his eyes. "I am a cripple."

Her gaze swung briefly to the boy's carefully wrapped foot. Its misshapen form revealed a clubfoot, a very resolvable problem in the future. What a pity! Still, it did not detract from the boy's handsomeness, though she could understand he would be sensitive about the subject.

"Where I come from, we do not use that word," she said.

"Where are you from?"

"A faraway land."

"The enchanted woods. Are you a fairy, then?"

There was such hope in his voice she hated to disappoint him, but though fairy sounded better than witch, she was neither.

"I am just a woman, Giles."

His little shoulders slumped, and his gaze shifted somewhere in the distance. Claire took the opportunity to examine him. He was small and thin, but he didn't look sickly. His face had a smudge or two, and his clothing wasn't exactly clean, but that was understandable since he was carrying firewood a few moments ago. "Where are your parents?" she asked.

"My father died when I was little, but my mother lives still. She is Lady Melissent, the only lady left at Delacroix," he said. "Besides yourself, now." Claire understood he meant *lady* as a social attribute, and not a gender, for she had seen many women in the castle.

"I must meet her sometime."

"Lady Claire, please do not let the ghost harm my mother." There was true fear in his voice.

"You need not worry about your mother, Giles. The ghost is interested in me, not her."

"Are you certain you are not a witch or fairy?" he insisted.

"Absolutely."

He sighed. "Pity."

"How so?"

"If you was a witch or fairy you could make me whole, and one day I could be a knight like my father once was, and I could take care of my mother in her old age."

Claire's heart tightened. Physical deficiencies were considered evil in the Middle Ages. She could only imagine the taunting Giles must suffer daily, not counting the fact he would be barred from pursuing his dreams. That he thought not only of himself but his mother's welfare as well showed character and endeared him to her.

"Giles!"

The boy spun around.

"Have you finished with your duties in the kitchen?"

"Aye, Mother."

"Then I shall see you in my bedchamber shortly. I have several tasks I need your help with."

"Can I go to the stables first, Mother?"

"You know Master Perry dislikes you being around the horses."

Giles nodded, dejected.

"You may take a quick peek, but do not delay. And do not get caught," she added.

He brightened, "Aye, Mother." He shot Claire a pleading look, then hopped out of sight.

"I apologize if my son has disturbed you."

"He didn't. He is a good boy."

The woman's face softened. She was probably younger than Claire was, but the faint lines creasing around her blue eyes spoke of a life of hardship aging her before her time. "I thank you for your kind words." She turned to leave.

"Melissent," she called, stopping the woman's retreat. "Maybe I could speak with Aiden about Giles. Find him something more interesting to do than help in the kitchen." Unless another insurmountable impediment, besides his clubfoot, prevented Giles from training for knighthood, Claire couldn't see why Aiden would refuse to help the boy. Unless he didn't have a heart. Which she refused to believe.

Hope and skepticism struggled on Melissent's face. "Why should you care about a cripple boy you have just met?"

"Why should I not?" Claire wasn't sure why she offered to help. Maybe it was her maternal instincts talking, or simply human decency. It seemed such a small thing to do for the happiness of one little boy who had probably suffered enough already.

Melissent took a step back. "I thank you for your kindness, but I ask you that you do not speak to Lord Aiden on Giles's behalf."

Claire was confused. "Why not?"

"My lady, I mean no disrespect, but since Lord Aiden took over Delacroix Castle, this has been a very unhappy place. My Lady Jeanne died, my husband lost his life in a freak accident soon after, my son was born a cripple. All of that in one summer. He is haunted, as you well know it, and thus so are all of us. I wish my boy nowhere near him."

"That's not fair," Claire said. "Aiden cannot be held responsible for the antics of a madwoman. A dead madwoman at that. Besides, you cannot blame everything that goes wrong in this castle on the ghost."

"Why have you come to this godforsaken place? Surely with your beauty you could have found a better husband."

"Surely, as a mother, you would want to give your son hope for the future."

Melissent's expression hardened. "I kindly ask you not to encourage my son to pursue his wistful dreams. His body is already broken; I wish not for his heart to be broken, too."

"What is a heart without a dream?" Claire asked.

"Dreams are for those who are born for them. The rest of us must accept our fate."

"That seems too fatalistic a view."

"Mayhap you shall think otherwise when the ghost comes to you demanding your demise. I pray your faith in Lord Aiden costs you not your life as it did my Lady Jeanne's." Melissent bowed respectfully, pivoted, and then left Claire to consider her words.

They all expected history to repeat itself, Claire realized. *Not if she could help it.*

AIDEN TOOK THE STEPS TO HIS BEDCHAMBER TWO AT the time, still reeling from yet another bothersome quarrel with Jasper in the garden. The man had hurled the same old accusations against Cherise, and Aiden had denied them, as always, in a futile attempt to knock some sense into Jasper's stubborn head. But Jasper would believe what he wanted to believe.

He pushed the thought of Jasper aside. Now that he was making headway with Claire, he felt hopeful for a future. For the first time, after her initial disagreeable reaction to his touch, she had responded to him with undeniable desire. A desire he intended to see burning again in her eyes.

The door to his bedchamber was open. He entered, expecting to find Claire. A cursory glance revealed she was not there. Where was she?

A shudder of worry skittered down his spine. Had Cherise appeared to Claire again? He hastened out of the bedchamber and down the steps, through the great hall, and outside into the bailey. No sign of Claire.

His heart lurched in his chest. She could not be in the garden; he had just come from there. Where on earth did she go? Was she in danger? Had Cherise found her? Just the thought congealed his heart.

Aiden marched across the bailey. As he passed the stables, he heard a commotion. He halted and swerved inside.

"I just wanted to help," a small boy cried as Master Perry carried him out by the scruff of his tunic.

"I told you before, boy. I do not want to see you near the horses. You spook them."

"What is the matter?" Aiden asked, annoyed. He had no time for small altercations between stable hands, but he could not turn his back on a little boy being mishandled.

Master Perry dropped the boy, who scurried to his feet, rearranging his tunic in a dignified manner.

"Naught, my lord. I was just getting this urchin out from under my feet."

Aiden inspected the scrawny boy of undetermined age. He did not remember seeing him before. His gaze settled on the wrapped foot that could not disguise its misshapen form. So that was the problem, Aiden realized, having wondered why Master Perry would turn away a willing helping hand. The man thought the boy possessed by evil spirits, as all cripples were said to be.

More and more Aiden wondered about matters of the netherworld. Was it not for Cherise haunting him, he would not even question all that he had simply accepted before. "What happened?" he asked again.

"I just want to help take care of the horses, my lord," the boy spoke out of turn. Master Perry was vexed, and rightfully so. "I am a knight's son, my lord," the boy continued. "I should learn about horses, I should be a page and train for knighthood, and not be allotted kitchen duty."

"There are worse duties," Master Perry said. "You could be a gong farmer, which is what you deserve for your insolence."

The boy wrinkled his nose in disgust. Aiden agreed. Laboring in the kitchen was infinitely more pleasant than cleaning latrines. "Do you have a name, boy?" Aiden asked.

"Aye, my lord. I am Giles, son of the late Sir Jules and Lady Melissent."

Giles. Appropriately named after the saint of cripples. Aiden vaguely remembered the boy's father, one of Jasper's father's knights, who died soon after Aiden had recovered Delacroix, which meant the boy was older than Aiden had first thought. His mother, he knew. Melissent had been one of Jeanne's ladies-in-waiting; the only one left at Delacroix.

"A cripple cannot become a knight," Master Perry spat, his voice laden with disdain.

Years ago, Aiden might have agreed with his stable master, but not these days. These days he was all too aware of fate's fickleness. He looked at the boy. So young, so battered already by fate. Born an outcast with no choice in his future.

Something inside Aiden rebelled. He had been born with privileges, and yet he had been stripped of them without warning. A kind lord had taken pity on him and fostered Aiden into knighthood. Without that chance he would never have served under King Richard, and he would not have regained his birthright.

The boy with his crippled foot had no chance of ever becoming a knight anywhere but in his castle. Aiden could give him that chance, did he prove worthy, and thus redeem a debt.

"So, you wish to be a knight like your father?"

"Aye, my lord." There was such eagerness in his voice, in the way he squared his scrawny little shoulders back. The boy was battered but not beaten. He possessed the needed courage to face Master Perry, and much more, to face Aiden, his lord, and make his wishes known. Courage must be rewarded.

"Then you must learn not to speak without leave, and to accept orders without gainsaying your master. I would also advise you to change into a clean tunic and wash your face."

As the meaning of Aiden's words sank in, the boy's big eyes grew immense. Still, he did not move; he waited for Aiden's final verdict as if his life depended on it. As it clearly did.

"Report to the great hall at dinnertime," Aiden said. "You shall begin your training as a page this day. And meet me in the stables at dawn on the morrow. I shall teach you a few things about horses."

Giles fell to one knee, head bowed, hands to his heart. "My lord, I render homage to you and to my Lady Claire."

Lady Claire? Did the boy know her? "Rise, Giles,"

Aiden ordered. "I accept your homage, and ask that you tell me whether you have seen Lady Claire this morn."

The boy rose. He seemed a little taller, his chest a little fuller. Aiden admired the wonders of hope. Of which he was beginning to benefit himself.

"Lady Claire left through the outer gates, my lord. I saw her going in the direction of the village church."

"Was she alone?"

"She and her familiar, my lord."

A familiar? What on earth was Claire plotting?

There was only one way to find out. Aiden headed for the outer gates himself.

Chapter 15

CLAIRE ambled down a graveled path flanked by tall grass and wildflowers outside the castle walls. The path led directly into the small village perched on the hillside like tree stumps. Farmland sprawled out in the valley below, and beyond that, a meadow stretched to the beech and pine forest from where she and Aiden had emerged yesterday.

A few white clouds sprinkled the royal blue sky on this balmy spring morning. Sun shone brightly, and a cool breeze fluttered the tall grasses, carrying from the woods the faint scent of pine.

The same scent that clung to Aiden earlier in the garden when she had almost lost herself in the briefest but most powerful kiss of her life.

Claire groaned and chased the memory away. She didn't want to dwell on her obvious attraction to Aiden.

She focused instead on finding her answers, perhaps hidden in a little medieval village church.

As she made her way down the path, her gaze glided over the undulating and verdant hills surrounding her. The landscape vaguely reminded her of a place she visualized when meditating.

Had she drawn her meditation image from the depths of her past?

Born and raised in the flatlands of Louisiana, she could as easily have pictured in her mind the beautiful swamp in the summer, with its bald cypress, overhanging Spanish moss, and mirror-surfaced rivers, which she loved.

Instead, she had chosen a foreign landscape almost identical to this one.

It was no coincidence.

This place held a special meaning to her, she was sure. She just wished she could remember what it was.

Coco—she had finally decided to name the cat—dashed ahead of her. No one seemed interested in claiming ownership of Coco, least of all Claire, considering medieval people's perception of cats and people together.

Coco, however, had ideas of her own. Much like her own cat in the future, Coco had claimed her. Claire could do very little about that.

Maybe there is such a thing as a familiar.

The scent of cooking food floated in the air as she ambled through the village. A pig and her piglets crossed before her in the direction of the meadow below. Claire stopped and waited for the procession to pass. Her gaze swept over goats roaming free and a couple of old women tending small vegetable gardens located behind their huts. Young children played in the dirt alongside clucking chickens. All able-bodied people should be laboring in the fields at this time of day.

A head or two rose in her direction, and Claire waved at

them. They waved back and then swiftly tucked their hands away, shooting suspicious glances at Claire and her feline companion.

Great! Claire thought. Like the boy, Giles, they were probably thinking she was a witch. She suppressed the desire to tell Coco, "You see the trouble you're causing me?" It would only confirm their suspicions if they saw her talking to a cat. Though Claire disliked having to watch what she said or did in the presence of others, she was bright enough not to disregard their opinions. At least while she remained in their midst.

Her gaze zeroed in on the small church. It might allay their suspicions if they saw her going inside.

The double wooden doors were wide open, and Claire walked through them unimpeded. Her soft leather shoes muffled the sounds of her steps over the stone floor as she approached the altar. The church was empty of people and the pews of modern churches. Claire was aware medieval people didn't sit for church services.

As she'd expected, there were no pictures or statues of saints, but a big wooden cross hung on the wall facing her, and before it, the altar was covered with a pristine white cloth. On top of the altar lay a small book in deep purple vellum.

A twitch of excitement ran through her. Guided by the remnants of her Catholic upbringing, she respectfully genuflected before the altar, made the sign of the cross, and then rose, reaching for the book.

"Have you come to confess your sins, my lady?"

Startled, as if she'd been caught red-handed, Claire hastily withdrew her hand, almost tipping the heavy metal cup resting alongside the book.

Inhaling deeply to calm her thundering heart, she turned slowly. Suddenly remembering Coco, her heart stumbled anew. Had Coco followed her inside? A quick glance revealed the cat lying just outside the church's door, still in plain sight. Had the priest seen her?

Claire forced a smile to her lips. "Good morning, Father Aubert. I was just admiring your book of prayers."

"It is a lectionary," he said. "Readings from the Scriptures. Mayhap my lady does not read Latin?"

"I did not have a chance to examine it closely," she said and stepped away from the altar. For some reason she didn't feel too comfortable around the priest. She had better get out of here ASAP. "I do not wish to disturb you, Father. I will be on my way."

He blocked her retreat. "Do not hasten your leave, my lady. I very much wish to speak with you, learn more about your person. After all, soon you shall be the lady of Delacroix. With your impending nuptials, surely you are eager to unburden the sins of your heart."

Realizing she couldn't avoid confession for long, Claire considered going through with it to be done with it. Of course, she intended to omit the more damning facts of her life. Her conscience nagged at her that creative confession wasn't exactly acceptable in the eyes of God. Her secular side reminded her it was necessary for her survival.

She was also well aware that she needed to come up with some innocuous transgression to satisfy the priest's need to give penance. Surely he would expect some sinful thought or action from her. The problem was, in these troublesome times, she wasn't quite sure what constituted a forgivable offense and what would mean grounds for heresy.

She'd better put it off a little while longer.

"It is kind of you to show an interest in me, Father, but I really cannot stay. Lord Aiden expects me shortly, and I do not wish to make him wait."

Technically that wasn't a lie. Aiden was probably looking for her right now, though they didn't have an appointment, per se. She took another step toward the door, but the priest's bony fingers clasped around her arm, impeding her retreat.

"Surely my Lord Aiden understands that matters of the spirit are more important than matters of the flesh," Father Aubert said.

The priest's persistence didn't bode well. How was she going to get out of this?

"Am I interrupting?"

Aiden!

Claire spun toward him, relief washing over her. The man had a great sense of timing. Without waiting for a response, he marched toward her with his customary purpose.

"I was just telling Father Aubert," Claire jumped in before the priest could speak, "that though I would love to stay and talk, I knew you were impatiently waiting for my return."

"And I was just telling Lady Claire," the priest countered, at last dropping his fingers from her arm, "that you would understand her delay if spiritual matters were at hand. I was just about to hear her confession."

Claire wanted to tell the priest that she didn't believe in confessions, that though she had great faith in God, she thought religion a human concept, and therefore, fallible. Of course, she said nothing of the kind. That would brand her as a sure agent of evil. She resorted to shooting a desperate look at Aiden. Maybe he would understand her dilemma, and knowing the priest better than she did, he would find a way to deal with him.

Aiden eyed her curiously for a moment, as if deciding what exactly she wanted him to do, and then turned his gaze on the priest. "I am certain my lady is eager to confess the small failures of her heart, but there are pressing and unavoidable matters that she and I must attend to before the wedding takes place. Surely, Father, you understand my haste."

Bless his heart! Claire could weep with relief at Aiden's understanding. Warmth filled her, and a sudden desire to jump into his arms and kiss him in eternal gratitude flooded her. She would have done it, too, were they not in a church, in the presence of a fire-and-brimstone priest who would most certainly frown upon such a display of affection.

She shot Aiden a grateful grin instead.

Unfortunately, Father Aubert wasn't a man easily convinced. "I mean no offense, my lord, but women are the seed of Satan sent to earth to tempt men. You should know that better than anyone."

To Aiden's credit, he didn't cringe at the priest's cheap shot at his predicament.

"What do you know about Lady Claire?" Father Aubert continued as if she wasn't there. "Where is her family? Where does she hail from? A woman who does not fear an evil spirit should not be trusted. She could be a Cathar, for all we know. Would it not be best to learn the secrets of her heart before the wedding takes place?"

By the look on the priest's face, Cathar wasn't a good thing. Claire could just picture Father's glee when he got a look at the contents of her purse, as he searched her belongings for proof of heresy and witchcraft.

"I place my trust in the Mother of God, Father," Aiden said. "When I visited Chartres Cathedral, I laid my petition for a bride in Her merciful hands. I cannot disregard the fact I met Lady Claire in Her cathedral's sacred labyrinth. Surely, the Virgin Mother would not have steered me wrong."

That seemed to shut up Father Aubert. Thank God!

"I shall hear both your confessions before the wedding takes place."

They let Father Aubert have the last word and hurriedly left the church.

"THANK YOU FOR COMING TO MY RESCUE," CLAIRE said as soon as they were outside.

"It was clear you were not eager to remain in Father Aubert's presence much longer." Aiden eyed the cat by Claire's foot with misgivings. He did not prescribe to the prevalent fear that cats were diabolical creatures, but he did wonder why it had suddenly appeared and attached itself to Claire. "I trust you have your reasons to avoid baring your soul to a priest." He just hoped those reasons were not insurmountable, did he convince her to become his bride.

"I do have my reasons, but I appreciate your understanding."

It troubled him that she did not even flinch, as if she had naught to hide, when he knew she held many secrets in her heart.

"Let it be known you leave me no choice, Claire. I would much prefer you trusted me, for surely, by now you must realize I wish you no harm."

"I don't doubt that—"

Finally, she trusted him!

"But perhaps my silence serves you as well," she added.

How would her silence serve him? Before he had a chance to inquire further into the matter, Claire turned and veered to the back of the church. Aiden followed her. She stopped a couple of steps ahead of him, near a big rock, and pivoted to face him, the cat no longer at her side.

Something in the way she looked at him, proud and fearless, struck him as very familiar.

He shook the eerie feeling away. It was not the time for fanciful thoughts. He had pressing matters in mind. Father Aubert's mention of the Cathar awakened a memory Aiden had buried long ago. Years ago, Cherise had shared her belief in the Cathar's dogmas with him. Certain that the Church would not tolerate such opposing views, he had demanded she speak no more of it. She had complied, and he had forgotten about it.

Until now.

Realization that those views could have played a pivotal part in her death—the Cathar believed suicide was not a mortal sin—dawned on him like crashing thunder.

Had he been wrong about Cherise all along? Could she have taken her own life? Did his disregard for her beliefs cause her haunting of him?

He could not repeat this mistake with Claire. He needed to know the truth; it was the only way he could protect her.

"Are you a Cathar, Claire?" he asked without preamble.

She shrugged. "What is a Cathar, anyway?"

Such nonchalance did not agree with Claire. Was she testing him? It was not beyond the realm of possibility that she might know naught about the Cathar, but it was odd, since they were well-known all over Christendom.

"It is a sect that the Church is fighting to smother."

"What are their beliefs?"

"Duality of God, disregard for the sacraments, contempt for the clergy, rebirth of the soul, amongst other things."

"Rebirth of the soul?"

Why had that particular belief caught her attention? Aiden eyed Claire intently. "A fanciful notion, is it not?"

She cocked her head. "Is it? Wouldn't you want another chance to right the wrongs of your life?"

The hair on Aiden's nape stood. He would give much for such a chance. But it was not possible. A person was given only one life; and thus far, he had mangled his. He could not undo the past, but maybe God would still give him a chance to right his wrongs now before his passing to the nether world.

"There is no point in entertaining the idea," he said and returned to the matter at hand. "The Church thus far has been tolerant of the Cathar, Claire, but I hear rumblings of persecution in the air."

"So it wouldn't be wise to side with them at this time," she said.

"It would be foolish beyond words."

"People are known to do foolish things when properly motivated."

Fear for her safety slid down his spine like cold water. "Are you a Cathar, Claire?" he repeated the question.

"What would you do if I were?" she asked in response.

Mère de Dieu, spare me that fate again!

"I would keep Father Aubert away from you," he said without hesitation.

She grinned, as if that was a matter of little importance. His outrage disappeared, however, as her smile transformed her face, made her seem attainable, carefree. For a moment, he forgot what had him so worried.

She reminded him. "You seem to know a lot about the Cathar."

"I knew someone once who was a believer."

"Are you a believer, Aiden?"

Her directness startled him. Was she trying to muddle his wits? He had not missed the fact that she had neither denied nor confirmed his suspicions. He chose to challenge her back. "What would you do if I were?"

"I would keep Father Aubert away from you, of course."

The lighthearted manner with which she answered him brought a smile to his own face. They shared a laugh together, and then quieted. Aiden was suddenly aware of a shift in their relationship, a pull that brought them closer together.

With new awareness, their gazes met and locked. Aiden's heart quickened, and his arms ached to draw her closer. He did not. He waited for her to reach out first, to set the boundaries between them.

She took a step toward him. "What do you believe in, Aiden?" she asked quietly.

The need to share his thoughts with Claire, and to have her share hers with him, filled him with longing. Would she see him as a weakling if he spoke of his doubts? He decided to dare.

"There was a time that life and death were uncomplicated matters to me. It was my understanding that depending on our worthiness, we went to heaven, hell, or purgatory after our demise."

"And now?" she urged.

"Since Cherise's death, I simply do not know anymore, Claire." He kneaded the back of his head. "Father Aubert believes Cherise to be a wicked, sinful soul doing the devil's deed on earth."

"And you?"

Cherise was not evil in life. Would her taking her own life make her evil? "It is best not to question such matters too deeply."

"Eventually, we all have to face the truth one way or the other."

He shrugged. "Who knows what the truth really is? I know naught of what exists in heaven and earth."

"I suspect there's more than we will ever know."

Had he not been watching her so closely, he might have missed her glide toward him. His heart quickened its pace. Her sweet honey scent wafted to him, and he almost groaned with the need to hold her in his arms. As she drew closer, his breath caught in his throat, his blood thudded in his ears, and his whole body tensed with unbearable expectation.

He could almost taste her, and having savored the

sweetness of her lips earlier, his hunger for her increased tenfold.

Still, he waited.

Finally, when he thought he could bear no more, she lifted her hand and placed it ever so lightly on his jaw. Bracing himself for the adverse reaction that never came, he watched his bewilderment reflected on her face.

Perchance, she wondered the same as he.

Where were the memories, the flashbacks? Claire wondered, dumbfounded. She had come to expect it every time she touched Aiden. And yet, this time it had not come. What had changed? Surely not her need for answers; she still wanted them. How else was she going to find out about her past? Disappointment settled in a thick knot in her throat.

About to withdraw from the contact, the slight shifting of his face against the palm of her hand stalled her. Awareness, akin to an electric shock, jolted her at his gentle caress, making her forget thoughts of the past, anchoring her in this very moment.

The combination of smooth skin as he slowly cocked his head one way, and the emerging of prickling stubbles as he moved back, drew gooseflesh over her body. On his next foray, his tongue reached out and touched the tip of her thumb. Claire's gaze riveted on that tongue as every new move drew her thumb deeper inside his generous mouth, until finally his lips closed over it, sucking it, nibbling at it, tasting it as if it was a delicacy he'd craved for a long time.

Heat surfaced to her neck, her mouth dried, and her heart quickened to an impossible tempo. Good God! The man had yet to lay a finger on her, and she was already panting with lust.

She couldn't keep on teasing him, and herself, this way. Eventually Aiden would expect more than she could give him, if he didn't already. And she would be too far into it to step back.

With much regret, she slid her thumb out, dragging her gaze from his tempting mouth only to be caught prisoner of his smoky blue eyes. Spellbound, she watched his face lower to her, aware she might be waging a losing battle against her attraction to him.

Still she fought. Indulging her senses would cause more harm than good to both of them. "Aiden—" she warned.

He stopped, his face a hairbreadth away from her, giving her a last chance to retreat, yet his gaze begged her not to.

She shouldn't do it. She shouldn't give herself and Aiden this moment in time. Their time was past. There was no future for them.

Damn her! She knew she would.

Claire lifted her face to him, parted her lips, and closed her eyes. His big hands cupped her head, and his mouth covered hers in a deep, ravenous kiss. As he slid one hand down the small of her back and pulled her closer, she laced her arms behind his neck and molded her body to his.

Waves of pure pleasure rippled through her, and an unbearable ache grew inside her. Having braved this far, she prayed the moment would last forever.

It ended much too soon.

As if struck by a lightning bolt, her whole body tensed and then went slack. The flashback came as the others had, the scene at the back of the church, but unlike before, she wasn't a part of it but a witness to it. She wasn't *living* it but watching it like a movie.

What Claire saw shook all her convictions to hell.

Through the maddening thumping of her heart, she watched Aiden kiss a woman who bore a remarkable resemblance to Cherise. She was watching it, and at the same time, she was feeling his mouth on hers.

The memory vanished as quickly as it came, leaving

Claire weak-kneed and clinging to Aiden in utter bewilderment.

Realizing she held his arms in a death grip, she let go of him and stumbled back to the big rock behind her, where she sat, supporting her quivering legs.

Aiden lowered his big body by her side on the rock and took her trembling hands into his. "What is the matter, Claire?"

He looked troubled, but no more troubled than she felt as she struggled to make sense of what she'd seen. Had she, as Jeanne, witnessed a moment between Aiden and his mistress in the past? But how had she felt the kiss? Did the present and past mix in Claire's mind?

Or had Claire *remembered* a moment between Aiden and Cherise?

The latter boggled her mind. That would mean all her assumptions so far had been wrong. And if they were wrong, then who had Claire been in her past life? It still bothered her that none of Jeanne's belongings had brought her any kind of memory or recognition or déjà vu. Still, she couldn't jump to the conclusion she had been Cherise. Cherise was a ghost haunting her, after all.

Unless . . .

Unless the ghost was someone else. Jeanne, maybe? It would go against everything she'd heard about Jeanne. A kind gentlewoman wouldn't become an evil spirit after death, would she? Maybe she would, if properly motivated. Being murdered by the ghost of her husband's mistress could do it.

But when Claire had described the ghost she'd seen in the garden to Aiden, he had recognized Cherise. How could that be?

A headache threatened to split Claire's head in two. She didn't know where she was going with all those suppositions, but it was obvious she had much to learn yet.

"What has you trembling so?" Aiden insisted. "Is it I? Is it my touch you abhor?"

Claire took a few calming breaths. She wanted so badly to share her thoughts with Aiden and be done with the subterfuges, but she wasn't sure he was ready to handle such a bizarre story just yet. Particularly when she wasn't even sure what was the truth. He was already going through a spiritual crisis; revelations of time travel and reincarnation would probably drive him over the edge.

Yet she couldn't keep on using him—yes, that was what she was doing, using him—to get her answers, and give him nothing in return. In these few days since she'd met him, she'd learned that Aiden was a good, honorable man, despite what had happened in the past between them, and she didn't want to deceive him anymore.

She just couldn't blurt out the entire truth, either.

"I'm not sure you would understand," she said.

He shot to his feet, letting go of her hands and leaving her bereft of his warmth. *"Mère de Dieu!* I am no witless fool, Claire, though you might think so, since only a fool would make a bargain with a woman who never once answers his questions."

She winced, knowing he was right. It was time she answered some of his questions. She couldn't let him keep on thinking he was doing something to cause her discomfort.

"I don't abhor your touch, Aiden." *Much the contrary.* "But it does affect me in a very strange way."

He shifted his weight from one leg to another, waiting impatiently for her to continue.

"I have . . . visions when I touch you."

His head snapped back. "Visions?" Obviously, that wasn't what he had expected to hear. "Are you a seer?"

"Not in the strictest sense and not with everyone. It only happens with you, Aiden."

His eyes became alert, interested. "What do you see, Claire?"

She took a deep breath, blew the air out, and then rose to her feet, knowing she was opening a Pandora's box she wasn't sure she could handle.

"I see you, Aiden. You and me."

Chapter 16

AS much as Aiden fought against it, hope unfurled in his heart. That he was glad she was a seer instead of simply abhorring his touch was a sign of his desperation. "Perchance the visions reveal a future for us?" he asked.

Claire shook her head, smiting his hope to pieces. "I'm afraid there's no future for us. Only a very troubling past."

"We have no past," he retorted a little harsher than he intended.

"I know we do." A plethora of emotions danced on her face. Remembering what they had spoken of before, his entire body tensed.

"You speak of another life, do you not?"

She simply nodded.

The ache began at the base of Aiden's skull and spread rapidly. Kneading the back of his head with more force than was warranted, his gaze swung from Claire to the church, then back to her. "So, you are a Cathar," he whispered.

"I am not," she denied, to his utter relief. "I hadn't even heard of the Cathar until you told me about them. But I do share some of their beliefs, particularly the rebirth of souls."

No wonder she had been reluctant to enter confession with Father Aubert. And with good reason. Cathar or not, the priest would not have taken her beliefs lightly.

For a moment, Aiden's thoughts veered to another woman, another time.

"Oh, Aiden," Cherise had said as they had lain together in bed, passion spent. "Would it not be wonderful if we could be together life after life?"

He remembered being annoyed at Cherise for bringing up the matter he had explicitly asked her not to broach again, but mellowed by their lovemaking, he had merely said, "Woman, one lifetime with you is enough to wear out a man's strength."

Understanding his warning, Cherise had said no more.

In that moment of levity, Aiden had indulged Cherise her whimsical thoughts, though he had never entertained her notions.

Now he faced the same troubles with Claire.

But there was no levity between him and Claire. The matter was far too serious for jesting. For the same sin, ten years ago, Father Aubert would have excommunicated Cherise. These days, the Church would demand Claire's life.

He must keep the priest from finding Claire out.

That Claire believed they shared a past life, however, did not exactly make it true. It was only a belief, after all. She could be mistaken. "How can you be certain the visions are of the past and not the future?"

"I am certain."

Unappeased by her brief response, he waited for further explanation.

"I know this is difficult to accept," she said. "You have just heard of this. I, on the other hand, have been struggling with this truth for years. Aiden, you invaded my dreams and disrupted my life before I was even sure you truly existed. When my ghost revealed a vision of you in the labyrinth at Chartres Cathedral, I jumped at the chance of meeting you. I have come to you seeking answers to my past so I can finally put it to rest and gain control over my life. Surely you can understand that."

He understood perfectly. Her quest had brought her to him, but it would not keep her by his side. It prickled him that every word she spoke was slanted against him. He haunted her dreams; he disrupted her life; she wanted to put the past behind her.

And him along with her past, no doubt.

It occurred to Aiden that her feelings for him were similar to his for his ghost. He, too, wanted Cherise gone. At least he had loved Cherise. Had Claire ever loved him in this past she thought they had shared?

There was a time in his life Aiden would have dismissed Claire's beliefs as fanciful notions of an idle mind. He had done thus to Cherise with grave consequences. Now, not so certain of his own beliefs, and mindful of Claire's safety, he could not be so careless.

Claire believed they had a past together. He would not counter her on that. Yet, whether they had lived a hundred lifetimes together, only one, or none at all, it mattered not to him. What mattered was the future she continued to deny him.

Clearly, she was not the answer to his prayer. Once again, he mourned the loss of what he could not have. But above all, he mourned the loss of Claire. He could not force her to remain with him, but he would not turn his back on her, either.

He had failed Cherise; he would not fail Claire.

He opened his arms wide and offered himself to her touch. "You may have your answers without fear of retaliation."

That much, he could give her. In sooth, it pleased him to be able to aid her in her quest. It was little in comparison to her willingness to help him with Cherise's ghost.

Claire was stunned at Aiden's offer. Yet she shouldn't be. Since they'd first met, she'd been making demands on him that he had fulfilled, regardless of what she gave him in return.

Just as he was doing now.

Awareness of Aiden's generosity struck her anew. She had put her life in his hands, and he had held it with care. She had no doubt he would keep Father Aubert from her, even though he wasn't obviously totally sold on her esoteric thoughts.

She was proud of him for his nonjudgmental attitude—many modern men had not reacted as well to her beliefs—and thankful for his acceptance.

Of course, he still didn't know the whole story.

Maybe the need for such revelations would never arise.

Maybe she could get her answers, free him from his ghost, and return to her life without further involvement with him or disruption to his life and hers.

Maybe.

For the first time, Claire realized what a great loss she would suffer when she returned to her own time. If she could return to her own time . . . But of course she could. She had to! She didn't belong here. She had come for answers alone, and once she got them, she would be gone. Despite his obvious misgivings, Aiden was offering her carte blanche to explore her past. She wouldn't waste the opportunity.

She took a step closer to him and then laid a hand on his

face. Nothing happened. Nothing but a tingling coursing through her body that had nothing to do with memories. She ignored it. Like her last flashback, this next one might only come after a longer contact.

For reinforcement, she added another hand, cupping his face, which brought her body even closer to his. Her gaze fell on his mouth, and she remembered the way his tongue had darted out to touch her thumb earlier, the wild, passionate kiss they had shared. Her heart stumbled in her chest. That wasn't the memory she was looking for.

She closed her eyes, chasing the thought away, and concentrated on her previous flashbacks, remembering each one distinctly, rearranging them in an attempt to put some order in the scenes.

Not only did the flashbacks not fit together, but they didn't fit in with her last memory at all. And no new memory came to elucidate her doubts.

Frustrated, she dropped her hands and flared her eyes open.

"No vision?" he asked.

She shook her head.

He circled her waist with his big hands and pulled her closer. "Give it another moment. It might still come."

Maybe he was right.

She eased her hands over his strong arms and wide shoulders, and rested her face against his chest. What triggered the flashbacks? she wondered. Obviously, they didn't come at her will. Then what? Her emotions, the right moment, the place where they were? Could it be Aiden's thoughts? Or maybe a combination of their thoughts in a given moment? Or was fate holding the strings of her memories as a puppeteer would a marionette?

Too many variables, including the seemingly evolving nature of the flashbacks, made it impossible for Claire to know. And she didn't rejoice in her lack of control.

As the moments trickled by, awareness of his thundering heart, the faint scent of pine mingled with his manly scent, and the feel of his fingers tracing circles on the small of her back slowly eroded her concentration, replacing it with bursting desire.

It felt so right to be in his arms, she wondered—

"Fire, fire!" A small boy ran up and down the hill, shouting the warning.

Aiden and Claire separated. The smell of burning wood wafted in the air. Why hadn't she noticed it?

The church bells began to peal, calling the attention of the villagers and castle people alike. Aiden dashed down the hill, and Claire followed close at his heels. Not too far, on the edge of the village, a small hut burst into flames much like a bonfire on St. John's Eve, spewing a dark cloud of smoke into the blue sky. From the fields below, men, women, and older children rushed up the hill.

By the time she and Aiden got close enough to see the very pregnant, very young woman—she couldn't be more than seventeen—sitting on the ground a few feet from the burning hut, wailing in desperation, she was already surrounded by many people. At the sight of Aiden, however, the crowd parted. Claire wasn't sure whether out of respect for his rank or in fear.

Not wanting to intrude, she remained behind as Aiden crouched beside the young woman. "Are you harmed?" he asked softly.

She shook her head, stopping the wailing but continuing to sob uncontrollably. A young man, looking more like a teenager than a grown man, surged forth and broke through the crowd to kneel by the young woman's side. He took her in his arms, cradling her like a baby. She calmed down, whimpering quietly against his chest.

She didn't appear hurt, Claire thought, just scared and heartbroken at the loss of her home. They were so young, and a couple already, with a baby on the way. Somehow, though, unlike in modern times, it seemed right. Life was short in these times, childhood almost nonexistent. She didn't know whether to envy or pity their blissful ignorance.

More people arrived—some from the fields, some from the castle—carrying buckets of water filled from a big communal barrel. A little too late, Claire thought. There was no saving the hut. Its highly flammable construction material—wooden walls coated with clay and a thatched roof—were already mostly consumed by the flames. At this point, they were probably just trying to contain the fire and prevent it from spreading to the rest of the village.

Apparently satisfied that the situation was under control, Aiden addressed the distraught couple. "You and your wife may seek shelter in the castle until your home is rebuilt."

The young couple exchanged an uneasy glance. It was obvious the offer wasn't appreciated. The young woman's eyes grew enormous with fear, and she gripped her husband's arms.

The young man shuffled in place. Unable to face Aiden, he bowed his head and kept his eyes lowered to the ground. "I thank you, my lord, for your generosity, but we do not wish to be a burden to you. If 'tis all the same, my wife and I will stay in the village with her family."

Slowly, Aiden rose to his feet. A muscle jumped in his cheek. Surely his displeasure wasn't at the couple's refusal but at the reason behind it. There was no denying fear mandated their actions. Fear of something Aiden had no control over: his ghost.

Heat surged up Claire's neck. She was outraged on Aiden's behalf. He could do no right in these people's eyes. Why didn't they see he wasn't the cause of their troubles? Not even Cherise could be blamed for all the misfortunes in their lives.

And yet, the thought struck her suddenly, hadn't she,

too, blamed Aiden for her unhappiness in the future? Hadn't she allowed his betrayal in the past to poison her heart for all time? But was his betrayal what haunted Claire, or the fact he apparently had not loved her?

"It is all the same to me." Aiden's voice rescued her from her never-ending mental questioning. He pivoted and marched to where she stood.

"My lord—" the young man called, jerking to his feet.

Aiden stopped. Claire saw his face assume an impersonal mask before he slowly turned around. Try as he might, he couldn't hide his hurt from her keen eyes, though.

And finally Claire understood the depth of his loneliness. Her heart constricted painfully for him.

Under Aiden's cool stare, the young man seemed to shrink back. He hesitated, swallowed hard, and flipped his gaze to his young wife who squeezed his hand in encouragement. He looked back at Aiden—or rather, at Aiden's boots—and cleared his throat. "My lord," he began again. "I beg your permission to rebuild my home a few paces from where it stood before it burned down."

He held his breath, waiting for Aiden's response. Utter silence fell like a mantle over the crowd, the crackling of burning wood the only sound filling the still air. Judging by the strain on everyone's faces, the matter was obviously far from trivial, though Claire couldn't fathom why.

Aiden took his time to answer, adding to the already high tension. His gaze glided over the crowd, taking each person's measurement. The young man who'd made the request flinched, others drifted their gazes, unable to sustain Aiden's scrutiny, but some stared at Aiden as if hypnotized. When Aiden finally spoke, his voice was strong and clear. "I grant you my permission."

There was a collective sigh of relief, but Aiden had already turned his back on them, his own face a mask of discontent.

"Thank you, my lord. Thank you." The young man fell to his knees again, and his wife began weeping quietly. This time, Claire thought, with relief.

"Come," Aiden said as he reached her.

"What was that about?" Claire spun around and took his arm with one hand while she gathered her skirts with the other.

She didn't get an answer until they had taken a few steps away from the crowd. "Apparently they believe the place is cursed."

"Cursed? Why would they think that?"

Aiden's hand tightened over Claire's. "Cherise once lived there."

Claire's feet locked; she couldn't take another step. She glanced back at what was left of the hut, and her entire body tensed. She knew what was about to happen. Quickly, she clutched Aiden's arm for support before her vision blackened completely, and she slacked against him.

She was inside the burning hut. The heat was unbearable, the room dense with smoke. She could barely breathe, could scarcely see as she fought her way to the door. She had to get out! Fear squeezed her heart, flames licked against her legs. Her skirts caught on fire. She screamed, desperately batting at the flames, fighting the panic threatening to overwhelm her senses. Blindly, she continued to move. Abruptly, the roof caved in, showering blazing reeds down on her. She spun to get away from it, her foot caught on the stool, and she lost her balance. She felt herself falling as if in slow motion; her legs lifted in the air, and her head hit the corner of the table.

Her last conscious thought was of Aiden.

The brightness of the sun made Claire squint. She could still feel the heat burning her skin, her lungs fighting for every breath. With every eye on her, she quickly turned away and leaned against Aiden.

"Did you have a vision?" he whispered.

Gasping, she nodded, though she wasn't sure what the hell had happened.

"It was but a moment," Aiden said, tightening his hold of her. "No one noticed. If they did, they probably thought you were distraught at the sight of the fire."

She *was* distraught at the sight of fire, but not this fire, she was sure.

Good God! What could this possibly mean? She needed to ask Aiden how Cherise had died, but she didn't dare have such a conversation within earshot of these people who already feared everything on earth. They might feel the need to cast her into the bonfire for good measure.

"Can you walk?" Aiden asked.

She eased away from him a bit, straightening her body, but her legs quivered so badly, she kept her hold on his arm. She took a deep breath, and another, and then finally nodded.

Slowly, they made their way through the village. They passed Father Aubert, standing at the church's entrance, and Claire caught the priest's guarded gaze as he followed her and Aiden's progress.

"Where are we going?" she asked, when Aiden veered to the opposite direction of the castle.

"We both need a little solitude, Claire. We will not find it in the castle. There is much we must discuss."

And very little she could tell him, Claire thought, though she had much to ask.

CLAIRE LEANED BACK, SINKING HER ELBOWS INTO THE cool grass for support, while Aiden sat by her, arms over drawn knees, rolling a blade of grass between his fingers. The melodic sounds of water rushing over smoothed rocks, carrying away fallen leaves on a journey with no return, bubbled beside them. Sunlight dappled through the trees like rays over a saintly figure, casting light but little warmth to the cool shade.

The soothing sounds and gentle breeze did little to dissipate the horrendous scene replaying incessantly in her mind. Only time and answers would dull that memory.

She pushed herself up to a sitting position and turned to Aiden. She was about to appease his curiosity about her vision, and find some answers in the process. "How did Cherise die?" she asked.

The blade of grass fell to the ground as Aiden jerked his gaze to her. His eyes narrowed, his answer took long to come. "Her home burned down. Why do you ask?"

Claire sighed. It was as she'd seen, or remembered, she wasn't sure anymore. For the most part, Claire had *lived* the episode of Cherise's death in the burning hut, but at the very end, for a split second, she'd seen Cherise lying unconscious amidst the flames, as if her spirit had detached itself from the flesh to look back before it departed.

Had she had a vision or flashback? The answer to that question would unravel the secrets to her past.

"Why do you ask, Claire?" Aiden insisted.

"I think I saw Cherise's death." Her voice choked; she had to pause, breathe deeply, and again ban the pictures from her mind.

Aiden took her hands into his and squeezed them tight in a show of support. She smiled gratefully at him. "She was battling the flames, suffocating with the thick smoke, trying to escape—"

"She was trying to escape?"

Why would he doubt that? "Yes, but the roof caved in, she lost her balance, and hit her head on the table, losing consciousness. Obviously, she didn't get out."

"But she tried," he whispered.

"Why would that surprise you?"

He blew out a breath. "For years I wondered whether she had taken her own life."

Claire swung a free hand to cover her mouth in shock. "Good God, Aiden! Why would you think that?"

"I was led to believe that was what happened, but I always doubted. Always . . ." His voice trailed.

"What, who led you to believe such a thing?"

"Words Cherise spoke to me that fateful day, her haunting of me since, her sister's accusation—"

"I thought her sister couldn't speak."

His gaze sharpened on her. "Do you know Meredith?"

"I saw her earlier on the castle's grounds."

"She can speak, but she chooses not to. In fact, the only time I heard her voice was on the day Cherise died, when she told me Cherise had chosen death over living without me."

"Maybe it was grief speaking."

"Perchance it was. Meredith was always a troubled soul. She was raped at a young age, and from that time on became a recluse. Even more so when she was partly disfigured trying to save her sister from the fire. What I know is that Cherise was deeply distraught and angry with me over my upcoming marriage to Jeanne."

Claire had never considered Cherise's feelings in the matter. All she had thought of was Jeanne's pain in having the man she had married love another woman. Still, Cherise had come first into Aiden's life; therefore, she also had the right to feel betrayed when Aiden married someone else.

How about Aiden? What did he truly feel about those two women in his life? About her in the past? Had he cared for them at all? Or did he merely feel guilty over their unnecessary deaths?

"Obviously, both Jeanne and Cherise loved you, Aiden. What did you feel for them?"

He stared into nothingness. "Jeanne and I met for the first time a few weeks before our wedding. I would not say she loved me. She was a gentle born lady, and understood her duty. Had our marriage lasted longer than a month, I would have proved myself a kind husband to her.

"It was different with Cherise," he continued. "We were together for over a year before I wedded Jeanne. After Guillaume's death in the Crusade—" He cast a sidelong glance at her, and Claire remembered Aiden thought she knew Guillaume. She decided now wasn't the time to point out she had misled him.

At her silence, he continued, "I journeyed to Brittany, where Cherise lived, to fulfill a vow I made to Guillaume to take his possessions back to her. By the time I reached Cherise, though, Guillaume had been dead for months, and she already knew it. Meantime, the Crusade was over, King Richard had been captured by Duke Leopold of Austria, and I had nowhere to go. Thus, I offered my services to Guillaume's liege lord and remained in his stronghold with Cherise until King Richard returned to England and fulfilled his vow to return Delacroix to me."

Aiden picked up a small pebble and cast it on the brook. It skipped three times over the water before it sank with a small splash. "Richard's boon came with a caveat, however. To take possession of Delacroix I had to wed Jeanne. And so I did."

He turned and faced her. "Cherise was a passionate woman, and I admired her joie de vivre. Had I been free to choose a wife, I would have chosen her without question."

Claire's insides churned, not with the expected jealousy, but with the deepest of doubts. She knew she had loved Aiden in her past life, but Aiden believed Jeanne hadn't loved him.

Cherise had, however, passionately.

Good God! Could she be the reincarnation of Cherise

and not Jeanne? Wouldn't that explain her memories of Cherise's death?

Her mind promptly rebelled against the thought. Cherise's soul was presently a haunting ghost. Aiden had confirmed her identity when she described the ghost to him in the garden—a detail difficult to dismiss. For Claire to even entertain the notion that she could have been Cherise in her past life, the ghost must be someone else. But who?

"You might think me a heartless man," Aiden said, wresting her from her thoughts. "But I had a choice to make, and I made it. *Mère de Dieu!* I made it, and I paid dearly for it." He fisted his hands. "I am still paying."

For once, the words of recrimination died unspoken in Claire's mouth. She knew enough about these times to recognize the value of property. A castle meant not only a home, lands, and income, but honor. Add to that a duty to recover what was stolen from his family, what he believed was rightfully his, and Aiden had made the only choice he thought he could have made.

Claire couldn't condemn him for that.

And yet, Cherise had.

Cherise had made it her purpose in death to punish the man she once loved, to condemn him to a life of loneliness and unhappiness, to kill his wife, and frighten away all others because he had jilted her.

Claire could not have done the same were she in Cherise's shoes.

She placed her hand on Aiden's arm, for once relieved no memory came to her. "For what it's worth, Aiden, I don't think you a heartless man."

His eyes softened and caressed her. Good God! If she didn't know better, she'd think there was love swimming in their beautiful depths. Of course, there wasn't. It was merely gratitude. A man who faced rejection every way he turned would appreciate her understanding.

She couldn't deny there was a potent, vibrant, consuming fascination between them, but love . . . ?

Unless she'd been Cherise, and she wasn't prepared to accept that yet, love had not been a part of their past. It was not a part of their present. And it could never be a part of their future.

Chapter 17

JOY and relief—emotions unknown to him for a long time—filled Aiden.

Cherise had not taken her life!

Claire did not condemn him!

The words replayed in his mind, mingling and meshing and thrilling, and making him shudder at their liberating effect. Claire's gifts to him.

Feeling more alive than he had in years, he pulled her into his arms and eased them down to the grass. She laid her head on his chest, her hand over his heart, her body alongside his. He laced his fingers through her soft curls, lazily caressing her nape. His other hand held hers over his heart.

A thrill of pleasure shot through him, and his heart stumbled in his chest. Knowing she listened to its maddening beat, he wished he could hold her like this until the end of time, until the rushing waters silenced in the brook and the leaves ceased to rustle in the trees above.

For a moment he indulged in the fantasy of winning her heart, to have her always by his side. Instinctively, his arms tightened around her, as if that simple action would make his wish come true. He inhaled her sweet honey scent, his lips brushed against her silky hair.

She eased back a little. Her face turned to him, and he lost himself in the depths of those velvety brown eyes that seemed to seek out his soul. For a maddening moment, it was as if he had always known her.

Mère de Dieu! Could Claire be right? Had they shared a past life together, after all? The thought struck him so suddenly, his heart skipped a beat.

Bewildered that he would consider the possibility, he wondered whether he had been bewitched, for no more unusual lady had he ever met than Claire.

Mystical forces or not, there was no denying the pull tugging him to her. A pull he had no urge to fight against. The past was no more, but the future was his to fight for and win.

He lifted his head toward her and brushed his lips over hers, a mere feather stroke that teased and promised and dared. She did not pull away. Encouraged, he went back for more, and more. Each new nibbling of lips, each thrusting of tongues, each slanting of mouths further wove a magical spell around his heart.

Half lying over his body, one leg raised over his right hip, dangerously near to his growing arousal, Claire whimpered against his mouth. Blood pounded loudly in his ears, briskly in his heart, and heavily in his loins. He slid his hand down her leg, burrowed underneath her skirts, and traced his callused fingers over the firm, smooth skin of her calf, until they cradled behind her knee. With his mouth devouring hers, he slowly trailed his hand up the back of her thigh, higher and higher.

He felt her shudder course through his own body.

The next moment, Claire pulled her mouth from his. Gasping for air, she rolled to the side, taking her warmth with her, leaving him bereft. She sat up. "Maybe we shouldn't be doing this."

It took Aiden a moment to clear the fog of desire clogging his mind. When it did, he saw her flushed face, her chest heaving, her breathing choppy. She flipped an errant curl from her face with a trembling hand, avoiding his gaze.

Had he offended her with his overtures? He reached for her, but she pushed to her feet, evading his touch. He rose to stand behind her. "Claire, I meant you no disrespect. I would not dishonor you. I would not force myself upon you. You know I would wed you this day, did you consent."

She shook her head, and then pivoted, settling troubled eyes on him. "You know I can't stay."

Heart beating wildly in his throat, he refused to accept the truth of her words. "Nay, I do not know. Why, Claire? Why can you not marry me? Perchance, are you already married?" The mere suggestion congealed his heart.

"I'm not married, but I don't belong here. This is not my time, this is not my place. Our connection lies in the past, Aiden. There is no present, no future for us."

His hand flew to the back of his neck. Why was she so adamantly bent on refusing him? It was clear she was not indifferent to him. What was she not telling him? "The past is no more. Why can you not leave it alone?"

"It haunts me, Aiden. The past haunts me."

The pain in her voice shook him. *The visions! Mère de Dieu!* That was the reason she wished no life with him. He was the cause of her pain. It was touching him that provoked her visions. Aching to offer her comfort, he balled his hands alongside his body. "Would that I could ease your burden," he said.

Claire shot him a resolute look. "Help me find the answers I seek."

"I do not wish to cause you pain."

She shrugged. "Pain is of no importance. It's the price to freeing both of us from the shackles of the past. Aiden, I think there's a connection between you, me, Cherise, and Jeanne."

"What could possibly tie us all together?"

"Cherise is my ghost."

Aiden's mouth slacked open. "Your ghost?" he breathed. "It cannot be. You told me your ghost had led you to me. Why would Cherise do so?"

"I'm debating her motivation, myself. After all, if her intention was to get rid of me, she could've done so in any of the countless times she appeared to me before."

That Cherise had appeared to Claire outside Delacroix Castle was a puzzle in itself. That she had drawn Claire to him was bewildering. "Perchance she lured you here to prove she means you no harm. She has appeared to you before several times without an incident. Your first encounter at Delacroix was harmless. And she has appeared to you in a vision, letting you and I know that she did not take her own life. Perchance, she even means to prove her innocence in Jeanne's death."

The more he thought about it, the more convinced he became.

"It is possible," Claire said, looking utterly unconvinced. "Or perhaps she hasn't threatened me before because she wants you to witness my demise, to suffer yet another loss, to know for certain that you will live the rest of your life alone. What better punishment for your betrayal of her?"

As much as he wished to deny it, the truth in Claire's words struck him like a sharp whip. Still, he fought against it. There must be another answer. Not only for Cherise's sake, but, more importantly, for Claire's. He could not bear it if Claire met a tragic fate because of him.

"Or perchance," he insisted, "you are mistaken, and your ghost and Cherise are not the same."

"I'm sure they are one. What I'm not sure is whether the ghost haunting us is Cherise."

Aiden's body snapped into full alert. "Who else could she be? You perfectly described Cherise to me when you first saw her in the garden. You even saw her in your vision of her death. Were they not the same woman?"

Claire reluctantly nodded. "That is what puzzles me." She paused. "Could another spirit be mistaken for Cherise, perhaps Jeanne?"

Aiden adamantly shook his head. "They looked naught alike. Cherise was voluptuous, Jeanne willowy. One had wavy, reddish gold hair, the other, straight flaxen hair. They could not be mistaken. Besides, Jeanne had no reason to haunt me, she—"

"I beg to differ," Claire interrupted. "Jeanne had ample reason to resent you. After all, your mistress killed her—" She lifted a hand, forestalling his forthcoming defense of Cherise. "Whether on purpose or not, Cherise was the cause of your wife's death. You can't deny that."

"I can and I shall. The only witness to that terrible incident was Jasper, whose motivation is suspicious in the least." And now it was his turn to forestall her denial with a lift of his hand. "Besides, you cannot have it both ways. If, as you suspect, Cherise is not the ghost, then she can have naught to do with Jeanne's death."

"And neither can you, Aiden. If Cherise *is* the ghost, there's a good chance she was involved in Jeanne's death."

"Then we must agree to disagree."

"No, we must agree to find out whether Cherise is the ghost or not. That should give us some of the answers we seek."

* * *

THE HALL WAS NEARLY EMPTY. THEY HAD MISSED MOST of the midday meal, but a few people still lingered. Claire's stomach rumbled, but she wasn't in the mood to partake of a meal with a dozen strangers scrutinizing her every move.

Before she had a chance to make her wishes known, however, Aiden took hold of her elbow and routed her in the direction of the high table where Melissent and Jasper shared a meal.

Did Aiden have a masochistic streak in him? Claire wondered. She didn't know how he bore these people's dislike. Then again, what else could he do? He could not avoid everyone in the castle for the rest of his life. And he could not dictate their feelings toward him. Well, maybe he could force them to be nicer to him, but Aiden didn't have a tyrannical bone in his body.

For what it was worth, at least for now, she wouldn't let him stand alone. He had gone out of his way for her. It was the least she could do for him.

Swallowing her earlier objection, she allowed him to lead her. She stole a glance at him. His jaw was tight, his face veiled with a stony veneer. It was how he protected himself from the pain of rejection, she realized, by remaining aloof and hiding his emotions.

She squeezed his hand in a show of support, and he turned a smiling gaze at her. Good God! The way his dark blue eyes sparkled when he looked at her did things to her insides she couldn't possibly describe.

Damn, but she was beginning to like this man far too much for her own good.

When she touched him, she was not only cursed with memories she didn't understand, but with physical and emotional needs she struggled to ignore. Clearly, the solution wasn't as easy as having a torrid affair with him. She was afraid that once she let Aiden inside her body, she would never get him out of her heart.

Their little sojourn into the village and woods had further complicated the dynamics of their relationship. She no longer thought of Aiden as merely the man with whom she had issues from the past. She was getting to know him as he was now, beginning to care for him in a whole new way that had nothing to do with whatever she felt for him in the past.

And that didn't bode well at all for her.

As they reached the table, Aiden bowed to Melissent and ignored Jasper, who stood up at their arrival.

"Claire, this is Lady Melissent," Aiden introduced.

"Nice to see you again," Claire said, brushing her thoughts aside and preparing to make nice.

Aiden's eyebrows rose. "Have you met before?"

"Earlier this morning," Claire explained. It had been a very long morning. So much had happened in such a short time, it was like one of those intense foreign language courses, where a student was sequestered for days at a time, immersed in the language and culture being learned.

Melissent rose and curtsied prettily. "My lady."

Claire inclined her head slightly in response, and then turned to Jasper, acknowledging him with a smile.

Niceties out of the way, they all sat down.

Suddenly Melissent sprang to her feet again. Claire's gaze followed hers, and she saw the reason behind the woman's blanched face. Her son, Giles, dashed across the hall, his face freshly scrubbed, his hair wet and combed forward, his shirt lacking the dark soot of earlier. Despite his gait, he carried a heavy-looking pewter carafe and two cups with an innate charm and speed.

He halted at the foot of the table, bowed to the occupants, then rushed to Aiden's side. His face was flushed, his eyes sparkling. Claire wasn't sure whether from the run or excitement.

What was he doing at the hall, anyway? she wondered.

"Giles!" Melissent cried, obviously wondering the same thing. Jasper refrained from commenting, and Aiden didn't look surprised.

"My lady." Giles bowed to his mother, and then immediately turned his attention to Aiden. "My lord. I have fresh wine to refresh your parched throat. May I pour you some?"

Aiden nodded. "For my lady, too."

Giles did so, barely containing his grin.

Slowly, Melissent sat. Her hands shook; she clearly didn't know what to make of her son's presence in the hall.

The boy set the carafe on the table and stepped back. "I shall return shortly, my lord. I must make certain they serve you the choicest cut of meat and the freshest of breads."

Grinning, Claire followed the boy's retreat. He was trying so hard to please Aiden. Still, how did he get to be here? Claire had understood he was persona non grata in certain places in the castle.

She returned her gaze to Aiden and saw that mask of indifference he often wore had slipped a bit. He, too, watched Giles retreat with amusement. It was clear he was pleased.

Not so Melissent.

"I thank you, my lord," Melissent said, looking quite disturbed, "for indulging Giles for this day. He shall return to the kitchen shortly and will not impose on you further."

"Giles will no longer do kitchen duty," Aiden said. "He is my page, now. His duties are to me alone."

"Your page! But my lord, with what intention do you order him thus?"

"With the intention of training him to be a squire, and one day a knight, if he is worthy of the golden spurs."

"He has no means to pursue knighthood," she interjected.

"I shall foster him."

Melissent darted a questioning glance at Claire. Claire shrugged. She had nothing to do with this. She didn't even know Aiden knew Giles. He had come to the boy's rescue without her interference. Claire couldn't be more proud of Aiden. But she wondered why the hell Melissent was so belligerent. Shouldn't she be happy Giles was given the chance of his lifetime?

"My lady," Jasper addressed Claire, deciding to put in his two cents worth. "What a benevolent influence you exert over Aiden. I am overly impressed. Had I regained my birthright, I would have offered to foster the boy myself. As it is, Giles must roll the dice with what is offered to him."

Claire wasn't too thrilled with the tone of Jasper's words. "I am sure—" Before she could defend Aiden, he squeezed her hand in warning.

"You need not concern yourself with Giles's fate, Jasper, or with aught else relating to Delacroix. However, just to ease my lady's mind, pray tell, were any of your needs not met when you lived under my fosterage?"

Jasper snapped his lips together. It was clear he'd like to ignore the question if he could. Claire pointedly stared at him, waiting for his response.

"You have provided well for my training, my lord," Jasper finally said, albeit begrudgingly.

"But Giles is . . ." Melissent's voice trailed off.

Aiden turned his attention to her, as if daring her to speak the words he knew danced in her mind.

"He cannot ride," she whispered.

"He shall learn. He has the interest and the desire, that is all that is required of him."

"He will hurt himself."

"That is a possibility, but you cannot protect him forever. He will grow to be a man, Melissent, whether you will it or not. And he must fight his own battles. There is more courage in that little boy than I have seen in many a grown man. Where have you kept him that I have never laid my eyes on him before?"

Melissent shrugged, looking unhappy. Why? Claire wondered again. She knew Giles's dream was to be a knight. Did she fear he wouldn't make it? Or that he would be ridiculed? She had said earlier she feared his heart would be broken as his body already was.

Couldn't she put her motherly protective instincts aside for a moment and give the boy a chance at his dream?

But what did she know about the powerful emotions linking mother and child? She wasn't a mother, after all. She would never be one, if she remained here.

Claire shook the thought away. It simply wasn't an alternative she would consider.

Melissent blew out a breath. "Why are you doing this?" she asked with less anger now, almost with resignation.

Aiden took a sip of his wine and met Melissent's eyes with an unwavering gaze. "Because he asked me to. Because he wants it badly. Because everybody should have a chance to fulfill their dream. And because I can."

WITH THE EXCEPTION OF A FEW COMMENTS ABOUT the fire in the village, the rest of the meal elapsed mostly in awkward silence. Aiden's and Jasper's circumspect countenances didn't seem to affect their appetite, though. Claire, however, picked at her food, while Melissent nursed her cup of wine as she stole glances at her son.

Giles seemed the only one enjoying his day. He hopped

from one side of the table to the other, ever so solicitous, and unable to hide his happiness.

If Claire didn't have so much on her mind, she'd surely have already contracted the joy bug from the boy. As it was, she could only be happy for him and proud of Aiden. A quick glance around her revealed her dinner companions were equally distracted with their own thoughts, and therefore impervious to what could be the first sign of joy in this old castle in a very long time.

By the time the meal was over, the morning had slowly edged its way into afternoon. Jasper didn't linger, called away by one of his men, and Melissent excused herself soon after. Claire was ready to remove herself to the bedroom and take a long, soothing bath to banish the tension stiffening her muscles.

She rubbed her neck, suppressing a smile as she remembered Aiden's often repeated gesture. The man could probably benefit from a professional massage. That thought led her to other dangerous ones that she quickly chased away.

"You look weary," he said.

She dropped her hands to the table. "This day seems to stretch unendingly." God! Had it been only a week since she traveled back in time? It felt more like a year. So much had happened, so much had she learned, and yet so little she still knew.

Aiden downed the rest of his wine. "The past ten years of my life have been like that: one endless moment stretching thinly before me."

Empathizing with the helpless feeling in Aiden's voice, Claire placed her hand on top of his and squeezed gently. "You will regain control over your life once the ghost is gone."

Reassuring words from a woman who constantly struggled for control, Claire thought. She couldn't even command her flashbacks, since apparently it wasn't a simple matter of merely touching Aiden, as she'd first believed. How could she make idle promises to him when she couldn't even predict when the ghost would next appear? It wasn't as if there was a set place or time for such occurrences. Cherise, or whoever the ghost was, had only made her presence known when she felt threatened by another woman's connection to Aiden, and she seemed to have preferred no witness to the deed.

Claire was definitely a threat to Cherise, since everyone thought she and Aiden were getting married. But she'd been quite busy since her arrival, and Aiden had not left her side for too long. Claire couldn't afford to wait for Cherise to make her move. She had to provoke the ghost's appearance somehow, to resolve this once and for all, for Aiden's as well as her own sake. She didn't think she could hold her emotions in check around him much longer.

But she couldn't draw the ghost out with Aiden around.

Placing his other hand on top of hers, he enclosed her hand between his. Warmth seeped through Claire, and that always tantalizing quivering.

"Aiden, you don't have to stick around me all the time. I'm sure you have plenty to do. I'll be all right on my own."

"I have neglected my duties of late," he said. "With the journey to Chartres and all, I have been away for over a week, but I do not wish to leave you unprotected. I shall assign a guard to escort you when I cannot be present."

That wouldn't do at all. Cherise wouldn't make her move with Claire heavily guarded. And yet, she understood Aiden's precaution and was thankful for his concern. She had to think of a way to circumvent the guard without putting herself in more danger than necessary.

"That is really not necessary. I can take care of myself. You know I don't fear the ghost."

"I do not doubt that, but I would rather take no chances with your life. You shall have an escort."

"I thought you believed Cherise was harmless," she taunted.

"As you said, we do not know whether the ghost is indeed Cherise."

She shot him a bemused smile. So, it wasn't above him to use her words to suit his needs. "Whoever the ghost is, judging by her previous appearances, she won't approach me unless I'm alone."

He shrugged, as if saying *That would suit me just fine.*

"What's the point of my being here, if I can't confront the ghost?" she demanded. "I might as well leave now."

That wiped the deliberate nonchalance from his face. "The matter is not debatable, Claire. When I am not with you, I will have a guard escorting you at all times."

God! She wasn't used to being dictated to. Her brother was the only one who meddled in her business, but he always backed off when he understood she wouldn't change her mind about some matter. Not so Aiden. He would not back down on this, she knew it.

"How close to me do you want him? Inside the bedroom while I bathe?"

A muscle twitched on his cheek. "He will remain outside your door. You need only to call out."

Claire blew out a breath. "As you wish, Aiden," she agreed. "As long as he stays out of my way and out of my sight."

"I thank you for understanding."

Suddenly all her irritation whooshed out of her. Aiden was only trying to protect her, she reminded herself. "Sorry. I guess I'm just a little on edge. It hasn't been the easiest of days."

"Perchance you should seek your rest."

"Perchance I shall," she said with a smile. "In fact, I

would love a bath. Who can I ask to help me with that?" She didn't want to order the servants around.

"Giles," Aiden called.

"Aye, my lord." He stood straight like a little toy soldier. "I shall order a bath be drawn immediately for my Lady Claire," he said before Aiden even had a chance to ask.

Claire laughed. "Keep this up, Giles, and you will become indispensable in no time at all."

Giles grinned, standing before them and basking in the obviously previously unknown praise.

"Why do you wait?" Aiden asked. "Do not let your lady's praise go to your head."

"Aye, my lord." He bowed. "My lady?" He bowed again and strode away, his step a little firmer, his gait a little straighter.

DESPITE CLAIRE'S PROTESTS, BEFORE AIDEN LEFT THE hall to attend to his much neglected duties, he assigned a guard to escort her. What Hughes lacked in height he more than made up in width, and not one ounce of that was fat. Resembling a short but sprawling oak tree, he seemed a quite capable defender, although how all that strength would play against a ghost was anyone's guess.

Still, realizing it'd be useless to try to convince Aiden of the bodyguard's ineffectiveness, she resigned herself to his presence and walked briskly ahead of him to the stairs. Obligingly, Hughes kept a healthy distance, though his gaze never left her. As she reached the stairs and was about to take the first step up, Coco dashed from behind her, brushing against her legs, and raced ahead of her without a pause.

Pressing a hand to her stampeding heart, Claire stopped and glanced up. The cat's habit of appearing out of nowhere, dashing here and there without apparent destination, took a little getting used to. At least her Coco in the future was a little more subdued.

Finding Coco at the top of the stairs, Claire's heart flipped in her chest. The cat wasn't alone. By her side, immersed in the shadows of the dark corridor, facing Claire's bedroom door, Cherise stood in profile, her chin slightly elevated as if posing for a portrait. She turned her head slightly, giving Claire a snooty stare, and then glided inside the room. Coco followed.

Gathering her skirts, Claire dashed up the steep stairs. It wasn't an easy or quick climb. Hughes, noticing her sudden hurry, dashed after her. Despite his cumbersome attire, he managed to swiftly overtake her and reach the closed door at the same time as Claire. He injected his body between her and the door and, drawing his sword, shoved the door open with his wide shoulder before she could tell him not to interfere.

The door gave way easily. It wasn't locked. Hughes rushed inside, and Claire followed, this time overtaking him. The room was in utter chaos, but the ghost was nowhere in sight. Coco sat calmly on the seat underneath the open window. Maybe Cherise was in the garden? Claire rushed to the window, but a quick glance down dashed her hopes. The garden was empty.

Frustrated, she stepped back. A little scrap of white linen caught between the slats of the window shutter distracted her. Claire picked it up, rolled the thin fabric between her fingers. Surely it wasn't part of Cherise's dress. A ghost was spirit and her clothing as ethereal.

She dropped the scrap. More likely it was torn from a cleaning rag.

She plumped down on the cushioned seat underneath the window. Hand absently scratching Coco's soft, furry body, she assessed the damage with a troubled gaze. Feathers from the disemboweled pillows littered the floor. The bed curtains hung in tatters on the four-poster bed. And above the fireplace, written in bold, bloody letters, an unmistakable message.

DEATH TO THE BRIDE!

Claire jerked to her feet. There was no more debating the ghost's true intention.

Chapter 18

TRY as she might to look at the message as a mere scare tactic, Claire just couldn't deny it unnerved her.

Hughes stepped into her line of vision, and with his back to her, poked inside the fireplace with the tip of his sword. That was when Claire noticed the smell of burning cloth and leather. With dread prickling her skin, she rushed over the feather-covered floor to the immense fireplace in time to see Hughes lift the remains of her sandals. Of her dress, lacy panties, and scarf, there was little left but a pile of ashes. And as her sandals were half consumed by fire, Hughes dropped them back into the fireplace. There was nothing in the fire that remotely resembled her purse.

Outrage filled Claire, hardening her resolve. If the ghost, whoever it was, thought she would send her hightailing out of Delacroix on account of losing her personal belongings and a melodramatic message, she had seriously underestimated Claire. The ante might have been upped a little, but the battle was far from decided.

"Hughes," Claire said. "Inform Lord Aiden what has just happened. I'm sure he would want to know about this immediately." She hoped once the guard was gone, Cherise would return. Claire was spoiling for a fight.

"My orders are not to leave you alone, my lady, unless another guard relieves me or Lord Aiden returns."

Claire bristled and then forced herself to be reasonable. She couldn't fault the man for following orders. However, every moment that delayed her confrontation with Cherise prolonged her stay in this time and drew her closer to Aiden. And the closer she got to him, the more difficult it would be for her to leave. She was already dangerously tempted to consider possibilities she had not entertained when she'd first met him.

"He also told you to keep your distance and respect my privacy," she reminded Hughes in a last attempt to ditch him. "Now, if you don't mind, I would like for you to wait outside."

Hughes didn't stir. "I fear Lord Aiden would not see it your way, my lady. Not under the circumstances."

Claire blew out a breath. No, Aiden would not see it her way. And with Hughes shadowing her, Cherise would not return now.

Curbing her annoyance, she turned around, taking in the senseless vandalism. Senseless in her mind; in Cherise's it had a definite purpose. Her gaze rested on Jeanne's trunk. On the outside it looked untouched, yet it couldn't be. Her clothes had been hidden inside, along with her purse and sandals.

She dropped by the trunk and jerked the lid open. Impatiently, she shuffled inside. Nothing of Jeanne's was missing, but Claire's purse was gone.

What the hell would a ghost want with her purse? Did she just make it disappear to annoy Claire?

Shoving the trunk lid closed, she rose. Her gaze fell on the ruined bed curtains, slashed to thin ribbons, swaying like tiny ghosts with the breeze blowing from the open window. A spot of blood caught in the sea of fluttering white caught her eye. She strode to the bed and pulled the strips of linen aside.

At the head of the bed, where her pillows should have been, lay the bodiless head of an unfortunate chicken, beady eyes staring into nothingness, in a garish mimic of a New Orleans voodoo scene. Claire gagged, snapped her gaze away.

And found her missing purse.

Tossed on a corner of the stripped mattress, its contents spilled out like a gutted animal. Credit card, hotel key card, and money leaked out of her wallet. The cell phone was on, the beach scene of her screen saver staring mockingly at her. Claire picked it up and flipped it off. Her small travel bottle of acetaminophen was open. She collected the white caplets and hunted for the lid, gathering the last three pieces of her Dove dark chocolate squares as well. Her lip gloss was there as was the small bottle of perfume she carried everywhere. The only missing item was her passport. Why had Cherise chosen to take that and leave the rest behind?

"My lady, what happened?"

Claire almost jumped at the sound of Giles's voice behind her. Using her body to obstruct his view, she swiftly shoved her belongings back inside her purse, then pivoted.

"Looks like I had a visitor," she said, stepping away from the bed, purse in hand, and as inconspicuously as she could, she dropped the purse inside Jeanne's trunk.

She noticed two older boys shuffling uneasily by the bathtub, wooden buckets of hot water for the bath she'd requested earlier by their feet, gawking at the message on the wall. Claire guessed they couldn't read, but the creepy red blood drippings surely gave them an idea of content.

"Not a very friendly one," Giles said as his big eyes roamed about the room to finally settle on her. Claire thought fleetingly that those dark, fathomless eyes would one day intrigue many a woman. "You are not harmed, are you, my lady?"

Claire smiled. "No, I'm not."

Giles relaxed for a moment, but immediately stiffened again. "I wish she would go away. I wish she would leave Lord Aiden alone."

There was such outrage and wistfulness in Giles's voice that Claire was moved. The boy's protectiveness of Aiden was a good sign. Apparently, he was Aiden's first supporter. Hopefully, the first of many to come.

"She will, Giles," she promised, patting his thin shoulders in reassurance. "She will."

A FEW MINUTES LATER, SUMMONED BY GILES, MELIS-sent arrived with a young woman in tow. She stopped a moment, darting her gaze around the room, then spoke quietly to the woman before sending her away. She turned a sharp gaze on Claire, and apparently satisfied she needed no medical attention, turned to Hughes. "I need your aid."

Following her instructions, Hughes carried the bench from the table to the bed. Melissent stepped on it and be-gan stripping the shredded curtains. Claire joined her on the opposite end of the bench.

"You need not bother yourself, my lady. Yvonnet will return shortly with another servant, and we shall have your bedchamber set to rights in no time at all."

Maybe Melissent thought that a woman in Claire's posi-tion shouldn't be doing menial work. What would she say if she knew Claire cleaned her own toilet in the future? "One extra pair of hands will finish the work faster. And please, call me Claire."

Melissent nodded, relaxing her shoulders a bit. The woman always seemed worked up about something. They worked in silence for a few more minutes, and then finishing that side of the bed, they stepped down so Hughes could move the heavy bench to the other side.

That was when Melissent saw the bodiless chicken. She exchanged a quick glance with Claire, then using one of the strips, wrapped the chicken head. "I shall dispose of this later."

"Thanks."

She put it aside and returned to work. Once the stripping was finished, she gathered the shredded bed curtains. "We shall have to make new bed curtains and pillow coverings."

Claire nodded agreeably. She was afraid Melissent would be on her own on this task. She couldn't sew, let alone weave. Besides, she wouldn't be here long enough to help with what looked to be a lengthy job.

Yvonnet and another servant returned with a pile of clean bed linens, a fur coverlet, and a couple of exquisitely embroidered pillows.

"Set them there for now." Melissent pointed to Jeanne's trunk. "We need to turn the mattress first."

While the two servants took care of that task, Claire picked up one of the pillows and traced the beautiful roses with her fingertips. "This is beautiful work."

"My Lady Jeanne embroidered them. It was part of her wedding gift to me."

Melissent and Jeanne had been close friends, Claire realized. Had Claire been Jeanne in her past life, shouldn't she feel something special for the young woman? A flash of recognition, an instant liking? She felt no closer to Melissent than she did to Yvonnet.

Claire put the pillow down. "Thank you, but I can't accept your generous offer. They are obviously precious to you. I can do without pillows for a while."

"I wish for you to make use of them. I . . ." She lowered her voice. "I thought ill of you when you first arrived. You seemed oddly detached from us all. Now I see I misjudged you."

It was easy to understand Melissent's reaction to her, Claire decided. She would have looked rather standoffish to them. She hadn't mingled, hadn't tried to get to know them, hadn't really cared what they thought of her. Not that they had welcomed her with open arms, which was odd, since if she succeeded in chasing the ghost away, she would be not only Aiden's salvation but theirs as well.

"You have been kind to my boy," Melissent continued. "And mayhap you shall succeed where others have failed." She looked around. "By the looks of it, though, you shall have a fierce fight in your hands." Her gaze returned to Claire. "However, you do not strike me as a fearful lady, and as Jasper, er, Lord Jasper said, you are a good influence on Lord Aiden."

However agreeable Melissent's words were toward her, Claire didn't like her inference that Aiden needed to be influenced. "Aiden is a good man. You and the people here do yourselves a disservice by thinking otherwise."

"I am beginning to see some truth in what you speak."

"Well, I'm glad. He does not deserve yours or anyone's contempt or anger. He's as much a victim of the circumstances as all of you are, and he's trying to make the best of the situation without blaming someone else for his misfortune. Maybe you should be doing the same."

Melissent lowered her gaze at the short tirade. Claire

wasn't entirely sure, however, whether in shame or disagreement.

It suddenly occurred to Claire she should do as she so righteously preached to Melissent. Shouldn't she be as forgiving of Aiden's role in her unhappy past? Hadn't he then made the choice he thought was best? Aiden had not intentionally set out to hurt anyone, she was sure. Life was full of difficult choices. Aiden had made his, and she would have to make hers in the very near future.

Forgiveness was liberating. It was as if an elephant had been removed from her back. For the first time that she remembered, it didn't hurt to think of the past.

Though the future was another matter altogether.

"You must love him profoundly." Melissent's words snapped Claire out of her musing.

Love Aiden? The thought struck her speechless. She knew she had loved Aiden in the past. She had come to admire his strength of character in the present. Even after such a short time she couldn't deny he was a good man. Her heart did jump joyfully every time she saw him, and constricted painfully when she thought of going back to her own time and never seeing him again.

Good God! Did that mean she loved Aiden?

Was she doomed to have her heart broken again? "He is a good man," she repeated, not trusting herself to elaborate.

"I saw a side of him in his dealings with Giles that I had not seen before," Melissent said. "I thought he did not care."

"Oh, he cares," Claire said. "He cares so damn much—" She ignored Melissent's flinch at her use of profanity. "—that if people weren't blinded by fear and superstition, they would notice Aiden doesn't retaliate when treated unfairly, when he's within his rights to do so." She knew enough about medieval life to know a lord had power of life and death over the people under his domain. And yet,

Aiden refrained from using that power, even when they goaded him. That showed admirable restraint, in her opinion.

The object of her heated defense appeared at the open archway. Predictably, her heart did its customary jig. He spotted her, and ignoring everything and everyone, marched in her direction. He swept a worried gaze over her, brushed a stray curl from her face. "Are you harmed?"

"I'm fine."

He blew out a breath, and then his gaze strayed briefly around the room, his face hardening when he saw the bloody message on the wall one of the servants was just beginning to wash.

He snapped his gaze back to her. His generous mouth was set in that stubborn line she was beginning to recognize. "From this moment on, you are never to be alone, Claire."

She didn't respond to his dictate, spoken in a tight, controlled voice. It would be useless to point out *again* that she needed to be alone to draw Cherise out, and that a confrontation between them was inevitable and necessary.

It was fear for her safety that drove him to make such an unrealistic demand.

And that thought warmed her insides more than she cared to admit.

WITH THE ROOM BACK TO NORMAL, THE CLEANING crew filed out carrying buckets, brooms, and rags. Claire thanked them for their quick work, though she suspected it was due more out of fear the ghost would reappear while they were still here than mere efficiency.

Melissent gathered Giles to her, probably knowing the boy would hang around Aiden as long as he could, and was about to leave as well when Claire stopped her. "Thank you again, Melissent, for all your help, and for lending me your beautiful pillows. I promise to take good care of them."

Melissent smiled in response and herded Giles on. As they passed Aiden, who stood near the arched doorway after dismissing Hughes, Giles stopped to speak with him a moment. Aiden listened, leaned down, and took something from Giles's hand. Claire couldn't see what it was, since the boy had his back to her.

And then there was only Claire and Aiden alone in the room.

He approached her with his usual purposeful stride. "What happened here?" His voice was low, gentle, despite the fact that his insides were probably churning. The more troubled Aiden was, the more control he exerted over his emotions. Claire had come to understand that about him.

"There isn't much to tell. I saw Cherise at the top of the stairs outside this room, and I followed her inside."

"Was she ever near you?"

Claire shook her head. "By the time I got here she was already gone."

He looked relieved. "Perchance it is a good omen."

Claire didn't think so, particularly after that unmistakable message on the wall, and yet, why had Cherise run? Despite her penchant for meeting her victims alone, she had missed a good chance to spook Claire away, or to try to do her harm. Hughes wouldn't be much of an impediment. After all, what could a sword do against a ghost?

"Unless she's gone for good," Claire said, "a short reprieve will not help us much."

"Then we shall wait and see. Time will tell whether her retreat is long lasting."

"Time is one thing I don't have in abundance, Aiden."

Probably understanding she meant she'd be leaving

soon, he changed subject. He opened his hand. "Does this belong to you?"

Claire eyed the small, red foil-wrapped Dove dark-chocolate square. "Where did you find that?"

"Giles gave it to me. He said he found it on the floor by the bed."

Damn! In her rush to hide her stuff, she must have dropped a piece of chocolate. She should just claim ignorance. Aiden wouldn't know any better, would he? Their gazes locked, and though his stare was steady and his face an unreadable mask, she knew he would know that odd little square could only belong to her.

"It is mine." *Why this sudden compulsion to tell him the truth?*

"What is it?" he asked as he handed it to her.

"Chocolate."

"Chocolate?" His tongue rolled awkwardly over the unfamiliar word.

"It's similar to one of your sweetmeats. Try it." She fumbled with the wrapping and offered him the dark square.

He looked at it, unsure. "I have never heard of such food."

To ease his mind, she took a small bite, savored the rich flavor, and then licked her lips. "It's quite delicious. A little bitter, a little sweet; it melts in your mouth, and it lingers in your mind."

"Like you."

She swallowed hard; her breath quickened. Remembering the taste of him, she licked her lips again. Suddenly chocolate fell to a distant second in her list of favorites.

Watching her, he reluctantly opened his mouth to her offering. Claire popped the chocolate inside. For a moment he did nothing, then as the rich flavor seeped into his mouth, he moved his jaw, and Claire knew he was working his tongue over the melting bar.

Desire pooled hot and demanding inside her. She wanted to taste that tongue again.

"Forbidden food from pagan gods," he whispered after a moment. "Is this from your homeland?"

Heart pumping faster, she nodded.

"Not Orléans."

She shook her head.

He waited for her to expound. She didn't.

"Where do you hail from, Claire?"

Just mention Castile, Rome, any place he would recognize, her mind screamed. "It is not a matter of where but when, not a place but time—"

"You speak in riddles," he interrupted her. "Speak the plain truth."

She lost some of her nerve. What was she thinking? Wasn't reincarnation mind boggling enough? Did she have to confuse him further with tales of her fantastic voyage through time? Soon she'd be gone. What good would it do for Aiden to know about a future he would never see or understand?

"What is the truth but our own perception of reality?" she said.

He blew out an exasperated breath. "You mistake me for a witless fool if you presume to pull the wool over my eyes with such drivel."

"That's not what I'm trying to do. I'm trying to explain, in a way that you might understand, the chasm that exists between us."

"Mère de Dieu!" His hand flew to the back of his neck, and Claire realized she might have sounded a tad condescending.

Damn! That was not what she intended at all.

"Do you think I do not see you are uncommon?" he asked. "No foreigner I know speaks as you do, or wears the odd garments I first saw you wearing, or eats the unusual food you have just offered me. I choose to ignore your eccentricities, Claire. You could be fay, for all I care, and it would matter naught to me."

Fay! That was a concept Aiden would understand. For a moment Claire considered latching on to the very convenient explanation he had just given her. Instead, she found herself rejecting the cop-out, at least partly. "I'm not fay, but you could say magic had a role in bringing me here."

"What manner of magic?"

"I can't explain what I don't understand myself, Aiden. All I know is that I went to the labyrinth in Chartres seeking answers to my past life, and there I found you."

He considered that for a moment. "I am beginning to believe we have indeed shared a past, for I feel I have known you forever, though I beheld you first only a few days past. But if the past ties us together, why do you not consider a future for us?"

Why didn't she?

She piled up the reasons in her mind: She didn't belong to this time, she couldn't bear the thought of causing her brother—her only family—pain by disappearing without an explanation, and she didn't want to give up her hope of one day becoming a mother, which could only happen in the future. And if that wasn't enough, she considered what it would cost her to leave behind her way of life, her business, her friends, and her home, all because of one man.

And yet wasn't that man the reason she had traveled through time? If she couldn't forget Aiden when she knew little to nothing of him, when he was only a vague memory, how was she to go on with her life after she'd gotten to know him, admire him, and—she finally admitted—love him all over again?

She'd always known, from the beginning, that if she allowed herself to get closer to Aiden, she'd be tempted to never leave his side. How would such decision affect the future?

Claire agonized over a decision that at first had seemed simple enough, but with the passing of time had embroiled her deep in doubts.

"I don't know, Aiden. I simply don't know what fate has in store for us."

He burrowed his hand in her silky curls, cradling her head. "Ah! Claire. I fear you shall disappear from my life in the same manner you came into it, with no forewarning." He rested his forehead against hers. "God have mercy on my soul, but I cannot abide the thought of parting with you."

Claire's heart swelled in her chest, robbing her of breath, as she fought to deny the undeniable.

She didn't want to part with him as well.

When he nudged her face up and closed his mouth over hers in a gentle yet desperate kiss, she desisted fighting against her heart.

She opened her lips to him, and their tongues met and danced and tasted, and she drowned in the pleasure of it. She would forever associate the rich taste of chocolate with the luscious taste of Aiden.

And she knew she'd never savor the sweet confection again without her heart breaking.

But that was yet to come, she told herself, banning the sadness enveloping her. There was no present, no past, and no future between them now. Just a stolen moment in time.

While she lost herself in the sensations his mouth elicited from her, she slid her hands up his hard chest. Finding the opening in his shirt, she burrowed underneath the collar. His skin burned as a furnace, searing her as she circled fingertips and raked fingernails up and down the back of his neck. She felt the gooseflesh rise over his taut muscles.

His arm pressed against her back, bending her. Though

she feared he would break her in two, she did nothing to ease the pressure. Instead, she melded to him, her soft breasts against his hard, naked chest, her pelvis pressed against his blooming arousal.

He pulled back a little, his eyes flaming, his breathing harsh. He gazed at her as if he was afraid she would disappear at any moment.

"Would you have me, Claire?"

Chapter 19

WOULD she have him?

Wanting him as she had never wanted a man in her life, Claire's entire body trembled with the need to join with Aiden. She was beyond fighting her feelings. "I will have no other."

Eyes smoldering, he took a small step back and removed his sword belt, allowing it to fall to the floor with a loud clank. Then he whisked his tunic and shirt together over his head. Claire drank in the sight of his naked muscled chest. She'd seen him undressed before, but only briefly. And that time she had swiftly turned her gaze away.

She was in no hurry to do so now.

And he was in no hurry to cover himself from her view.

For once they were in accordance.

Hands itching to touch him, to rake her fingernails through the dark hair in his chest, to rub her breasts against the hard planes, she watched him while he fumbled with his boots.

Belatedly remembering she was still fully dressed, she undid the lacing on either side of her gown and then pulled it over her head.

When he lifted his gaze to her and saw her standing before him in her thin undergarment, he drew in a sharp breath. For a moment he froze in place, then in one swift move he scooped her up and carried her to the bed. He propped her against the pillows and knelt by her side, his gaze gliding over her, arousing her as surely as if his hands roamed her body.

"Your beauty steals my breath away," he whispered.

Then why am I the one unable to breathe?

She watched him remove her shoes, toss them to the floor, and then run his fingers over her painted toes. She could guess the doubts roaming in his mind, and yet he said nothing. Odd as she must seem to him, he accepted her without reservation.

What was his motivation? Love or desperation?

Hand trailing up her calf, he burrowed underneath her chemise, unveiling her and capturing her wayward thoughts as he slowly made his way to her knee. "You have such smooth skin," he whispered.

Glad she'd had her legs waxed before she undertook the trip to France, Claire sucked in a breath as goose bumps spread over her skin. She should have had a Brazilian bikini wax as well, she thought wickedly, picturing Aiden's reaction to that, but she'd chickened out at the last minute and only gotten a trim.

The self-satisfied grin fled swiftly from her face like air from a busted balloon when his rough fingers skittered over the sensitive skin of her inner thigh. She gasped and raised her knees, shifting them slightly apart. Her undergarment pooled in her lap, exposing her to him.

His breath quickened, and his midnight-blue eyes blazed as he looked at her, giving her some satisfaction. She wasn't the only one overcome with desire.

Eyelids half closed, Claire waited for him to touch her where she ached. To her chagrin, however, he removed his hand from her thigh. Leaning over her, he placed a hand on each side of her head and lowered his mouth to hers. He kissed her lightly, again, and again, and again. His day-old beard rasped against her chin, and his chest rubbed against her breasts every time their mouths touched. With each new touch he deepened the kiss a little more—a harder suckling, a deeper thrusting of tongue—savoring her, delighting in her, drawing her closer.

She did no less for him.

Lost in this soul-mating kiss, he lowered his body alongside hers, partly pressing his weight on her, one leg between hers, his hardness pressing against her hip. He entwined one hand in her hair, caressing her scalp, while the other sought her breast. He cupped it, kneaded it gently, and rubbed the palm over the sensitive nipple until it strained against the thin fabric of her chemise.

Fingers digging into his shoulders, Claire moaned against his mouth, relishing the building pleasure tightening her insides. When his hand ventured farther down her body, her stomach muscles clenched in anticipation, and she arched against his seeking hand. Cupping her mound, he pressed the heel of his hand against her clitoris, parting her with one thick finger, pressuring but not entering, moving his finger up and down her cleft, sliding easily in her wetness. Juices flowing, muscles contracting, blood pulsing hot and furious, Claire bucked when he finally thrust a finger inside her.

Her entire body was one mass of coiling sensations as the waves of pleasure slammed ever so close with each plunge of his finger. Blindly, she reached down between their bodies with her hand. Damn! The waistband of his pants was too tight to allow more than a couple of her fingers inside. She could only touch the rounded tip of his engorged member, a drop of moisture sleeking the smooth head. Frustrated, she withdrew her hand and pressed it against his hardness through the fabric of his pants, dying to close her fingers on his naked flesh.

Aiden recoiled abruptly, leaving her bereft and confused.

Moaning a complaint, she tried to focus on his taut face. Hard to do when her whole body thrummed with need, fogging her mind.

Kneeling by her, wearing an expression of almost pain, Aiden looked as if he was about to enter into battle and not lovemaking.

"Lady," he breathed. "You shall be the death of me."

"Oh please, Aiden, do not die on me now," she cried, half joking, half serious.

The deep, raspy sound that escaped his throat was a mix of groan and laughter. Then his voice lost any hint of humor. "Ah! Claire. Not even death could take me away from you."

How appropriate! she thought, also sobering up. Death had separated them once, and yet they had found each other again. Would fate be kinder to them this time around? Claire was afraid to believe. It would be best to accept this moment as fleeting and unique and not start building castles in the air.

She pulled herself up, kneeling before him. Touching his face as she'd done so many times before, she ran her fingers over his jaw. "We have this moment, Aiden. Let's make the most of our time together."

He covered her hand with his, kissed her wrist, his lips lingering on her skin, his gaze glued to her face. "I want you so desperately, Claire, I fear I would hurt you with my need."

Hurt her? When she was about to jump him and have her way with him? Or did he mean hurt her emotionally? She was afraid she would cause him as much pain. "I want you, Aiden, just as desperately," she reassured him. "And I have no fear." At least not fear of a physical joining. The other fear, the emotional fear, she chose to ignore at this time. She would take whatever Aiden gave her, and give him whatever she could.

The corner of his lips curled into a small grin. "Nay, my lady, you would have no fear."

She smiled, too. "Then would you have me, my fair knight?"

Take me to paradise, my fair knight. Aiden swiftly chased away the distant memory. Cherise was the past, Claire was his present, his future.

"I would have no other."

And he would not. No other woman compared to his Claire. *His!* That was how he thought of her. A fierce possessiveness took hold of him. She might be under the misguided notion she would take her leave of him eventually, but he would have none of it. He would not part with her, now or ever. Having known love once, and having lost it at a great cost to him, he knew the devastation it had caused to his life. God in His infinite grace had granted him to know love again. He knew not why he deserved such a blessing twice in a lifetime, but he would not be so cavalier with His gift this time around.

Did he persuade Claire to remain by his side a little while longer, he would eventually conquer her heart, he was certain. She would not be sharing his bed did she not care a little for him. He would take this moment she granted him, and all the others surely to come, one at a time.

He was a patient man. He had waited ten years for Claire to come into his life.

He let go of her hand and grabbed the hem of her chemise, sliding it up her body. She raised her arms, and he pulled the flimsy garment over her head, revealing her magnificent body.

Disrobed, Claire ran both hands through her dark tresses threading the glorious curls away from her face, the movement jutting forward her full, round breasts. Aiden remembered how they felt under his hands, soft and yet firm. His fingers itched to touch them again. He swallowed hard as his gaze strayed down her slim waist, her flat belly, and her dark womanly triangle, trim and enticing.

Though he refused to accept the wall Claire's secretive ways could erect between them, if he pushed her for an explanation he feared he might lose her. And that he could not chance. She would tell him when she was good and ready, if ever. That much he had learned of her. Only if her secrets stood in the way of their being together did he need to know them.

Otherwise, he accepted her as she was. This goddess of unknown parts, this woman so beautiful he trembled just thinking he was about to make her his. He was humbled she would give herself to him. Honored she would do so.

"You have me at a disadvantage," she said, pulling him out of his trance.

He looked up at her uncomprehendingly.

"You still have clothes on." She gave him an unabashed smile and a pointed stare.

A brief moment of apprehension skittered down his spine. Could he please her well? Claire was no untried maid. Her brazen behavior proved it, had her lack of maidenhead not already alerted him to that fact when he had buried his finger deep inside her. He quickly chased away the thought of another man loving her, though his guts coiled inside.

Ignore the past, he reminded himself. Secure the present, and God willing, there would be a future for them together.

There was so much he wished to say to her, but he could not trust his voice not to tremble, so he said naught.

Fumbling with the ties of his breeches, he tore at them when they knotted. Swiftly he disposed of what was left of his garments. He turned to her, his wanting clearly exposed.

"Wow!" she whispered. "*You* take my breath away."

Heat of lust and pleasure flushed up his neck. With a groan, he pulled her down with him. She laughed, the sound resonating oddly in this place where joy had been absent for far too long.

Keeping most of his weight off her, he wedged himself between her thighs. She shifted to accommodate him better, her gaze clouding as he slowly slid into her. Warm tightness enveloped him, almost making him lose control and spill his seed too early. He halted, fighting not to shame himself. Blood pounded so loudly in his ears, he thought he would go insane. She shifted again under him, taking another inch of him, and without recourse he plunged into her in one deep thrust.

Buried to the hilt like a well-sheathed sword, he remained still for another moment. His heart pumped so hard in his chest, he feared it would escape through his throat. Through half-closed eyelids he saw Claire lift her face to his. She bit his chin teasingly, ran her tongue under his chin, over his throat and jaw, nibbled on his ear, flicking her tongue inside for a fleeting moment. Aiden jerked.

Groaning, he captured her mouth, savoring her sweet taste while he began moving inside her in slow, deep thrusts. Raking his back with her long fingernails, Claire wrapped her legs around his waist and arched demandingly against him.

"Don't hold back," she whispered against his mouth.

Mère de Dieu! If he did not hold back, it would all be over too soon. It had been too long since last he found comfort in a woman's body, but this was beyond comfort.

He was where he should be, with whom he should be.

He drove into her harder, faster, spiraling out of control when her sheath tightened around him and her body began jerking under his. He tried to rein in his own pleasure, to prolong hers, but he was too far along already.

He careened out of control, and his entire body trembled with the intensity of his release. He cried out Claire's name, a deep, husky sound that rumbled like a thunder from deep within his exploding heart.

In that brief moment that seemed to last an eternity he knew there would be no other for him.

BODY THRUMMING, CLAIRE RODE THE LAST WAVES OF her release. Breathless, she finally slid open her eyes and, looking up at Aiden, was struck by an emotion so intense, tears stung her eyes.

She smiled at him, but in the next moment, her entire body tensed, the smile disappeared as a light flashed before her eyes. She knew what was about to happen.

Damn! Not a vision. Not now!

But it was already too late.

THE PIERCING BLUE SKY SPREAD ENDLESSLY ABOVE HER head as she paced impatiently on uneven ground. How dare the day be so beautiful when her heart was breaking in a thousand shards inside her chest? A tempest should be raging, a torrent of rain crying from the heavens!

Stomping away, she pressed her hands over her ears to muffle the sound of church bells singing in the crisp air, inviting all to the joyous occasion. Each peal tore deeper at her soul.

By the time Aiden appeared around the church's corner, dressed in his finery, she had already worked herself into a snit. She halted, pivoted, and watched his purposeful stride toward her, his generous mouth lacking the usual wide smile, his deep dark blue eyes troubled and arrowed on her. The anger that had so easily spilled from her moments ago cowardly retreated as passion overtook her, mining her resolve and tainting her heart with sorrow.

God in heaven, how she loved that man!

How could he expect her to share him with another woman? How could she bear the thought of another knowing his touch?

"The wedding is moments away. What do you here?" he asked as soon as he reached her. He was not pleased with her demand to see him before the wedding took place, but she knew there would be no time for talk later.

And yet, now that he was here, words failed her. The need to feel his arms around her, his lips on hers, almost overpowered her senses.

Nay, she told herself. She needed to speak with him now. What she told him could change everything between them.

She would have all of Aiden or naught at all.

"I have tidings," she said.

He stole an impatient glance behind him. "Could this not wait? It is not the most appropriate of times."

"Nay. It is vital you know now before the wedding takes place." She took a deep breath. "I am enceinte."

Aiden's mouth slacked open. His hand reached behind his neck, as was his way. He drew in a breath. "Are you certain?"

She nodded.

"Mère de Dieu!" He pulled her into his strong arms, and his mouth sought hers in a passionate kiss. He held her so tight she was afraid he would tear her asunder. She cared not. Her heart sang with hope. All would change now. She kissed him back with all her love, all her passion,

*all her need, as she embraced the hope, let it swell inside
her until it encompassed every inch of her heart.*

Then gently he pulled away. Bereft, she stared at him.

*"You know this is not how I would have wished it to be
between us," he said. "Yet there is no other way. I vow that
you and our child shall want for naught—"*

"I shall not become your paramour," she spat.

*He shook his head, exasperation showing in the hard
setting of his generous mouth. She knew what he was thinking, that she was already his paramour, sharing his bed
without the benefit of marriage. But that was different. She
was free to share her passion with him as he was free to
share his with her. Once he was wed, everything would
change.*

"That is all I can offer you," he insisted.

*Anger rose so swiftly, she thought she would explode.
Raw pain lacerated her heart. "That is not enough for me.
You shall regret choosing a pile of stones over me and your
own flesh and blood."*

*"Delacroix is not a pile of stones to me." His voice rose
in anger. "It is my birthright. My family honor demands I
recover it. I vowed to my dying father I would do so, and by
God, I shall honor my word."*

*As quickly as his temper rose, it vanished. He blew out a
breath. "Why must you fight me in this? You have my heart,
is that not enough?"*

*"I would rather die than see you with another," she spat.
"I cannot accept it."*

*"You have no say in the matter. Do not make demands
of me that I cannot fulfill."*

"Even after what I have just revealed to you?"

*His gaze softened. He sighed. "That changes naught,
and you know it."*

Tears stung her eyes. Her chest compressed with pain.

She couldn't breathe. Heart wrenched with sorrow, she allowed anger to overtake her again. It was easier to hate him than to ache for him.

"Bastard," she cried, and slapped him so hard, his face slammed to the side. As it sprang back, he stared at her with troubled, saddened eyes. Then, without a word, he pivoted and walked out on her.

"You cannot get rid of me," she shouted to his retreating form. Tears spilled from her eyes, blurring her vision. She took a blind step forward, lost her balance, fell to her knees. "You hear me, Aiden?" she cried. "You shall never get rid of me. You are mine!" Her voice lost strength. "You are mine!"

But Aiden did not respond, he did not turn back. He continued his sure stride until he disappeared behind the village's church. Out of her sight, out of her life.

CLAIRE OPENED HER TEAR-FILLED EYES AND FOUND her face resting against Aiden's chest. She remained quiet, gathering her composure. Though the flashback had ended, her heart ached as if the moment she remembered had happened not hundreds of years ago, not ten years ago, but this very instant.

Finally learning who she'd been and what had torn them apart didn't free her as she'd hoped. It shackled her with greater sorrow instead.

Good God! She had loved Aiden so desperately, and though he professed to love her back, he had rejected her summarily and married another. Rejected her when she carried his child, for God's sake, a child she never birthed.

A child she might never be able to conceive again.

Claire moaned. The truth was too painful to bear.

Realizing she had come out of her episode, Aiden tightened his hold of her. She was relieved he had withdrawn from her while she was still in the throes of her flashback. She didn't know how she would've reacted had she found him still throbbing inside her. But she wasn't in the mood to be thankful. Her insides were too raw with the pain of his betrayal and what it had cost her.

What it would still cost her.

She pushed against him and rolled off the bed.

"Claire," he called, but she slipped away, ignoring the worry in his voice. Her anguish was too powerful, her anger too vivid. If she spoke to him now, all her words would be of accusation. She needed to put some distance between them.

Damn! Intellectually she understood Aiden's motivation for marrying Jeanne all those years ago, but emotionally . . .

Ah, emotionally she was a wreck.

Particularly when she thought of the child she lost.

Her inability to conceive in the future was no cosmic joke but karma, directly related to what had happened in her past life.

Knowing that didn't make it any easier to accept her fate.

Besides, why was she being punished? She was the one who lost it all.

Claire picked up her chemise from the floor and slipped it over her head. Covered, she ambled to the table and sat on the long bench. Keeping her gaze away from the approaching Aiden, she stared at the spot above the fireplace mantel where she'd found the ghost's message, now a barely visible blotch on the wall.

And the ghost was another matter she still had to contend with.

"What has your vision revealed that has you so upset?" Aiden asked as he straddled the bench beside her, utterly oblivious to his glorious nakedness. Claire's body stirred when his knee slightly touched her behind. She scooted away. Annoyed at herself, at her body, for responding to him so promptly, she tried to flee, but Aiden pulled her down between his thighs, wrapping his arms around her.

She glared at him, but he looked so worried, so damn in love with her, she just couldn't stand. She fought him, absurdly holding on to her anger, to her pain, but he would not slack his hold of her.

Why hadn't she learned the truth in her own time? Why had she to travel back in time, meet Aiden, get to know him, love him all over again?

Lose him all over again.

"I cannot bear that you are in pain," he said, burying his face in her hair. "Whatever the vision has revealed to you, Claire, know that you need not face it alone. I am with you. I shall never leave you."

"You have left me already," she whispered.

He gently pushed her away, holding on to her shoulders and turning her to face him. "What is your meaning?"

Time to set the cards on the table.

"The visions I have when I touch you, Aiden, are in fact memories of my past life," she said. "Until now these memories were unclear, mere fragments of a moment in time. Today I have finally understood what happened to me. Finally found the answers I have been looking for."

He beheld her unsmiling face for a moment, his eyebrows furrowing in confusion. "I take it the answers were not what you had expected."

"Not exactly."

She had expected pain, she had expected betrayal, but she had expected closure as well. She hadn't expected for her past to continue to hurt her, to continue to be a factor in her future.

"Do these memories pertain to me as well?" he asked.

"Directly."

He rubbed the back of his neck. "I have wronged you, have I not?"

The knot in her throat prevented her from speaking. She nodded instead.

"Then I humbly beg your forgiveness."

Anger rose swiftly again, mingling with and feeding from the pain. "A blank apology for past misdeeds will not do it," she spat, pulling away. Rising, she took a couple of steps away from him.

"Then tell me what I have done so I can beg your forgiveness properly."

She pivoted, finding him standing behind her, a stricken look on his face. "You betrayed me," she cried. "You broke my heart and abandoned me without a second thought."

He opened his mouth, snapped it closed. His eyes narrowed. He looked at her differently. Was he thinking of Cherise? He couldn't even begin to guess she stood right before his eyes.

There was a long moment of silence before he spoke again. "I am certain I would not have intentionally hurt you—"

"Oh, so if you didn't mean to hurt me, I should just forgive and forget, right? To hell with my wasted life." She stomped away, not bearing being near him. Good God! How was she going to get past this pain? She didn't want to hate Aiden. She didn't hate him. She loved him still; more than she did in her past, if that was possible.

She knew she was being irrational. His betrayal had happened in another lifetime. She couldn't keep on blaming him forever. She had to let go of the past. She had to forgive him. Not for his benefit, but for her own.

Heart aching as if an iron fist clutched it, she took several calming breaths.

Aiden came to stand before her again, towering above her.

"Claire," he called, and she turned her face to look at him. Look at the man who had wronged her, the man she loved more than life itself. Her body and heart ached, battered as if she'd been hit by a truck.

"I understand not why you insist on clinging to a past that has no significance to our lives now," he said. "A past I remember not. A past I cannot undo or apologize enough for." His voice shook with frustration. He took a moment to compose himself. Claire knew he didn't entirely share her beliefs of a past life, and still he tried to understand her.

Her heart softened a little.

"All I can offer you is my heart and my life now." He opened his arms as if offering himself to her. "Do with me what you will."

A great sigh escaped from deep within her lungs, her heart, her soul. Tears spilled hotly down her cheeks. Hell! Aiden made it difficult for her to hate him. How could she hate a man who offered himself to her as he did? He loved her. She couldn't dispute that. But was love enough? It hadn't been in the past.

She didn't know what to do. She didn't know what to say. Sensing her indecision, he pulled her into his arms and rested his face against her hair.

"Forgive me, Claire," he whispered, mining the last of her resistance.

She relented, wrapping her arms around his waist and burying her face in the crook of his neck, inhaling the piney scent of his skin.

When he sought her mouth, she tasted her salty tears on his lips and their mutual desire in the dueling of their tongues, in the desperation of their kiss. All the passion she had ever wanted with a man, she had found with Aiden. There was no point in denying it.

"I love you." She whispered the words she had longed to say, the emotion she had longed to feel her entire life, relenting to the truth that could not, would not be denied.

He pulled her back gently. His generous mouth curled

in a tentative grin as his dark blue gaze sought hers. "Ah! Claire. You are my life. Will you consent to be my bride?"

If only it were that simple!

There was so much yet to be disclosed, explained, accepted.

With regret, she stepped out of his embrace and watched his grin disappear. "There is still much I need to tell you."

"I have no need to know."

"I have the need to tell," she insisted. "There can be no more secrets between us."

He sighed, relenting. "Very well. If that is your wish, speak your mind. But know that whatever you have to say shall have no bearing on the way I feel about you."

That remained to be seen.

Claire took a deep breath, choosing to begin telling her tale where she thought it would be easier for him to understand. "I was Cherise in my past life."

Chapter 20

MÈRE de Dieu! Had Claire lost her wits?

Openmouthed, Aiden stared at her. Unblinking, she calmly bore his stare. Claire and Cherise, one and the same? Aiden shook his head. Impossible! Even if he was inclined to believe in the rebirth of souls, as Claire clearly did, it still would make no sense. Claire and Cherise were of a same age.

Surely Claire was mistaken, misguided, confused.

She looked naught but determined, convinced, assured.

Unable to fathom the inconceivable notion, Aiden marched past her to where his breeches lay crumpled on the floor. He pulled them on, tying the torn lacings with gauche fingers. Breathing deeply, he vainly commanded his wayward heart to halt its maddening flips in his chest.

"Cherise has been dead for only ten years," he said.

"You are near the age she would be were she alive today. Her soul could not possibly have been reborn in you." The reasonable argument momentarily arrested the dread skittering down his spine and the absurd hope inching its way into his heart.

Could there be a chance to make up for his past misdeeds?

He immediately sequestered the wayward hope. What was he thinking? It was impossible!

Claire ambled to where he stood, rooted to the floor. "You're right," she said. "Had I been born thirty-three years ago, it would have been impossible for Cherise's soul to be incarnated in my body. The fact, however, is that although I'm a grown woman, my actual birth won't occur for another seven hundred years or so in the future."

Blood pounded loudly in Aiden's ears. Surely he misheard Claire. Surely she did not say that she was not yet born.

Unable to form a coherent thought, Aiden just stared at her. Perchance *his* wits were addled.

"I know it's difficult to believe such a fantastic story, let alone comprehend it." Her voice was soft, cajoling. It broke through the ringing in his ears but did naught to ease his mind. "As bizarre as it sounds, I'm telling you the truth. I came from a time hundreds of years in the future to find my past and you."

Anger rose hotly and swiftly in Aiden's gut. For his own sanity, he latched on to it. "Do you think so little of me that you feel the need to concoct this outrageous tale to avoid wedding me? You have rejected my proposal before without so much as an explanation. Why the ruse now?" He could not understand. Why would she conceive such a lavish tale when she could as easily tell him she was a witch or fay? Or tell him naught at all? He had not forced her to reveal her secrets.

"Believe me, it's not a ruse, it's the truth. I don't want any more secrets between us."

Aiden's head swam. It confounded him to realize that despite her outrageous tale, he wanted to believe her. In shock, he glided his gaze away from her loveliness. He could not think while his emotions were so engaged. Sighting his shirt, he marched to it and snatched it from the floor, snapping it over his head, almost tearing the soft cloth. His boots suffered the same ill handling.

His aching chest struggled for air. He needed to get out, clear his mind. Without a word, he headed for the door, buckling his sword belt along the way.

"Aiden, don't leave me like this," Claire cried. "Let me explain, please."

At her beseeching voice, he halted. He drew in a big gulp of air before slowly turning to face her.

That was his mistake.

Claire's beautiful eyes, still bright with shed tears, held him captive, mining his resistance as they begged his understanding. A memory of Cherise those many years ago begging him to reconsider his marriage to Jeanne flashed in his mind. He had turned his back on her then. Regardless of whether or not Claire had been Cherise in her past life, as she believed, he could not turn his back on her now.

As swiftly as it arrived, his anger abated, leaving in its place a chaos of emotions. He watched the sway of Claire's hips, the bouncing of her soft curls as she approached him, and his heart tightened.

Mère de Dieu! How he loved this woman. Loved her even more than he had loved Cherise, if that was possible. He had been too young then, too cocksure he could have it all. Ten years of loneliness had taught him there was no certainty in life.

"You noticed my strange ways, and still you accepted me," Claire said quietly. "You didn't share my belief in a past life, but you didn't condemn me. When you learned about my visions, you stood by me and tried to help me. Had I told you I was a witch or fay, I have no doubt you would have understood. Why can't you acknowledge that I might be telling the truth when I tell you I come from another time? That I believe I was Cherise in my past life? Are these truths any more bizarre or any less believable than what you were willing to accept?"

Aiden could not dismiss the verity of Claire's words. He had remarked upon her oddness, had even entertained the thought she might be fay or witch, though he admitted to being relieved when she denied being either. But a journey through time was so utterly bizarre it was unfathomable. And the thought of a past life, downright eerie, if not profane.

And yet, for those precise reasons, what Claire told him could very well be true, for naught concerning her had ever made much sense.

Aiden had always known Claire's secret would be deep and inscrutable. He had not counted on it being so utterly unbelievable.

Her eyes suddenly brightened. "I have proof," she said, and without waiting for his response, dashed to the garment chest by the wall. She pulled the lid open and withdrew her satchel from inside.

The muscles on Aiden's shoulders knotted even more as he watched Claire take the steps that separated her from the bed. She opened the satchel and spread its contents on the ruffled mattress where moments ago their bodies writhed with passion, then pivoted and waited for him to approach.

Aiden hesitated only for a brief moment. Even as dread swelled in his chest, he decidedly marched to her side. There was no avoiding what was yet to come.

His gaze took in the numerous unidentified objects with trepidation.

Claire picked up a small white receptacle with odd inscriptions on it, pulled the red lid off, and spread the contents in her hand.

"These are pills," she said, naming the white drops. "They are medicine for pain. You ingest them with water."

She replaced the pills into the small receptacle and picked up a small square flask, this one with a visible amber liquid inside. She unstoppered it, and the sweet smell of honey wafted to him.

"This is perfume. Though you might say smelling oils are not out of the ordinary, notice the container. Touch it." He did. Besides its unusual shape, it felt hard and cool to the touch. "This is glass, the material found in cathedrals' windows."

He knew what glass was. He had never seen it so clear and in such a small form, though.

She handed him a couple of small, very thin pieces of what he thought was parchment engraved with odd inscriptions. They were hard and somewhat flexible at the same time. "One of these is a door key card, and the other a credit card, which serves to purchase things, same as money. They are made of plastic, which is a hard, resistant material that hasn't been invented yet. Many things are made of plastic in the future. They are almost indestructible."

She took the cards from his hand, and Aiden scooped a few coins from the bed. He turned them in his hand but did not recognize either the inscription or the images inlaid in them. There were also a few sleeves of thin, colorfully illuminated parchment, only they felt naught like parchment to the touch.

"Money," Claire explained.

And then she picked up the oddest object of all. It was shiny black and silver with a small white inscription he could not decipher. She flipped it open, and Aiden felt the blood drain from his face. The inside was silver with a small dark square on the top part, and at the bottom, several tiny silver squares with unknown black symbols. Some of them resembled letters, others he could not even guess their meaning.

"Brace yourself," she warned, and he dug his feet on the rushes. She pressed one of the tiny squares. For a moment nothing happened, then the black square on the top part turned white, and a loud sound resonated from it.

Startled, Aiden staggered back. *Mère de Dieu!* What manner of magic did Claire release?

But the magic was far from over. In another moment, what he thought was a diminutive person flew inside the little square to abruptly disappear and turn into trees and blue sky. At the same time the etchings on the tiny squares at the bottom changed colors from black to glowing blue.

Aiden's heart stammered in his chest. Claire touched his arm. "It's harmless."

It looked anything but harmless to him. He blinked, tried to speak, but managed only to croak.

Meanwhile, the small square went black again.

Aiden cleared his throat. "What is it?"

"It's called a cell phone. People talk to each other through it."

"You need this to talk?" He was baffled.

"Only from a great distance, and the other person must have a similar machine."

"Can you talk with the future?"

She shook her head. "It doesn't work here."

"Ah!" He was pleased to hear that.

Claire offered the odd object to him. He rejected it. Whatever it was, he had no need for it.

"Aiden, I am no witch, or the devil, or anything equally nefarious, though it might look like it." She smiled nervously. "I'm a perfectly ordinary person, and these items are perfectly ordinary in my time. In the future, most people possess them, make use of them in their everyday life. They are just a product of man's ingenuity, like . . ." She sighed, clearly frustrated in her attempt to explain the unexplainable. "Like better plowing equipment or the development of the crossbow. There is no magic about that."

Aiden begged to differ. There was naught ordinary about the things Claire showed him or about Claire herself.

He had always known she was different; he had not fathomed she was from another time, though.

"Now do you believe me?"

How could he not? He either believed in her tale or concocted another bizarre one in his mind, for what other possible explanation could there be for such unusual objects?

Still, did he accept her tale of journeying through time, would that mean he also accepted she was Cherise?

For some reason, the latter troubled him more.

Aiden settled his gaze on Claire, seeking a trace of resemblance, but she looked naught like Cherise. She did possess the same passion, the same power to evoke emotions in him no other woman, save Cherise, had.

He remembered Claire calling him her fair knight in bed. Cherise used to call him thus. Claire had also called Delacroix Castle a pile of stones, just as Cherise once had. But that hardly proved Cherise's soul lived inside Claire's body.

Did she possess irrefutable proof of this matter as well? Needing to be convinced, he asked, "Tell me something that only Cherise and I would know."

She shuffled her feet in place. "That's tricky, since I don't actually have all the memories from my past life. All I remember is one scene behind the church right before your wedding to Jeanne was to take place. I can tell you everything about that moment. Cherise told you she carried your child, hoping to sway you from marrying Jeanne, but you still went through with the wedding." Her voice faltered.

"This proves naught," he said.

"I know, but I don't have all the answers. I do believe, though, deep within my soul, that I was Cherise, that I once loved you, and that you wronged me. Hundreds of years later, the memories of my past life erased from my mind, I still couldn't forget you, Aiden, couldn't stop loving you."

Aiden's heart burst with gladness for Claire's words. Words he longed to hear for so long. Still, uncertainty gnawed at him. And then a dreadful suspicion blinded him with a powerful blow. "Did Jasper hire you to get me out of the way so he can take over Delacroix?"

"I have nothing to do with Jasper. I've only met the man the day I arrived here. Besides, what would my telling you I was Cherise in my past life or that I came from the future accomplish?"

"Perchance you wish to muddle my mind, drive me to insanity with such affirmations. Given my association with you, such unholy matters would cast grave aspersions on my person. I am certain the church would eagerly persecute me, stripping me of my holdings. And that is Jasper's ultimate purpose." Those were much more reasonable explanations than Claire's tale, though infinitely more devastating than her truth.

"And what would I gain by casting suspicions on my own person as well? Wouldn't I be as severely or even more seriously penalized than you? After all, I'm the one making these unholy claims. I can only imagine what Father Aubert would do if he got hold of such incriminating information. I have put my life in your hands, Aiden. Isn't that proof enough of my sincerity?"

There was no denying the verity of Claire's words. She trusted him with her life. He could do no less for her.

"I shall not betray you," he said.

"I know that, but do you believe me?"

Whether he shared Claire's beliefs mattered not. What mattered was that he trusted she was telling the truth as she perceived it.

"I believe you, Claire."

Closing her eyes momentarily, she bit her lower lip and let out a sigh of relief. Then she grinned at him. "Thank you."

"And you, Claire. Do you believe in my deepest regret for having caused you pain in the past?"

She nodded. "You said so before, Aiden. The past is no more."

And with those words, Claire unfettered Aiden from the shackles of his guilt.

He pulled her into his arms and sought her mouth. He thought of Cherise for a brief moment, and then let go of the memory forever. Cherise was the past; Claire was his future.

Their children would inherit Delacroix Castle and the children of their children after that, fulfilling his deepest longing.

Joy, absent for so long, finally filled his heart to over-flowing as he carried Claire to his bed. Ruthlessly, he thrust away the insidious doubt germinating in his mind.

Claire had forgiven him. She had declared her love for him. But she had said naught about giving up her future filled with wondrous machines and magic to remain here with him.

On the morrow it would be soon enough to speak of their future. There had been enough revelations for one day. This eve, he wanted Claire all to himself with no doubts hovering over them.

"MY LORD JASPER," FATHER AUBERT CALLED. HIS VOICE was barely audible amidst the clash of sword against sword. "I must speak with you."

Parrying a swinging blow, Jasper used all his strength to

push his opponent back and prevent the cleaving of his head.

"Can it not wait, Father?" he managed to say before John was upon him again. Damnation, but his knight was as strong as an ox, Jasper thought, glad the man was friend and not foe.

"Nay, my lord, it cannot."

The priest's voice echoed the urgency of his words. Noticing that, and the fact that his sword arm had just gone numb with John's latest strike, Jasper thought it best to call a halt to the practice. It was almost dark, anyway.

He dismissed his knight, and fearing a lecture from the priest on his pitiful confessional habits, Jasper turned to Father Aubert. "Speak your mind, Father."

Father Aubert darted a suspicious glance about the almost empty bailey. "Can we adjourn to your bedchamber, my lord? What I have to say must not be eavesdropped by prying ears."

Curiosity piqued, Jasper nodded, bemused at the priest's secretiveness. As he began to walk, the priest fell into step with him. He had known Father Aubert since he was a child, and even then the priest had been a feisty old man with dreams of grandeur at odds with the humility demanded of a man of the cloth. Jasper stole a glance at the wrinkled face. He must be ancient now, but still he walked with the sure step of a young man. He looked almost excited.

In silence they headed for the castle, crossed the great hall, and walked into the adjoining chamber that Jasper called his own. Behind closed doors, Jasper poured wine into two chalices, offering one to the priest.

Father Aubert drank greedily, whether seeking courage or merely enjoying Aiden's fine wine. He swiped a clothed arm over his thin lips while Jasper perched a hip on the table edge.

"My lord," he said, setting the empty cup down. "I have

the key to deliver Delacroix castle back into your rightful hands."

His attention effectively grabbed, Jasper feigned nonchalance and continued to sip from his cup. "And what could that possibly be?"

"I am in possession of very damning information that I am willing to turn into your hands."

"I assume this information pertains to Lord Aiden."

"Not directly but very closely."

Jasper concealed his excitement. He had waited long enough to take his revenge on Aiden. He would never forgive the man's role in Jeanne's death. Would God finally deliver it to him? Still, no one gave anything for naught. Not even a priest. "And why would you turn this information over to me?"

"I served your father faithfully for many years, my lord." Jasper refrained from pointing out that a priest served God and not an earthly lord. "He was a great warrior who knew he owed his great fortune to God. He respected the Church, always having God's representative on earth with him on his campaigns. We traveled far and wide, and very successfully together. My greatest wish is to visit Jerusalem again before my death."

"It seems a reasonable request, Father. Why have you not shared your desire with your new lord?"

"I have, my lord, on two occasions, but each time he dismissed my wish as unneeded, refusing to furnish the escort of men I would need for such an endeavor."

Ah! Jasper smiled. Now he understood Father Aubert's dislike of Aiden, though he thought it petty. For a priest, he was not very forgiving. And now Father Aubert had the means to obtain his wish and revenge on the man who had denied him.

And so would Jasper, it seemed.

"I have a few men I could spare," Jasper said. "You

shall have what you ask, Father. Now, tell me your won-drous tidings."

Instead of speaking, Father Aubert reached inside the folds of his robe, withdrew a small, thin book and handed it to Jasper.

Curious, Jasper brought it closer to the light of a candle and examined the dark cover. Odd words and a bird with flaring wings, a branch of some kind in one claw, and ar-rows in the other were engraved in gold on the cover. The heraldry of an unknown lord. His fingers detected no wax of a seal, merely the smoothness of some unknown parch-ment.

He opened the book. Inside there were more words he could not decipher, though some resembled French, others English. But Jasper recognized not only Claire's name but her likeness as well, the likes of which he had never seen in his life.

A shiver slithered down his spine.

Witchcraft! Damning evidence, indeed.

He flipped through the pages with more undecipherable words and seals without wax.

"What do you make of it?" Father Aubert asked, his dark eyes narrowed with unconcealed glee.

"I know not," Jasper answered cautiously.

"It is evil, I have no doubt."

"Still, it pertains to Lady Claire, not Aiden."

"Their association should be incriminating enough. Let us not forget the haunting ghost and the despair that befell Delacroix Castle since Lord Aiden usurped the holding from your family."

Jasper wanted Delacroix Castle and his revenge badly, but if he used this odd little book against Aiden, he would be signing Claire's death sentence. He had no quarrel against her, and the thought of causing a woman's death sat heavily in his gut.

He was not certain he was willing to go that far. Despite the fact she might be a witch.

"How did you get this?"

"I found it in the church."

In the church, of all places, Jasper mused. Who would have put it there, knowing exactly what would ensue? And who was the intended victim? Claire or Aiden?

Jasper rubbed his jaw. "Who else knows about this?"

"I showed it to no one."

"Speak of this to no one, Father," Jasper warned. "I shall take care of it myself."

Chapter 21

CLAIRE awoke, startled.

Her gaze fell on the empty spot beside her. The indentation on the embroidered pillow brought to mind the incredible night she'd spent with Aiden.

She gently touched the spot. It was still warm. He had just left.

Her heart constricted. Despite the intense passion and joy they'd shared last night, unspoken doubts had hovered between them in a portent of doom. Aiden had not pressed for an answer to his proposal, though she knew it was ever present in his mind, and she hadn't broached the subject.

The fact was, she wasn't sure anymore what to do. The early certainty that she'd traveled through time to exorcise her past and free herself from Aiden's haunting image stood on very shaky grounds after he conquered her heart and inflamed her body all over again.

The impossible choice she would have to make between Aiden, her only love, and her life in the future, her beloved brother, and her only chance at motherhood, loomed ever so much closer. And she wasn't any more prepared to make that choice today than she was yesterday.

A chill coursed through her body, and she pulled the covers to her chin. Unimpeded by the absent bed curtains, her gaze wandered to the open window. Wisps of fog floated in with the gray light of dawn.

Below the window, Coco lay sprawled on the cushioned seat, quietly licking her paws.

Claire wasn't surprised to see the cat back in her room after she had disappeared so quickly yesterday. Coco had the uncanny ability to come and go as unobtrusively as a ghost.

Ghost!

That was another matter still to be resolved.

Suddenly, Coco jumped up from the seat to balance precariously on the windowsill. Surely she wasn't thinking of jumping out. Even for a cat, it would be quite a long fall. Wrapping the fur cover around her body, Claire rose and ambled to the window. Quietly, so as not to startle Coco, she scooped her up. Her mind returned to the ghost, and she peered down into the garden.

And there the ghost stood, a mere white blotch in the quivering fog. Who was she?

Last night, amidst the tumultuous revelations, heartfelt acceptances, and frenzied lovemaking, the subject of the ghost's identity had simply been ignored by Claire and Aiden.

It was time to put that question to rest.

Claire put Coco down and hurriedly dressed, wondering

whether a ghost had the ability to assume different forms. More and more she was inclined to believe that Jeanne was the haunting ghost taking the form of Cherise. Of course, that wouldn't explain Jasper's allegation that Cherise's ghost had caused his sister's death. But perhaps Jasper was mistaken. After all, he'd been only ten years old at the time. Perhaps shocked at witnessing the accidental death of his beloved sister, and with the subsequent appearance of a ghost in the castle, he mixed the two things together. In his grief, he looked to put blame on someone, and Aiden and Cherise were the chosen victims.

It was possible.

As it was also possible the ghost could be an entirely different entity.

There was only one way to find out.

Dressed, Claire bolted out of her room. As she reached the bottom of the stairs, she heard Aiden's voice in the great hall, ordering Hughes to set guard outside her door. Flattening her body against the wall, she disappeared in a dark corner. After Hughes passed her, she slipped out of her hiding spot and scurried after Aiden.

The hall was beginning to stir for the day. Ignoring the servants' curious glances, she stepped outside in time to see Aiden disappear into the fog.

She headed in the opposite direction, to the garden.

Fog slipped and slid in waves, revealing a patch of green here and there, veiling Claire's body with a fine mist in the chilly dawn. She trembled with cold, mentally cursing herself for not grabbing a coat on the way out. Her thin velvet gown was no protection against the chill in the air, particularly when she hadn't bothered with an undergarment.

Doing her best to ignore the cold, she vainly searched the grounds.

Disappointment and annoyance gnawed her insides. Why

did the ghost keep playing hide and seek with her? Why not face her once and for all, whoever she was, and end this stupid game?

A wisp of white fluff by the castle wall snapped Claire's attention. She rushed in that direction. She found Coco buried in the thick foliage, head poking through the low branches of an ornamental tree.

How had the cat gotten here before her without being seen?

"Come on, Coco. I have no time to play peekaboo."

But the cat didn't move. Her meows sounded stressed, though. Was she trapped? Claire tried to dislodge Coco's head, but from where she stood, she couldn't get her hands through the vines snaking through the branches. Stepping on the raised plot, her ankles buried in deep wet leaves, she tried to work her way around the tree and reach Coco from behind. She found herself in a tunnel of vines and branches wide enough for a thin person to walk through. She wasn't exactly thin, but she squeezed herself in enough to try to grab the cat, which promptly backed away.

Claire wasn't in a mood to play games. If Coco could move, she could get out on her own. Claire stepped back. Her foot got entangled on a vine, and she bent to free it, propping one hand against the wall for balance. Her hand went through the vine covering the stone wall and touched wood.

Claire straightened. She parted the vines, pulling and yanking until they yielded, revealing a door no more than four feet tall. A hole in the wall or a secret passage? Was Aiden aware of its existence?

Curiosity piqued, she pushed against it, and it opened with a creaking sound.

A musty smell wafted to her. Claire wrinkled her nose.

And Coco dashed past her inside.

Damn that cat!

"Coco," Claire called, as if the cat would know she'd been so named and respond. "Come out right now." God knew what kind of creepy crawlers resided inside the dark hole.

Coco neither answered nor came out.

For a moment, Claire considered leaving the cat to fend for herself. Still, just to ease her conscience, she decided to take a peek inside.

With some difficulty, she lowered herself to her knees and half crawled in. The place was dimly lit, musty and drafty. The floor was packed dirt, and little pebbles drove into her palms and knees. Shifting in place, she sought Coco out. No sign of the cat.

Not about to chance being face-to-face with a rodent or worse creature, Claire began to crawl out when she caught sight of the ghost appearing to hover above the ground a few feet away to her right.

Startled, Claire jerked up, hitting her back on the low threshold. With a muffled groan, she fell back down, rubbing her scraped back. When she lifted her gaze again, the ghost was gone.

For a moment Claire considered the wisdom of going after the ghost alone, but if she went back for help, Aiden would probably crowd her, set Hughes on her, and she'd lose precious time and the opportunity to resolve this situation.

Decision made, Claire crawled all the way in. Slowly, hands above her head, she stood. There was plenty of room upward. She wasn't so sure what lay ahead, though.

Hands extended before her, she took a step forward and hit a wall. She spread her hands on the cold, damp wall and slid them in opposite directions. The left side was solid for at least the breadth of her open arms. The other side ended shortly in a sharp corner. Realizing the tunnel bifurcated into two corridors, she took the one to the right, since there was where she'd glimpsed the ghost, and promptly hit her foot on a step.

Her toe throbbed through the thin leather shoes. Biting another groan, Claire cautiously began to climb. The passageway was barely double the width of her body. Thank God she wasn't claustrophobic.

Hands serving as her eyes, since the only illumination came from a smoke-spouting torch on the top middle of the wall, Claire counted the steps as she climbed. Five, then a short landing, then another five steps, and yet another landing, and so on. She pictured the passageway running alongside the thick inner walls of the castle. Though totally unrelated, the absurd image of Jacob's ladder came to her mind. This surely wasn't her stairway to heaven.

At some point the corridor veered to the left, still climbing. Where would that lead? To the roof? Another torch flared halfway up that wall. Who would leave lit torches inside secret passages? Not that she worried such puny lights would be much of a fire hazard. Those damp stone walls wouldn't burn too easily. The motivation behind the action was what bothered her.

Maybe there was another common entrance, and these passageways were used by servants, she thought, ever ready to speculate. She knew the ground floor of the castle was used for storage. Maybe even a dungeon?

Once again the narrow corridor veered to the left. Claire's legs began to burn. The climb was stiff, the air dense and cold. And then, finally, the light at the end of the tunnel. She smiled, remembering her brother's perennial joke about that. "Watch out for the train."

Thinking of what waited outside for her, Claire climbed the last steps that led up to an open trapdoor on the roof. Knowing she might be walking into an ambush, she cautiously poked her head through the opening. Her eyes, accustomed to the darkness, squinted at the natural light.

Blustery wind hit her in the face, stealing her breath momentarily. Hair flapping madly in her eyes, Claire blindly stumbled out of the tunnel and onto the parapet of Delacroix Castle. With one hand she gathered her curls away from her face while she placed the other hand against the wall to steady herself.

Vision unobstructed, she straightened her body and faced the ghost.

Gown and hair flapping wildly with the wind, the ghost's white figure stood starkly against the gray crenellated stone wall with its jagged, gaping-tooth top. Behind it, the rising sun fought its way up, bathing the top of the forest trees in the distance with a warm glow, while wisps of fog still crawled just above the ground.

Claire's heart stumbled madly in her chest when she realized she'd been wrong all along.

In her arrogance, she'd pitied the medieval people for fearing what they didn't understand, while making blind assumptions based on her *enlightened* knowledge of the spiritual world.

Not once did she consider any other possibility for the ghost's identity but the one she had in mind. And like everyone else, including Aiden, she'd failed to see the truth staring her in the face.

"You should have left." The regretful tone of the ghost's voice, and the fact she no longer hid the disfigured side of her face, didn't bode well. Meredith no longer pretended to be a ghost in this time, though she was a real one in the future. Obviously, she didn't expect Claire to leave the parapet alive.

"Was that why you killed Jeanne? Because she wouldn't leave Aiden?"

"That was her fault. I only wished to frighten her, to make her regret having caused my sister such pain. But instead of being frightened, she became enraged and pushed against me. I pushed her back, and she fell. It was her fault."

There was a naïve quality to Meredith's words, a cold calmness that proclaimed the woman wasn't all there. But of course, she wasn't. Who, in their right mind, would impersonate a ghost for years, scaring people literally to death?

Instead of horror, however, Claire's heart constricted with pity. Meredith had been her sister once. She tried to remember their past together, but though no memory came to her, Claire felt sympathy tugging at her heart.

Realizing Meredith had lured her to this dizzying height to do away with her, Claire pushed her sympathy aside. "Doesn't it bother you that because of your actions everyone thinks your sister was evil?"

Meredith shrugged. "They always thought the worst of us, anyway. We were strangers here. They wanted us gone from their lives. Where would we have gone?"

"Aiden would have provided for you and your sister. Didn't he do so even after Cherise's death?"

"It was his guilt. He knew Cherise had taken her life because of him. He meant to atone for what could not be atoned."

"Meredith, Cherise didn't kill herself," Claire said, hoping that knowing her sister's death was an accident would make a difference and stop her vengeful ways.

But before she could explain further, Meredith cried, "Aye, she did. She took her life and left me alone. She was all I had. And if it were not for Aiden, she would still be here with me. But I made him pay. He is as lonely and unhappy as he deserves to be."

"Cherise wouldn't want that. She loved him, and he loved her."

"Bah! Men love no one but themselves and their land.

They take what they will where they will, and are more apt to care for their horses than for the women in their lives. To them we are mere chattels, a means to an end. I warned Cherise that Aiden would never take her as a wife, but she would not listen to me. She kept saying that as soon as King Richard returned Aiden's birthright to him, he would wed her. Instead, he wed another."

"He had no choice," Claire said.

"We always have a choice. I was with Cherise on the day of Aiden's wedding. After meeting with him to beg him to reconsider and being rejected yet again, she returned home disconsolate. I held her while she cried. I allowed her to fling to our walls every breakable possession we owned. I held her back when in a fit of rage she threatened to disrupt the wedding festivities. And I chided her when she professed she could not live without him. I reminded her he was unworthy of her devotion and gave her a potion to calm her nerves. Only after she fell asleep did I leave her alone. When I returned later . . ." Her voice choked. "The hut was in flames, and Cherise was dead. I tried to save her. I tried . . ."

"Meredith." Claire took a step toward her. "It wasn't your fault. It was no one's fault. It was an accident."

"How would you know?" she retorted angrily.

Would Meredith believe her if she told her the incredible truth? But what proof did she have to offer? It'd be better to appeal to whatever vestige of reason was still left in her, rather than confuse Meredith further.

"Think, Meredith. Cherise wouldn't have killed herself. She wouldn't have killed her baby." As her sister, Meredith would know that.

But Meredith snorted. "There was no baby. Cherise was barren."

Claire's stomach sank to her toes. No baby? Cherise had lied to Aiden. She'd never been pregnant with his child!

Claire covered her mouth with her hand, holding the cry inside, her world once again rocked out of its axis. Good God! How many times would she be wrong? In her self-absorption, she'd solely blamed Aiden for her pain, not once considering she was as fallible and as responsible for her own fate.

Lost in her sorrow, she failed to see Meredith's move until the woman was already upon her.

"He wants you," Meredith spat, closing her fingers around Claire's throat like octopus tentacles. "I can see it in the way he looks at you, the way his eyes shine at the sight of you. It was the same with Cherise. But you shall not take my sister's place at his side. No one shall take Cherise's place at his side."

Claire gasped for breath as she fought to break Meredith's hold. Like a couple of drunks, they staggered about the parapet in a graceless dance made more awkward by the castigating wind.

When she found her back against the crenellated wall, Claire dug her feet down, realizing Meredith was trying to push her through the gap. From this height, a fall would be fatal.

Terrified, bent back over the hard stone, with the wind slapping at her face and the pressure on her throat increasing, Claire vainly pushed at Meredith. Madness seemed to be giving the woman superhuman strength.

Soon, black spots began dancing before Claire's eyes as blood pounded deafeningly in her ears. If she passed out for lack of oxygen, she'd be as good as dead.

She wasn't ready to end her life this way.

Surely that wasn't what was meant to happen.

Meredith's ghost in the future wouldn't have led her back in time to be the cause of her death.

As consciousness began to slip away, Claire felt the

pressure on her neck suddenly ease. She drew in great gulps of air through her burning throat and into her starving lungs. Her vision and hearing began to clear, but by that time, her buttocks were already hanging over the wall, with Meredith crouched precariously over her, one knee by her side, pushing her farther back.

In desperation, she grabbed Meredith's arm, pulling her down with her as she lost her balance.

One moment Claire was falling in slow motion. In the next, she was being yanked back with the speed of light.

Had she a voice, she would've screamed. As it was, she merely choked when wind gushed into her gaping, silent mouth.

BODY TWISTED IN AN IMPOSSIBLE POSITION—UPPER body bent over the wall, lower body desperately trying to gain purchase and not flip over, along with the two women—Aiden grabbed Claire's hips with one arm, while he managed to hold on to a sliver of Meredith's gown with the other.

He should just let the damn woman fall, Aiden thought of Meredith, the cause of all his troubles, even as he stubbornly held on to her.

"Cease your struggles," he told Meredith, and both she and Claire froze in the air. Any abrupt move could tear the flimsy material asunder and plunge Meredith to her death.

Down below in the bailey, people began to gather, their curious faces turned up to the skies, expecting a dramatic rescue or death, probably satisfied with either.

Mère de Dieu! Aiden chased away the fear he felt when he broke into the parapet and saw Claire and Meredith falling over the wall. Without a thought he had lunged for them, barely making it in time.

Had it not been for Giles seeking him out in the stables to tell him he had seen the ghost up here, his Claire would be splattered on the ground below.

The mere thought made him shudder.

"Can you pull yourself up?" he asked Claire. He did not move for fear he would lose hold of her.

She flapped her arms like a wingless bird, trying to bring head over body, but she couldn't reach his arm, and her fingers barely touched the side walls, unable to gain a hold.

"Aiden. Let me help."

For the first time, Aiden was relieved to hear Jasper's voice.

"Take Claire," Aiden ordered. "I know not how long I can hold on to both of them."

Jasper reached over Aiden and, grabbing Claire's hands, pulled her up. Aiden did not let go of her waist until he was certain she was out of danger.

Meanwhile, Meredith started struggling again, trying to get hold of Aiden's arm.

"Nay," Aiden warned, feeling the gown tearing even as he reached for her with his other hand. But it was too late. The gown tore, and Meredith rolled off Aiden's grasp, plunging seventy feet down to her death in eerie silence.

CLAIRE PUSHED THROUGH THE THRONG OF GAWKING people to fall to her knees by Meredith's broken body. Tears flowed freely down her face as she rearranged the dress over her sister's bloody limbs. An immense sorrow filled her as she thought of all the stupid mistakes people make. All the people they hurt, sometimes unwittingly, sometimes with the best of intentions.

She wished she'd had the chance to get to know Meredith again, to give her a chance to redeem her faults. But there was always next time. It was comforting to know there would be a next time for all of them.

"Till we meet again, Sister," Claire whispered and then rose.

Chapter 22

THE news of the ghost's death spread fast and wide. In the span of two weeks, Delacroix had seen an endless procession of visitors interested in hearing firsthand accounts of Aiden's ordeal and triumph. After so many years of being a social pariah, Aiden didn't seem too thrilled to be so in demand. And neither did Claire, who would rather put the painful past to rest.

A sentiment not shared by the castle people, however, who delighted in the sudden attention. Laughter echoed within Delacroix's walls once again, a sense of immense relief as if a dark cloud had been lifted and the sun shone brightly after a long, tempestuous time.

Which was an apt metaphor for what they'd just gone through.

And with the lifting of the curse, speculation ran rampant about a wedding. Everyone expected the announcement soon, though Claire and Aiden had yet to speak of their plans for the future. Granted, with all the people descending upon them like vultures over a dead carcass, they'd hardly had much time alone. And for days after the ordeal, Claire's throat had been so sore she could hardly speak. But she was better now, and the time for a decision drew near.

Fumbling with the scarf she wore to cover the necklace of purple and yellow bruises around her neck, Claire chased Coco off the table in her bedroom and then rearranged the fresh wildflowers she'd picked from the fields in a makeshift vase. She'd arranged for a meal to be brought in this evening for her and Aiden. They both could use a little solitude and time together.

Shortly after, Aiden entered her room, striding to her in that assured manner of his. Her heart did its customary flip in her chest. She was surprised, however, to see Jasper behind him.

After Meredith's death, Aiden and Jasper had stopped their bickering, making a taciturn agreement to put the past to rest, though they never spoke of it. Claire figured that unlike women, men chose action over words.

They'd even joined forces on the occasion of Meredith's death, when Father Aubert had created a little commotion, not wanting to give Meredith the last rites. At Claire's insistence, to the bafflement of both men, Aiden and Jasper convinced the priest otherwise. She didn't know whose idea it was to send the priest away after that, but Father Aubert had left for Jerusalem two days ago with an escort worthy of a king. Claire wished him Godspeed.

"I have come to say my farewells," Jasper said.

"So soon?" Somehow just the sight of Jasper made her feel closer to her brother, Nick. Although she had no proof, she couldn't chase away the feeling they were one and the same.

"My presence at Delacroix is no longer warranted or needed."

Claire took Aiden's hand and squeezed.

After a pregnant pause, Aiden said, "There is no need for a hasty departure."

Jasper grinned widely. "Ah! What great changes a good woman can effect in a man's heart."

His sardonic comment didn't get the rise out of Aiden it usually did. Jasper seemed almost disappointed. "Nevertheless," he continued. "However welcomed I might be here, it is time I find my own way."

"Will you visit and send news from time to time?" Claire asked.

"You shall hear of my great spoils, fear not."

Aiden snorted. Claire laughed.

"I have a gift for you, my lady." Jasper handed her a small velvet-wrapped parcel.

As she began to unwrap it, Jasper stopped her. "I ask that you wait until after my departure."

She stilled her fingers. "As you wish."

"This was given to me by Father Aubert," he explained, "who I expect never to see again. Jerusalem is quite far and the priest quite old." He smiled. "As far as I know, no one else is aware of this object's existence. I hope that shall bring you peace of mind."

Then he bowed respectfully and left.

Aiden eyed Claire curiously as she unwrapped the gift. She was surprised to find her passport between the soft velvet folds.

"What is it?" Aiden asked.

"This is one item that was missing from my purse when Meredith ransacked my room. I wondered what she'd done with it."

"He was protecting you," Aiden whispered. "Now I understand Jasper's generosity toward Father Aubert. He asked me to give the old priest leave, which I did quite willingly, but he provided the escort for the priest's journey to Jerusalem."

"As payment for his silence, maybe?"

"It seems thus."

"Then I owe him much."

"*We* owe him."

He pulled her into in his arms in a tight embrace and buried his face in her hair. They stood quietly like that for a few moments, thankful for just being together. Then suddenly he said, "I see you prepared a feast."

"Oh, it's just a little nourishment for the body."

"I take it that means food." Holding her hand he headed to the table. "How terribly kind of you to teach me your ways, Lady Claire of the future."

Aiden's joking manner surprised her. He wasn't usually in this good of a mood. "Not kind, just necessary," she explained as she took the chalice of wine he was handing her. "I need you to understand my needs."

He tilted her head. "And what does my lady need?"

Now, action would speak louder than words. Claire put her chalice down, stood on tiptoes, and kissed him ravenously, delighting in the taste and feel of him. His hand burrowed under her hair, squeezing a little too tightly, and she winced.

Immediately Aiden pulled back. "Forgive me."

"It is all right. My neck is still a little sore."

"When I think of what could have happened had I been a moment too late—"

"But you weren't, and I'm fine." She stepped closer to him again, placed her hands on his chest. "Everything is well now, Aiden. No more haunting, no more secrets. You're free. Free to make your choice."

His blue eyes darkened to pitch, narrowed to a slit. "I have already made my choice known. Several times, in sooth. It is you who has yet to decide."

"And so I have."

He drew in a deep breath. "Tell me what I wish to hear, Claire."

Claire smiled. Sometimes even men had need for words. "I love you, Aiden. I cannot envision my life without you. I have thought long and hard. You and I have suffered enough in the past, and we have both made mistakes. I wish that meant we are foolproof now, but we both know that's not how life works. God knows that fate has laughed at us enough times—"

"Claire," Aiden interrupted, a tad impatient, sliding a curl from her face with a flip of his finger. "You need not spin a tale for my amusement. Merely tell me that you agree to become my bride."

Well, maybe men needed *fewer* words than women. Still, she had to make sure. "I'm not your last chance at a bride, anymore, Aiden. Are you sure it's me you want?"

Aiden groaned. He pulled her roughly to him. His gaze glued on her face. "Damnation, Claire! Just say it! Say it!"

Claire laughed, her heart so light she thought it would fly right out of her chest. "All right. I would love to be your bride, Aiden. That is, if you'll have me."

For a moment, he said nothing. He just stared at her with a dumbstruck expression on his face as if he wasn't sure he'd heard her right, and a light in his dark blue eyes that said he knew he had. Then, with a groan, he closed his lips over hers in a kiss as passionate as it was desperate.

"Ah, woman," he said, when they finally came up for breath. "You shall be the death of me."

They both laughed, and Claire couldn't remember when she'd been this happy.

"I vow to love you, Claire," he said, then kissed her lips

lightly. "And cherish you." Another peck and a quick nip. A leg gently introduced between hers. "And protect you." A little flick of tongue, a teasing stroke of hips. "Forever." His mouth slanted over hers in a deep kiss. Then he began moving her backward toward the bed. "I cannot wait to fill Delacroix with the laughter of our children."

Children! Claire stopped so abruptly, Aiden almost toppled over her. Good God! Caught up in her fantasy world of perfect happiness, she'd forgotten the little flaw chipping away at her illusions. "There's something I need to tell you, Aiden."

He groaned, his mouth sliding down her throat. "Nay, not now. I wish to hear no more about the past or the future. We have now, Claire, and that is all that I am concerned with."

She stepped away from his embrace. His tongue near her ear was undermining her resolve. "That's not true. You are concerned with the future. Our future together." She considered telling Aiden that as Cherise she'd lied to him that she'd been pregnant but decided against it. In the scheme of things, that was no longer important. The truth about Claire's inability to conceive, however, was.

"How important to you is having children of your own?"

He frowned. "A man without offspring is a barren land. Of course I wish to beget children of my own. Besides, it is the only way I may keep Delacroix in my family. It is what I have fought for, for so long." He paused. "Claire, what are you trying to say?"

There was no going around it. "I cannot have children."

Aiden's silence lasted just long enough to tear at her heart.

"How can you be certain? You might not have had them yet, but there is still time. You are still within childbearing years."

"I cannot have children," she repeated. "Never could. Never will."

His hand fell from her and shot to the back of his head, a stricken look on his face.

A knock on the door interrupted the uneasy silence. "What?" Aiden roared.

Giles's little voice broke through the thick oak. "My lord, there is a messenger from the king waiting to see you in the great hall."

Aiden blew out a breath. "I shall be there shortly," he shouted to Giles, then turned to Claire. "We shall speak of this later." He pivoted, but Claire held on to his arm.

"I think we should speak of this now."

"I have a king's messenger waiting for me, Claire."

Sensing his anger, Claire hesitated. She wasn't sure if it was directed at her or at fate in general. She considered postponing the conversation until later, but that would solve nothing. She could simply take matters into her own hand and leave Aiden, Delacroix, and this time in the dead of the night, sparing him the agony of making such a decision.

But then she remembered how she'd felt when he'd made a similar decision without consulting her, and she knew she couldn't do it.

Claire didn't know what scared her the most: that he'd want to marry her out of a sense of obligation, to atone for past mistakes, or that he would once again reject her when she couldn't give him what he wanted.

Life was filled with difficult choices, and it seemed they'd been saddled with more than their fair share. However, having faced a similar dilemma before, and mangled it miserably, it was time for them to reach a decision together.

"The messenger can wait, Aiden. This is too important for delays."

Aiden's guts twisted and coiled. There he was again, at the same bifurcation in the road of his life, being pulled in different directions, knowing that whatever path he took would make him the poorer for it.

He sought the clarity of purpose that once had made such difficult decisions bearable, but all he found was an immense need for what he could not have.

And this time Claire would not be denied her say.

He finally nodded his agreement. She pointed to the bench by the table, and they headed there. He straddled the bench, and she perched by his side.

"You are certain of what you have just told me?" he asked quietly. Perchance she was mistaken.

"Yes, this can be determined with reasonable certainty in the future."

"And there was naught they could do for you then?"

She sighed. "There's a small possibility the problem can still be fixed in the future, but there are no guarantees. It would require both our presences for a lengthy period of time and complicated medical procedures. I'm not even sure *I* can go back to my own time, let alone the two of us. Besides, even if we succeed in traveling forward in time, we might not be able to travel back, which means we would have to live there. The future is very, very different, Aiden. The contents of my purse is only an insignificant sample of what you would have to get used to."

"You think I could not adapt?" He feared he could not. But if there was a chance, did he not owe her to try?

"I think it would be very difficult. But that's not the point. Why would you want to give up your life here for a place you know nothing about?"

"Do I not ask you to do the same for me?"

She smiled. "It is a little different, though, but yes, you have a point."

"Thus we have two choices. We can journey to this future of yours, knowing there is a good chance we may not return, and that I might not adapt, and that we still might not have children. Or we can remain here together and accept there will be no children from our marriage. Either way, the future of Delacroix is at risk."

She nodded. "There's a third option," she said. "We can go our separate ways. You can find yourself a suitable bride and have your family and your castle, and I can return to my own time. Which perhaps was what we were meant to do all along. Maybe our time has not yet come, Aiden. Maybe we will find our happiness together in another lifetime."

Aiden pulled her closer, edging her between his thighs. "I am not willing to wait another lifetime for you, Claire. I have waited long enough."

"So have I, Aiden. Still, that doesn't change the fact that what you want and need I cannot provide."

"Do you want a family, Claire?"

She nodded.

"Seems to me we both have much to lose and much to gain."

"It's true. Still, what you feared most will happen if we stay together. Delacroix will fall into someone else's hands. Maybe even Jasper's."

Suddenly the thought was not as abhorrent as it once was. What was unbearable was to live the rest of his days without Claire. Ten years ago he had chosen with his head. It was time he followed his heart.

"Bah! What is Delacroix but a pile of stones?"

Epilogue

THE smell of mulled wine wafted to Claire as she in-
spected the frenzied activity in the great hall of
Delacroix Castle on this Christmas Eve, the year of our
Lord 1205.

Aiden and Jasper walked in carrying the Yule log—a giant section of a tree trunk that would fill the huge fireplace
and supposedly burn for all the twelve days of Christmas.

Heart stumbling in her chest, Claire's gaze followed her
husband across the hall. She knew how lucky she was to
have found Aiden again. Sensing her stare, he turned and
his lips curled into a knowing smile. He, too, felt as she
did. They had suffered enough; they would never again
take their love for granted.

"Lady Claire," Giles called, drawing Claire's attention
from Aiden. "Where do you want the mistletoe?"

Giles was growing quite nicely into his thin frame,

Claire noticed. At thirteen, he was beginning to lose his boyish face, though he still looked at her adoringly like a puppy dog. She was glad Melissent didn't feel threatened by Claire's loving relationship with her son.

"Right above the door post, Giles."

"Make certain you center it right," Michael, the latest addition to their ever-growing family, chimed in. As the youngest son of an impoverished lord, the twelve-year-old Michael had been destined for the Church, until the funds that would accompany him mysteriously disappeared. Aiden had found him starving in the woods a year ago and had brought him home.

Claire thought he was more suited to knighthood than priesthood, anyway, given his commanding attitude.

"Leave Giles to his task, Michael. Did you collect the pine cones I asked for?"

"Aye, my lady."

"Then go hang them on the tree."

Lily, the three-year-old Claire had adopted when her mother—a maid in the castle—had died giving birth to her, pulled at her skirts. Claire scooped her up, keeping the girl's sticky hands off her face. Claire had no doubt she'd find a pot of honey somewhere under a table. She just hoped Coco wasn't immersed in it.

Finishing with his task at the fireplace, Aiden came to her, fussed with Lily's hair for a moment, and then kissed Claire's lips.

"Is there anything else my lady wishes?" he asked invitingly against her mouth.

He knew exactly what she wished, but that would have to wait until later. "You can hang this last decoration." She handed him a star of Bethlehem fashioned out of a thin sheet of copper.

He let out an exaggerated sigh like a long-suffering husband, kissed her again, and then hopped on a ladder to affix the star at the top of the huge Christmas tree. The one anachronism Claire indulged in for the thirteenth-century Delacroix Christmas.

Humming "Silent Night" quietly to herself, Claire hugged Lily and spared a loving thought for Nick, her beloved brother in the future. She could only hope that the iron box containing her personal belongings would find its way to him one day. And then he would know what had happened to her. Thoughts of Meredith, her poor sister of the past, also filled her mind. She said a silent prayer for her and then turned her attention to the members of her new family: Giles, Michael, Jasper, and Aiden. Some of them would stay with her for just a while, some would remain with her until she drew her last breath in this life, and still others would follow her in her journey through eternity.

The threads of fate tying them all together were strong and unbreakable. And she was mighty thankful for that.

Dreams of Stardust

by
Lynn Kurland

From *USA Today* bestselling author Lynn Kurland—"one of romance's finest writers"*—comes a magical love story about a modern man who's swept back into medieval England and the beautiful woman he yearns to possess...

"[Kurland] consistently delivers the kind of stories readers dream about."
—*Oakland Press*

"A vivid writer...She crafts an engrossing story."
—*All About Romance*

Jane's Warlord

by Angela Knight

The sexy debut novel from
the author of
Master of the Night

The next target of a time travelling killer,
crime reporter Jane Colby finds herself in the
hands of a warlord from the future sent to
protect her—and in his hands is just where
she wants to be.

"CHILLS, THRILLS...[A] SEXY TALE."

—EMMA HOLLY

0-425-19684-4

Available wherever books are sold or at
penguin.com

BERKLEY SENSATION
COMING IN SEPTEMBER 2005

Too Wilde to Tame
by Janelle Denison
New in the *USA Today* bestselling Wilde series. "No
one does hot and sexy better" (Carly Phillips) than
Janelle Denison.

0-425-20528-2

The Angel and the Warrior
by Karen Kay
"Karen Kay's passion for Native American love shines
through" (*Publishers Weekly*) in this sexy new novel.

0-425-20529-0

Someone to Believe In
by Kathryn Shay
Kathryn Shay steamed up your nights with her
firefighter romances. Now she's back with a story of
love on opposite sides of the political fence.

0-425-20530-4

Touch Me
by Lucy Monroe
A debut historical from "a fresh new voice in
romance" (Debbie Macomber).

0-425-20531-2

Personal Assets
by Emma Holly
From *USA Today* bestselling author Emma Holly, "one
of the best writers of erotic fiction" (Susan Johnson).

0-425-19931-2